A SISTER'S HOPE

.

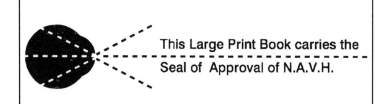

This Large Print Book carries the
Seal of Approval of N.A.V.H.

A SISTER'S HOPE

WANDA E. BRUNSTETTER

THORNDIKE PRESS

A part of Gale, Cengage Learning

GALE
CENGAGE Learning

Detroit • New York • San Francisco • New Haven, Conn • Waterville, Maine • London

GALE
CENGAGE Learning

Copyright © 2008 by Wanda E. Brunstetter.
All scripture quotations, unless otherwise noted, are taken from the King James Version of the Bible.
All German-Dutch words are taken from the *Revised Pennsylvania German Dictionary* used in Lancaster County, Pennsylvania.
Thorndike Press, a part of Gale, Cengage Learning.

Thorndike Press® Large Print Christian Romance.
The text of this Large Print edition is unabridged.
Other aspects of the book may vary from the original edition.
Set in 16 pt. Plantin.
Printed on permanent paper.

LIBRARY OF CONGRESS CATALOGING-IN-PUBLICATION DATA

Brunstetter, Wanda E.
  A sister's hope / by Wanda E. Brunstetter.
    p. cm. — (Thorndike Press large print Christian romance)
  (Sisters of Holmes County ; bk. 3)
  ISBN-13: 978-1-4104-2200-2 (alk. paper)
  ISBN-10: 1-4104-2200-3 (alk. paper)
    1. Amish—Fiction. 2. Dog breeders—Fiction. 3. Ohio—Fiction.
  4. Large type books. I. Title.
  PS3602.R864S56 2010
  813'.6—dc22
                                      2009040304

Published in 2010 by arrangement with Barbour Publishing, Inc.

Printed in the United States of America
1 2 3 4 5 6 7 14 13 12 11 10

DEDICATION/
ACKNOWLEDGMENTS

To my dear friends,
Jake and Sara Smucker,
whose hope is fixed on Jesus.

With great appreciation,
I wish to thank the following Ohio
friends who shared information with me
related to Holmes County, Ohio:
Esta and Melvin Miller,
Monk and Marijane Troyer,
Tom and Connie Troyer,
Lori Schlabach, Marlene Miller,
and Sig and Evie Kobus.
I also want to thank Rebecca Germany
and Becky Durost Fish,
my helpful editors.
Most of all, I thank my heavenly
Father, who continues to give me the
inspiration and desire to write for Him.

Be of good courage,
and he shall strengthen your heart,
all ye that hope in the LORD.
PSALM 31:24

CHAPTER 1

Ar-ou-ou! Ar-ou-ou!

Piercing howls roused Martha Hostettler from her sleep, and she rolled over in bed.

Ar-ou-ou! Ar-ou-ou!

There it was again. That couldn't be Polly. The beagle had a high-pitched howl, not deep and penetrating. Polly's mate, Beau, must be making that awful noise.

Martha turned on the flashlight she kept on the nightstand and pointed the light at her battery-operated clock. It was three o'clock. None of Martha's dogs ever barked or howled during the night unless something was amiss. Could Heidi have had her pups? The sheltie wasn't due for another week or so. Maybe Beau had sensed what was going on and wanted to let Martha know.

She shook her head, trying to clear away the cobwebs of sleep. *That's ridiculous. Beau might be able to sense that Heidi's having a problem, but I doubt he's smart enough to let me know. Something else must have disturbed the dog.*

Martha thought of the day she'd found her sheltie Fritz tied to a tree. One of his legs had also been tied up, and a bowl of water had been placed just out of his reach. Another time, Martha had found one of her puppies in the yard with its neck broken. She had wondered if whoever had been vandalizing her family's property and attacking them in other ways could have been responsible for the puppy's death.

A tremor shot through her body. What if someone was in the barn right now? What if they planned to hurt one of her dogs?

She pushed the covers aside and jumped out of bed. Dashing across the room, she slipped into her bathrobe, stepped into her sneakers, grabbed the flashlight, and rushed out of her room.

When Martha stepped outside, she shivered as a chilly breeze rustled the leaves. Martha hurried across the yard. As she approached the barn, she tipped her head and listened. Beau had stopped howling. The dog could have been spooked by one of the horses on the other side of the barn. She was probably worried for nothing.

Holding the flashlight with one hand and grasping the handle of the door with the

10

other, Martha stepped into the barn. *Clunk! Splat!* Something cool and wet hit the top of her head. The sticky liquid dripped down her face and oozed onto her neck.

Martha aimed the flashlight at the front of her robe and groaned. She was covered in white paint! She flashed a beam of light upward and gasped. A bucket connected to a piece of rope had been suspended above the barn door. Someone had deliberately set this up! Was it a prank by some unruly kids? *Or could this be another attack?*

She reached for a cardboard box on a nearby shelf and fumbled around until she located a clean rag. She blotted the paint from her face the best she could. The ammonia smell identified the paint as latex. At least it would clean up with soap and warm water.

Martha hurried to her dog kennels in the back of the barn. Relief swept over her when she saw that all of the dogs — Polly, Beau, Fritz, and Heidi — were okay. And Heidi still hadn't delivered her pups.

When Martha reached through the wire fencing and patted Beau on the head, he looked up at her and whined.

"Go back to sleep, boy. Everything's fine."

But it wasn't fine. Someone had sneaked into their barn and rigged up the bucket.

How long ago had it been done? Could they still be in the barn?

Martha swept the barn with her flashlight but saw no one. Satisfied that nothing else seemed to have been disturbed, she hurried outside. Glancing down, she noticed an empty pack of cigarettes on the ground.

Rustling sounded in the distance. She aimed her flashlight toward the field of dried corn behind their house. A man was running through the fields. She sucked in her breath. It was hard to tell much from this distance in the dark, but it looked like he wore a straw hat, the kind Amish men used.

Martha shuddered. *If I tell Dad about seeing the man, he'll think it was Luke.* For some time, her father had suspected Luke of attacking their family, but she was convinced Luke was innocent. At least, she hoped he was.

Martha hurried to the house and headed straight for the shower. She needed to get the paint washed off. She needed time to think.

When she stepped out of the bathroom a short time later and saw a man standing in the hallway, her breath caught. "Dad! What are you doing here? I . . . I didn't think anyone else was up."

"The sound of the shower running woke me." He frowned and pointed to her clothes lying on the floor outside the bathroom. "I've heard of folks sleepwalking during the night, but I never knew anyone who liked to paint in their sleep."

"I wasn't. I —"

"What's going on?" Mom asked as she joined them in front of the bathroom door.

Martha quickly explained what had happened in the barn.

"*Ach!*" Mom gasped. "Was this another attack?"

"I . . . I don't know," Martha stammered. "It's hard to say."

Dad looked over at Martha, his brows furrowing. "Did you see anyone?"

"I . . . uh . . . thought I saw someone running across the field, but I didn't get a good enough look to tell who it was."

Ruth showed up on the scene, rubbing her eyes and yawning. "It's the middle of the night. What's everyone doing out of bed?"

Martha recounted her story again and ended by saying, "I'm sorry I woke everyone."

"We needed to know what happened." Mom slipped her arm around Martha's waist. "It's not safe for you to go to the barn during the night."

"I just wanted to check on my *hund*. Besides, it's not right that we can't feel safe on our own property." Martha looked at Dad. "Will you let the sheriff know about this?"

"What's the point? Sheriff Osborn hasn't done a thing to prevent any of the attacks from happening. It's not likely he'll start now." Dad shrugged. "What's done is done. Notifying the sheriff won't change a thing."

As Luke Friesen headed down the road in his open buggy, the pungent smell of horse-flesh filled his senses. Despite the fact that he owned a pickup truck he kept hidden in the woods because his folks wouldn't approve of it, Luke preferred horse and buggy transportation. He'd only bought the pickup because some of his Amish friends, who were also going through their running-around years, owned a vehicle. Luke figured it was expected of him. Besides, having the truck gave him the freedom to travel wherever he wanted. And it gave him an in with Rod and Tim, the English fellows he'd been hanging around for a time. Luke's folks didn't approve of his rowdy English friends, and they'd been after him to settle down and join the Amish church for some time. But he wasn't ready. Some things he wanted

14

to do, he couldn't do as a member of the church. Besides, there was no point in joining the church when he wasn't ready to get married. He would consider it if and when he found the right woman.

A vision of Martha Hostettler flashed across Luke's mind. She was spunky and daring — the complete opposite of her sister, Ruth, who never liked to take chances and had seemed so subdued during the time they'd been courting. Under the right circumstances, Luke might consider courting Martha.

Luke gritted his teeth as he thought about the way Martha's father, Roman, had fired him for being late to work a few years ago, and how, after the Hostettlers had come under attack, Roman had pointed a finger at Luke. Even though Luke had denied having anything to do with the attacks, Roman had given him the cold shoulder ever since. If the man had any idea Luke was interested in his youngest daughter, Luke was sure he and Martha would both be in trouble.

At least I have a job working for John Peterson. Guess that's something to be grateful for. Luke snapped the reins to get the horse moving faster. *If I'm not careful, I'll end up being late for work because I'm allowing my horse to plod along while I think about*

15

someone I can't have.

The buggy jolted and leaned to the right. "Whoa! Steady, boy." He pulled back on the reins and grimaced when he saw his left buggy wheel roll onto the opposite side of the road. Good thing there were no cars going by at the moment.

Luke guided the horse and buggy to the shoulder of the road, jumped down, and sprinted over to the buggy wheel. "Great," he muttered. "Now I will be late for work."

Luke lugged the wheel over to his buggy and spent the next several minutes looking for the nut that had come off. When he couldn't find it, he reached into his toolbox in the back of the buggy and took out another nut. He'd just squatted down in front of the buggy to set the wheel in place, when Sheriff Osborn's car pulled up behind him.

"Looks like you lost a wheel," the sheriff said as he sauntered over to Luke.

"That's what happened, all right." Luke grimaced. "It's gonna make me late for work."

"Need any help?"

"Sure, I'd appreciate that." Luke's nose twitched as Sheriff Osborn knelt on the ground next to the buggy wheel. The sheriff's clothes reeked of cigarette smoke,

16

which made Luke think the man was either a heavy smoker or had recently been around someone who smoked.

"Are you still working for John Peterson?" the sheriff asked as he helped Luke lift the wheel and set it in place.

Luke nodded. "Sure am."

"Do you like working for John better than you did Roman?"

"John's a good boss — always patient and fair with me," Luke said without really answering the sheriff's question. "Of course I don't know how he'll react to me being late today."

"I'm sure he'll understand when you tell him what happened with your buggy wheel."

"I appreciate your help," Luke said once the wheel had been securely fastened.

Sheriff Osborn reached into his pocket, pulled out a pack of gum, and popped a piece into his mouth. "No problem. Glad I came along when I did. If you'd had to fix the wheel yourself, you'd be even later for work." He turned toward his car. "Guess I'd better get back to the business at hand. I got a report that there have been too many cars going over the speed limit on this stretch of road, so I figured I'd better nip it in the bud."

Luke shuffled his feet a few times, trying

to think of the best way to say what was on his mind.

"You're looking kind of thoughtful there," Sheriff Osborn said as he chomped on his wad of gum. "Have you got something on your mind?"

"I . . . uh . . . was wondering if you've had any leads on who's behind the attacks against the Hostettlers."

"Nope, sure don't. As far as I know, there haven't been any more attacks at their place in some time." The sheriff stuck another piece of gum in his mouth. "I might have caught the culprit responsible for the attacks if Roman had let me know about them sooner." He kicked a pebble with the toe of his boot. "From what I understand, it's not against the Amish religion to notify the police, so I can't figure out why Roman kept quiet about most of those attacks."

Luke shrugged. "I guess he figured it was best to turn the other cheek and not involve the law unless it became absolutely necessary."

"You're probably right." The sheriff turned toward his car again. "I'd better be on my way and let you get to work. Wouldn't want to see you lose your job on my account." He waved as he climbed into his car.

Luke checked the wheel over once more

for good measure, gave his horse a quick pat, and stepped into his buggy.

When he arrived at John's shop, he found John sitting behind his desk, talking on the phone. Figuring it best not to disturb him, Luke hurried to the back room to put away his lunch box. When he returned, John was off the phone.

"Sorry for being late," Luke apologized. "One of my buggy wheels fell off, and I had to stop and fix it."

"Of course you did." John smiled. "Your being late's not a problem. Some things happen that we can't control."

Luke wiped the sweat from his forehead as he drew in a quick breath. "I appreciate your understanding. I was afraid you might fire me the way Roman did when I worked for him."

A deep wrinkle formed above John's slightly crooked nose. "No one should be punished for something that isn't his fault."

Luke nodded. Working for John was sure easier than working for Roman had been. Nothing had ever seemed to be good enough for that man. Every time Luke had an idea about how something should be done, Roman had vetoed it.

"What would you like me to do this morning?" Luke asked as he moved toward John's desk.

John motioned to several cabinet doors stacked against the wall. "You can begin sanding those while I go over to Keim Lumber to pick up some supplies." He stood. "I shouldn't be gone long. If any customers show up, go ahead and write up the orders."

Luke nodded. It felt good to have John's trust. Roman never trusted him. He grimaced. *Why do I keep comparing John to Roman, and why can't I stop thinking about how things used to be when I worked for Roman?*

When John left the shop, Luke began working on the doors. John's beagle, Flo, who'd been lying on an old rug near John's desk, ambled over to Luke with a pathetic whine.

He bent down, and the dog licked his hand. "You don't miss John already, do you, girl? Are you craving some attention?"

The dog responded with a low whimper then flopped on the floor a few feet from where Luke stood.

As Luke plucked a piece of sandpaper, he thought about Martha and wondered how her dog business was doing. She'd sold Flo to John because the dog was barren, and she'd used the money to buy another dog she hoped to use for breeding purposes.

Luke wished he felt free to stop by the Hostettlers' to see Martha, but he knew if Roman saw him talking to her, he wouldn't like it. Luke and Roman would probably end up having words. He thought too highly of Martha to cause trouble between her and her dad. Luke figured it was best if he stayed away from the Hostettler place. Besides, there were other things he needed to do today.

CHAPTER 2

Martha stood in front of the counter in Irene Schrock's kitchen, rolling out dough for the pies they would serve when a busload of tourists came for supper the following evening. Her thoughts wandered as she pushed the rolling pin back and forth. She couldn't forget about the incident in the barn. Even though Martha had been the one who'd gotten doused with paint, Mom had been so distraught that her hands shook all during breakfast, and poor Ruth had seemed equally shaken. Dad hadn't said more than a few words. He'd gulped down his oatmeal and rushed out the door, saying he needed to get out to his woodworking shop because he had a backlog of work.

A trickle of sweat rolled down Martha's forehead, and she lifted the corner of her work apron to wipe it away. Who had put that bucket of paint above the door, and why had they done it?

She drew in a deep breath and closed her eyes. *Dear Lord, please make this insanity stop.*

Someone touched her shoulder. Martha dropped the rolling pin and whirled around.

"Are you okay?" Irene asked. "You're not feeling *grank,* I hope."

"I'm . . . uh . . . no, I'm not feeling sick. At least not physically."

Irene's dark eyebrows furrowed. "What do you mean, not physically?"

"Something happened at our place early this morning that left us all feeling troubled."

"What happened?" Irene's eighteen-year-old daughter, Carolyn, asked.

"Someone rigged up a bucket of white paint and hung it above our barn door. When I went out to check on my dogs, the paint spilled on me."

Irene gasped. "Ach! Who would do such a thing?"

"We have no idea." Martha wasn't about to mention the Amish man she thought she'd seen running through the field. No point in giving Irene something to talk about with others in their community. There had been enough talk already as to who might be responsible for these attacks.

"Did your *daed* notify Sheriff Osborn?"

Carolyn asked.

Martha shrugged. "I doubt it. Just like most of the other times when we've been attacked, Dad thinks he should turn the other cheek and say nothing to the sheriff."

"Do you agree with that, Martha?"

Martha wasn't sure how to answer Carolyn's question. Even though she had her own opinion, she didn't want to say anything that would make Dad look bad. "I think whoever has been doing the attacks will keep on doing them until they are caught," she replied.

"But how will they ever be caught if your daed refuses to notify the sheriff?"

"The best thing for all of us to do is to pray about the matter," Irene intervened. She patted Martha's arm. "In the meantime, we have some pies that need to be baked."

"You're right. I should get busy." Martha grabbed the rolling pin. She would keep her hands busy when she was working for Irene or caring for her dogs, but during her free time, she hoped to find out who was behind the attacks. She only wished she could talk to someone about this. But who could she trust not to say anything to Dad?

I'll begin by making a list of every attack, she decided. *After that, I'll make a list of suspects, which will include a motive and any opportunities they might have had to attack.*

"I guess it won't be long now until your sister gets married," Irene said.

Martha nodded. "Ruth and Abe's wedding will be two months after Sadie and Toby's. I'll have a part in both."

"What will you be doing?" Carolyn asked as she reached into the cupboard for a bag of flour.

"I'll be an attendant at Ruth's wedding and a table server at Sadie's."

Irene slipped two apple-crumb pies into the oven and shut the door. "It's nice that Ruth and Abe have found love again. I think they'll have a good marriage and Ruth will make a fine *mudder* to Abe's *kinner.*"

Martha couldn't argue with that. Ruth had talked about becoming a mother ever since she was a little girl playing with her dolls. Sadly, Ruth's hopes had been dashed on Christmas Eve, nearly a year ago. Her husband's buggy had been rammed off the road, and Martin had been killed. Ruth's injuries had left her unable to have children.

Irene touched Martha's shoulder. "Will your aunt Rosemary be able to attend Ruth's wedding?"

"I hope so. She found a buyer for her house in Boise, Idaho, so if she gets everything wrapped up soon, she should be moved here to Ohio in plenty of time for the wedding."

Irene smiled. "It's nice that Rosemary's part of your family again. I'm sure your daed missed her very much when she was gone those thirty-some years."

Martha nodded. Dad had missed his sister, but until a few months ago, he'd never admitted it.

"Since Rosemary will be moving back to Holmes County, maybe she'll consider joining the Amish church."

Martha made another pass with the rolling pin over the dough and turned to face Irene. "I think if Aunt Rosemary had it to do over again, she wouldn't have left the Amish faith and married an Englisher. But she's been English most of her life, so I doubt she'd be willing to give up all the modern conveniences she's become used to." She lifted the dough and placed it in an empty pie pan. "Besides, her son and his wife are English. It might make it hard on their relationship if she went Amish again."

Irene smiled. "I see what you mean."

"Will Rosemary's family be coming to Ruth's wedding?" Carolyn asked.

"As far as I know. I'm anxious to meet them, too." Martha smiled. "Until Aunt Rosemary's surprise visit to Holmes County several months ago, I didn't even know I had an English cousin." Martha smiled.

A knock at the back door interrupted their conversation, and Carolyn scooted to the other side of the kitchen to answer it. A few seconds later, Martha's brother-in-law, Cleon, entered the room, carrying a cardboard box.

"These are for you," he said, smiling at his mother. "I figured with all the dinners you've been hosting lately, you might be running low on honey."

"*Danki,* son." Irene motioned to the counter. "Why don't you set the box over there? Carolyn can put the jars of honey in the pantry after we finish with the pies."

"Sure thing." Cleon set the box down then turned to face his mother. "If my bees keep producing the way they are now, eventually I might be able to build a small store on my property. I'd like to have a place close to home where I can sell some of my honey, as well as those nice beeswax candles you and Carolyn make."

Irene smiled. "I think that's a good idea."

Cleon moved closer to Martha. "I heard about the dousing you got in the wee hours of the morning."

She nodded. "Dad wasn't too happy about having to clean up the mess in his barn, and

I wasn't happy about the mess all over me."

"I suggested that Roman keep the barn locked. That's what I've been doing with my own barn since I discovered one of my new ladders had a broken rung." Cleon grimaced. "I'm sure someone cut it."

"What did Dad say?" Martha asked.

"He said he'd think about locking the barn at night."

"Why only at night?" Carolyn asked.

"I guess he figures no one's likely to come around during the day — especially since someone in the family is usually around."

"That's true," Irene said. "Most of the attacks against your family have occurred at night."

"Or when we've been away from home," Martha quickly added. "Truthfully, I doubt that Dad will take Cleon's suggestion about locking the barn, but I hope he will. After what happened last night, I'm worried about my dogs."

As Luke left John's woodworking shop and headed toward home, he spotted another buggy ahead of him and realized it was Martha Hostettler's. He flicked the reins to get his horse trotting and pulled into the oncoming lane to pass her. As his buggy came alongside Martha's, he slowed the horse and motioned her to pull onto the shoulder of the road. Once her rig was stopped, he pulled in behind her, hopped down, and skirted around to her side of the buggy. "*Wie geht's,* Martha?"

"I'm fine now, but I wasn't doing so well in the wee hours of the morning," she replied.

He tipped his head in question.

"I got doused with a bucket of paint when I went out to the barn to check on my dogs."

Luke's mouth dropped open. "How did that happen?"

"Someone rigged the bucket so it would spill when the barn door opened."

"You weren't hurt, were you?"

Martha shook her head. "Just looked a mess, with white paint all over me and my clothes." She grunted. "It's a good thing the paint was water based, or I'd probably still be wearing a white face."

Luke grimaced. "I suppose your daed will blame me for what happened."

"Why would you think that?"

"Because he's accused me of doing other things to your family." Luke shook his head. "I'd never do anything like that. You believe me, don't you, Martha?"

She stared at her hands, folded in her lap. "*Jah,* I do."

A feeling of relief washed over Luke like a fresh spring rain. If Martha believed Luke was innocent, maybe she could convince her dad that he had nothing to do with the attacks. If Luke could get Roman to see the truth, he might have a chance at courting Martha. Truth was, ever since he and Martha had shared a pizza together a few months ago, she'd been on his mind.

"I had a little calamity myself this morning," Luke said.

"What happened?"

"I was heading to work, and my left front buggy wheel came off."

Her forehead wrinkled. "Did you have the tools you needed to fix it?"

Luke nodded. "Sheriff Osborn happened along, and he helped me put the wheel back on. Even so, I was late for work."

"Did you get in trouble with John?"

"Nope. Not even a harsh word." He grunted. "Not like when your daed jumped all over me for being late a couple of times. He was after me for just about everything I did when I worked for him."

Martha's mouth turned down. "I'm sorry about that, Luke. I truly am."

He shook his head. "It's not your fault your daed's so hard to please."

She gave no reply.

30

"I hope I didn't offend you," Luke was quick to say. "I probably sound like I'm griping. It's not right for me to be bad-mouthing your daed — especially not to you."

"It's okay; I'm not offended. I know how difficult my daed can be at times."

Luke figured it was time for another topic. "How are things going with your dogs these days?" he asked.

"Fairly well. My sheltie Heidi is due to have her *hundlin* any day, and Polly, the beagle I bought at the dog auction some time ago, is also expecting."

"That's good to hear. If you're going to raise dogs, you need some puppies you can sell."

Martha smiled. "I enjoy working for Irene, but I hope someday I'll make enough money with my kennel business to support myself."

"Speaking of kennels, did you read the article in the newspaper this morning, accusing some Amish folks of running puppy mills?"

Martha shook her head. "I didn't have time to read the paper. What did the article say?"

"It said that some Amish are raising puppies without a kennel license and that a few of them have been investigated and accused

31

of neglecting and even abusing their dogs."

Martha shook her head. "I would never neglect or abuse any dog. No one I know who raises dogs would, either." She sucked in her lower lip. "Did Gary Walker write the story? It would be just like him to write something like that."

Luke shrugged. "I can't remember who wrote the article. Fact is, I was so disturbed while reading it that I didn't pay any attention to the reporter's name."

Martha sniffed as though some foul odor had permeated the air. "Gary Walker is so arrogant and pushy." She leaned toward Luke. "Between you and me, I think my sister might be right about him being to blame for the attacks against my family."

A sense of relief shot through Luke. *If Martha thinks Gary is responsible for the attacks, then she must believe I had nothing to do with any of them. Maybe there's some hope for us. Should I ask her out? Would she think I was being too bold?*

He stared down at his boots, unable to make eye contact with her. "Uh . . . remember the day we had pizza together?"

"Jah."

"I enjoyed being with you."

"I enjoyed our time together, too," she said in a near whisper.

32

He lifted his gaze to meet hers. "I was wondering if you'd like to go out for pizza again."

She hesitated and stared at her hands. "I'd like that, Luke, but —"

"Are you worried about someone seeing us together and telling your daed?"

She nodded.

"How about we meet at the pizza place in Berlin this Saturday at noon? If anyone sees us there, we can just say we happened to meet and are sharing a table."

"I . . . I guess that would be all right."

"Great. I'll look forward to seeing you then." Luke turned and sprinted for his buggy. He liked Martha's spunky attitude and thought she was fun to be with. Now if he could only gain her daed's approval.

CHAPTER 3

As Martha sat across from Luke at a table in the pizza place on Saturday, her heartbeat picked up speed. She could hardly believe Luke had suggested they meet for lunch. Did his invitation mean he had more than a casual interest in her? She hoped it did. There was only one problem: Dad. Martha was certain he would never give his blessing for her to be courted by the man he thought might be responsible for the attacks against their family.

"After we met the other day, I went home and read that newspaper article you'd mentioned about the puppy mills," Martha said, pushing her thoughts aside.

"What'd you think?"

"I was right — the reporter was Gary Walker. It made me wonder if he's trying to make all Amish look bad."

"Why would he want to do that?"

She shrugged. "It could stem from his

anger when Grace broke up with him during her *rumschpringe* years."

"Do you really think that he's still carrying a grudge about something that happened during your sister's running-around years?"

"Grace thinks he is. She's sure Gary's responsible for every attack, even though she has no proof." Martha fingered the edge of her water glass. "I keep hoping the attacks will end, but it's beginning to look like they never will — at least not until we know who's been doing them and they're made to stop."

"I agree," Luke said with a nod. "But since there's nothing we can do about that at the moment, how about we order some pizza?"

"Sounds good to me."

"What kind would you like?"

Martha studied the menu their young English waitress had brought to the table. "With the exception of anchovies, there isn't any pizza topping I don't like." She smiled at Luke. "Why don't you decide?"

"How about sausage and black olives? Does that sound *gut* to you?"

"It sounds real good."

"Should we get a pitcher of root beer to go with it?"

"That's fine with me."

When the waitress returned to the table, Luke placed their order. After the waitress walked away, he leaned across the table to say something but was interrupted when Toby King and Sadie Esh entered the restaurant and sauntered up.

"I didn't expect to see you two here today — especially sittin' at the same table." Toby thumped Luke on the shoulder. "Are you and Martha courting?"

Luke's face turned bright red. Martha figured hers had, too, for her cheeks felt as hot as fire. "Luke and I are just sharing a pizza together," she was quick to say. No point in giving Toby something to gossip about.

Toby gave Luke's shoulder another good whack; then he pulled out the chair next to him and sat down. "Mind if Sadie and I join you?"

"Looks like you already have," Luke mumbled.

Toby looked at Sadie, who stood beside Martha's chair with a bewildered expression. "Aren't you gonna sit and join us?"

Sadie shuffled her feet and glanced at an empty table across the room. "I . . . uh . . . sort of figured —"

"Aw, I'm sure Luke and Martha don't

mind if we join 'em. Besides, we'll be alone plenty after we're married." Toby gave Sadie a quick wink. "Have a seat."

Sadie hesitated but finally sat down.

Martha reached over and touched Sadie's arm. "November will be here in a few more weeks. It won't be long until you and Toby are married. How are your wedding plans coming along?"

Sadie's face relaxed. "Pretty well. My *mamm* and I have begun cleaning the house for the wedding meal, and —"

"If everyone who got an invitation shows up, we might have over three hundred guests," Toby interrupted. "Since my daed's the bishop in our church district, I figure we'll have a real good turnout."

Luke cast Toby a disapproving look, and Martha grimaced. She didn't think Toby should be bragging about how many guests might be at his wedding. Truthfully, she'd never understood what Sadie saw in Toby, but then she guessed love was blind when it came to certain things. *Look at me,* she thought ruefully. *I've allowed myself to foolishly fall for Luke.* Martha refused to let herself believe Dad might be right about Luke. If only she could prove Luke's innocence. *Maybe I can. If I keep notes and study that list of suspects I made the other night, I might discover who the attacker is and clear Luke's name.*

Toby nudged Luke. "Do you still have that truck you keep hidden in the woods? I think everyone but your folks knows about it."

Luke's mouth dropped open. "Well, I —"

"You oughta sell that truck, find yourself a nice young woman to marry, and join the church." Toby grinned over at Sadie. "It took me awhile to realize I wanted to get married, but once I made up my mind, there was no stopping me from proposing."

Sadie's eyebrows furrowed. "Excuse me? If you'll recall, I was the one who asked if you'd be willing to marry me."

Toby gave her a sheepish grin; then he elbowed Luke again. "So what do you say? Are you gonna sell that truck and settle down to marriage soon?"

"I'll sell it when I'm good and ready." Luke's dark eyes flashed angrily. "It's not your place to be telling me what to do!"

Martha swallowed hard and reached for her glass of water. She took a quick drink and stood.

"Where are you going?" Toby asked.

"To the ladies' room."

"I'll go with you." Sadie rose from her chair and glanced down at Toby. "When the waitress comes, would you please order a medium-sized pizza with Canadian bacon and mushrooms?"

He squinted. "I thought you only liked pepperoni and cheese."

She shook her head. "It's *you* who likes pepperoni. I prefer Canadian bacon with mushrooms."

He lifted his shoulders in an exaggerated shrug. "Jah, okay."

Martha scurried off toward the restroom with Sadie beside her. Once they were inside, she turned to Sadie and said, "I just can't figure out what the problem is between Toby and Luke."

"I don't know. Toby and Luke used to be such good friends. I first noticed some problems between them when Luke was dating Ruth." Sadie groaned. "It made me wonder if Toby might be jealous."

Martha squinted. "Why would Toby have been jealous of Luke dating my sister?"

"For a while, I thought maybe Toby might be interested in Ruth, but when I asked him about it, he said he had no designs on Ruth. When she broke up with Luke and started dating Martin Gingerich, Toby said he was glad — that he thought Martin was a better choice for Ruth and he hoped they'd be real happy." Sadie frowned. "Ruth was happy, but for such a short time — until Martin's life was taken by whoever rammed their buggy last winter."

Martha nodded as the memory of that fateful night invaded her mind. She and her family had been waiting for Ruth and Martin to show up for Christmas Eve supper, but they never came. Dad and Cleon had gone out looking for Martin's buggy and discovered they'd been in a horrible accident. At the hospital, they'd been told that Martin was dead and Ruth needed a hysterectomy. Ruth had been devastated when she'd learned that she'd not only lost her husband of two months but would never be able to have any children of her own, either.

"I'm glad Ruth's found love again," Sadie said. "She deserves to be happy. I know she'll make a fine *fraa* for Abe and be a good mudder to his kinner."

Martha nodded. "All of Abe's children, especially Esta, have taken a liking to Ruth."

"So, are you and Luke courting?" Sadie whispered.

"Of course not. I told you at the table that Luke and I are just sharing a pizza." Martha slid over in front of the mirror to be sure her *kapp* was on straight.

"I can tell you like him. It's written all over your face." Sadie stood beside Martha. "I think Luke likes you, too."

"What makes you think that?"

"I never saw Luke look at Ruth the way he looked at you out there."

Martha felt the heat of a blush sweep across her face, and she covered her cheeks with her hands. "Even if I do feel something for Luke, and even if he returns those feelings, there's no hope of us ever being together."

"Why not?"

"Unless someone can prove that Luke's not responsible for the attacks against our family, Dad would never give his blessing for Luke to court me."

Sadie's eyes widened. "You don't really think Luke had anything to do with those horrible things, do you?"

"Not me. But my daed suspects Luke."

"He has no proof, right?"

Martha shook her head. "There's no proof of Luke's innocence, either."

"What are you going to do?"

Martha shrugged. She wasn't about to tell Sadie that she planned to do some investigating on her own. Sadie might tell Toby. Knowing Toby, he'd probably blab it to his dad or someone else. For now, Martha would tell no one what she planned to do.

Luke leaned his elbows on the table and

stared at Toby. "Are you trying to make me look bad in front of Martha?"

Toby's eyes narrowed. "What do you mean?"

"I think you know what I mean. You brought up my truck, made it sound like I wasn't a good person because I hadn't joined the church, and suggested I marry Martha."

"Huh?" Toby's eyebrows shot up. "I never said that."

"Jah, well, you said I should find a good woman to marry, and you looked right at Martha when you said it." Luke grunted. "What were you trying to do, give her some hope of something that's never going to happen?"

"Does that mean you don't like her?"

"Jah, I like her; Martha's very nice. But that doesn't mean I'm going to marry her."

Toby ran his index finger around the middle of his glass. "If you started courtin' Martha, you might fall in love and decide to get married, jah?"

Luke shrugged.

"Is there something holding you back?"

"Of course there's something. Martha's daed, that's what's holding me back!"

Toby gave him a knowing look. "That's right. You're not one of Roman Hostettler's favorite people these days, are you?"

Luke shook his head. "Unless I can prove I'm not responsible for the attacks that have been made on Roman's family, I'll probably never be accepted by him."

"How you gonna prove that?"

"I don't know."

"If you ask me, the best thing you can do is sell that truck and —"

Luke held up his hand. "Enough about my truck. Like I said before, I'll sell it when I'm ready."

Toby wrinkled his nose. "You always did like to have the last word, didn't you?"

Luke opened his mouth to defend himself but closed it again. What was the point of discussing something with someone who obviously wanted to goad him into an argument? For some time, Toby seemed to need to make Luke look bad. Ever since they were twelve years old and Luke had been declared the winner of a game of horseshoes Toby thought he should have won, there'd been a competitive spirit between them. Could Toby still be holding a grudge because Luke had always been able to do things better than him?

Luke balled his napkin into the palm of his hand. *Can I help it if I'm better at playing ball, buggy racing, and fishing than Toby? He ought to grow up.*

Martha and Sadie returned to the table just then, and Luke pushed his thoughts aside. He didn't want his lunch with Martha to be ruined, so he would do whatever was needed in order to keep the peace with Toby.

Luke was glad when their pizzas finally came. Now he could concentrate on eating.

By the time they'd finished their pizza and Sadie and Toby had left the restaurant, Martha's nerves were taut. Not only had she and Luke not been able to visit during their meal, but there'd been such tension between Luke and Toby that it had been hard to think of anything to talk about. She hadn't enjoyed her pizza that much, either.

"What was the problem between you and Toby?" Martha asked Luke as they walked out the door and approached her buggy.

Luke leaned against the driver's side of the buggy and folded his arms. "I think Toby is *falsch*."

"Resentful? Why do you think that?"

"Ever since we were *kinner*, I've been able to do things better than him."

She pursed her lips. "Lots of people can do things better than me, and I don't feel *falsch* toward them."

44

"Jah, well, Toby's the bishop's son. I think he feels he has to live up to his daed's expectations to be perfect."

"That's *narrisch*. I doubt anyone expects Toby to be perfect just because his daed's the head minister in our church."

"It might seem crazy, but if Toby thinks he's expected to be perfect and knows he's not . . ." Luke reached under his straw hat and scratched his head. "And if he's struggling with issues concerning me . . ."

"Then he needs to get over it," Martha interrupted. "He needs to be the best person he can, not compare himself to you or anyone else."

"That's what I think, too." Luke moved away from the buggy and reached out to stroke Martha's horse behind its ear. "I've been thinking about the attacks at your place. I wonder if someone might be trying to make me look guilty in order to get even with me for something."

"Like who?"

He turned his hands palm up. "I don't know, but I'm aiming to find out."

"How?"

Luke shrugged. "Haven't figured it out yet."

Martha drew in a deep breath and decided to say what was on her mind. "Would it be all right if I asked you a personal question, Luke?"

"Ask away."

"Would you mind telling me where you were around three o'clock on Thursday morning?"

"In bed, of course. Where else would I be in the middle of the night?"

She swiped her tongue over her lower lip as she struggled for the right words. Should she tell Luke that she'd seen a man dressed in Amish clothes running across the field?

Luke took a step closer to Martha. "Why did you ask where I was early Thursday morning? You don't think I had anything to do with you getting doused with that bucket of paint, I hope."

She swallowed hard. "When I left the barn, I shined my flashlight on the field behind our house, and I saw a man who looked like he was wearing Amish clothes running through the field."

Luke slapped his hands together, causing Martha to jump and her horse to whinny. "I told you someone's trying to make it look like it's me!" He shook his head vigorously. "It wasn't me, Martha. You've got to believe me."

"I want to believe you, and I'm hoping to do some investigating so I can find out who's responsible."

Luke's face blanched. "You're kidding, right?"

She shook her head.

"Snooping around could get you in trouble with your daed, not to mention that it could be dangerous if the culprit finds out you're onto him."

"Or her. It could be a woman, you know."

Luke grasped Martha's arm. "Promise you won't do anything on your own?"

"I can't make that promise. I —"

"How about we work together on solving these crimes?" he suggested. "After all, 'two heads are better than one.' "

She nodded as a sense of relief flooded her soul. If Luke wanted to help her find out who was responsible for the attacks, then he couldn't be responsible.

CHAPTER 4

"Where are you going?" Mom asked as Martha headed for the back door. "If we don't get this kitchen cleaned up right away, we'll be late for Sadie and Toby's wedding."

Martha grabbed a shawl from the wall peg near the door. "I know, but I want to check on Heidi's puppies."

Mom sighed as she lifted her gaze toward the ceiling. "You and those hundlin. I wouldn't be surprised if you weren't late for your own wedding because you were checking on some dog."

"Heidi's puppies are only a couple of days old, Mom. I need to be sure all five are getting plenty of milk. One of them's a runt, you know."

"I'm sure everything will be fine. Heidi did well with her last batch of pups, didn't she?"

Martha nodded. "Except for that one pup I found dead in the yard."

"Accidents happen," Mom said.

"I know."

"My point is," Mom said in a patient tone, "that you spend too much time with your hundlin and not enough time socializing. You'll never find a husband if you don't take an interest in courting."

"I'd need to find someone interested in courting me first."

Mom reached for the dishwashing liquid. "I'm sure the right man's out there. You've just got to look for him."

I've already found him; I just can't tell you who he is, Martha thought as she draped her woolen shawl across her shoulders. *Besides, Luke may never come to like me the way I do him.* "I'll dry the dishes as soon as I get back from the barn," she said.

Ruth entered the room just then. "I'll dry the dishes so Martha can check on her hundlin." She grabbed a sponge from the counter and began wiping off the tablecloth. "I know she wants to be sure they're all right before we leave for the wedding."

"Danki, Ruth."

"You're welcome." Ruth made a clicking noise with her tongue as she wagged a finger in Martha's direction. "Just make sure you're not checking on puppies the day of *my* wedding. I can't have my main attendant

49

being late to the service."

"I promise I won't be late." Martha slipped out the door and hurried for the barn. She found it unlocked, but that was no surprise since Dad had done his chores earlier that morning. Ever since the paint episode, he'd been locking the barn door at night. It remained unlocked during the day, but Martha wasn't too concerned because someone was usually at home.

When Martha entered the dog run where she kept Heidi and her pups, she gasped. One of the puppies was dead! Her thoughts went to the day she'd found one of Heidi's first batch of pups with a broken neck. It was the puppy she'd promised to give Grace's daughter, Anna. The child had been devastated, refusing the offer of another pup. Martha had never figured out the reason the puppy had broken its neck, but she had a hunch someone might have done it on purpose.

"I'm sorry, Heidi," Martha said, patting the sheltie's head. "I hope this puppy wasn't the victim of another attack."

Heidi whimpered and lifted her head as Martha reached into the box and picked up the dead pup. It was the runt of the litter. Maybe it hadn't been foul play, after all. The barn door had been locked last night.

Perhaps the puppy hadn't been getting enough milk or had gotten stuck under its mother and smothered. Now she was down to only four puppies, which meant one less pup to sell. Would she ever get her kennel business going well enough to make a decent living? Hopefully, Polly, her female beagle who was due to have a litter soon, would deliver a healthy bunch of pups. Most shelties sold for anywhere from $300 to $350, but beagles only brought in $200 to $250 if they were trained to run rabbits. Martha would be grateful for whatever she made from either of her female dogs.

She glanced down at the limp pup in her hand. *Maybe I'm not supposed to raise hundlin. Maybe I should look for a full-time job.* She shook her head. *No, I'm happiest when I'm caring for my dogs.*

"What do you mean you've got to work today?" Luke's mother asked when Luke announced that he wouldn't be going to Sadie and Toby's wedding.

"It's Thursday, Mom," Luke said around a mouthful of oatmeal. "John wasn't invited to the wedding, and he's open for business as usual."

"Couldn't you have asked for the day off

51

to attend your friend's wedding?" she persisted.

"I didn't feel like I could. We've got a lot of orders. John needs me in the shop while he makes some deliveries. Besides, Toby and I aren't getting along so well these days. I doubt he'll even miss me."

"Of course he will." Mom reached over and touched Luke's arm. "You and Toby have been friends since you were kinner."

"We used to be friends. Here lately, though, all we do is argue."

"Can't you bury your differences for one day? You know what the Bible says about —"

"If the boy says he has to work today, then he has to work," Luke's dad said as he stepped into the room. "We should be grateful our son has a good-paying job, Betty."

Mom's dark eyebrows furrowed as she took a sip of her tea. "I am grateful. I just think Luke should be at Toby's wedding."

Luke opened his mouth to comment, but his dad cut him off. "It's not as if he's one of Toby's witnesses, you know."

"That's true. Even so —"

"We'd better drop this discussion and eat our breakfast, or the two of us will be late for Toby's wedding," Pop said as he sat at the head of the table.

Mom nodded. "Jah, okay,"

The spicy aroma of cinnamon wafted up to Luke's nose as he poked his piece of toast into the oatmeal and dipped it up and down. Mom always seemed to be fussing about something these days. She wanted him to join the church, find a good woman, and get married. Luke had other things on his mind right now, and marriage wasn't one of them. At least it hadn't been until he'd taken an interest in Martha.

I need to do something to fix things between me and Roman, he thought. *I need to find a way to get back into his good graces and remove my name from the list of suspects Martha's working on.*

Martha had a hard time concentrating on Sadie and Toby's wedding as she sat on one of the backless wooden benches with some other women her age. All she could think about were Heidi's pups and whether the four surviving ones would be all right. She'd been relieved that Dad had agreed to lock the barn before they left home that morning. At least she didn't have to worry about anyone breaking in while they were gone.

She glanced over at the men's side of the room, searching for Luke. He wasn't in sight. Had he stayed home from the wed-

53

ding because of the disagreement he'd had with Toby the other day, or had he been expected to work for John? Probably the latter, she decided. Luke might not appreciate the way Toby got under his skin, but Martha didn't think he would deliberately skip out on the wedding because he had a grudge against Toby.

Martha clutched the folds in her dress. *I hope he's able to be at Ruth and Abe's wedding in January. It's going to be a joyous occasion, but it won't be nearly as joyous for me if he's not there.*

When Toby's father called for the bridal couple to step forward, Martha's attention was drawn to the front of the room. Her eyes misted when she saw Sadie look lovingly at her groom. Toby looked happy, too, wearing a smile as wide as the Ohio River.

If Luke would only look at me like that. If he would just ask to court me.

Anxious to get out of the stuffy house where a third group of guests had been served their wedding meal, Roman stepped onto the Eshes' back porch for a breath of fresh air. The sun shone brightly on this crisp November afternoon. A group of children frolicked on the lawn, while several young people milled about.

"You're looking kind of wistful," Bishop King said as he stepped up beside Roman and motioned to the children in the yard. "Are you wishing you were young again?"

Roman shook his head. "Although I'd be happy to have half their energy."

"Me, too."

"How's it feel to have your youngest *buwe* married off?"

"It feels rather good. I'm happy my boy's found a nice fraa and will soon be starting a family of his own." The bishop grunted. "Not like Toby's so-called friend, Luke, who didn't care enough to come to the wedding."

"Maybe he had to work today."

"Humph! You'd think he could have taken the day off to see his friend get married."

"Could be his boss had lots of work and wouldn't give Luke the day off." Roman didn't know why he was defending Luke. Truth was, he didn't trust the fellow any further than he could throw one of his buggy horses. The whole time Luke had been working for him, he'd acted cocky, like he thought he knew more than Roman did about woodworking. Luke had been late to work on more than one occasion, too, which made Roman think he was lazy and undependable. If Luke were his son, he would lay down the law and tell him he either had to settle down and join the Amish church or move out. But no, Luke's folks simply looked the other way while Luke pretty much did as he pleased.

Roman grimaced. *Who am I to talk? My oldest daughter took off for a time during her rumschpringe, and we didn't even know where she was. Then there was my sister, Rosemary, who left the Amish faith when she was eighteen years old. For the next thirty years, we never heard a word from her.*

The bishop nudged Roman's arm. "What's wrong? You look like you've just been given a hefty dose of cod liver oil."

"I'm fine. Just thinking about the past, is all."

"How far back were you thinking?"

"Back to when Rosemary left home."

"But she came back last year, and the two of you have made your peace. I don't see why you'd be brooding about that now."

Roman stretched his arms over his head then lowered them and reached around to rub the small of his back. His muscles always tightened up whenever he felt overly stressed. "Sometimes, even when I think I've let go of the past and given everything over to God, something happens or someone says something that brings it all to light again."

Bishop King's bushy eyebrows drew together. "I hope it wasn't anything I said that got you mulling over the past."

Roman shook his head. "I guess the mention of Luke Friesen is what set me off."

"You don't still think he's responsible for the attacks against you, I hope."

"I don't know." Roman shrugged. "I guess several people might have a grudge against me, but Luke seems the most likely."

The bishop leaned against the porch railing and stared into the yard. "I've never really believed Luke was capable of doing any of those things to your family, but after a couple of discussions I've had with him and his folks, I'll have to admit that I am a bit concerned."

"You think Luke's the guilty one?"

"It's not that. What's got me concerned is that Luke is twenty-two years old and still hasn't decided to join the church." The bishop grimaced. "From what Toby's told me, Luke's still running around with a couple of wild English fellows."

Roman nodded. "So I've heard."

The bishop's voice lowered as he leaned closer to Roman. "Toby also told me that Luke's got a truck he keeps hidden in the woods because he doesn't want his folks to know."

"Puh!" Roman waved his hand. "A lot of young Amish fellows who haven't yet joined the church own a car. Many keep 'em right on their folks' property."

"That's true, but Luke's parents have always been very strict about that kind of thing. They've never let any of their kinner keep a car on their property, so I'm sure they won't abide by Luke doing it, either."

"You're probably right."

"Toby's told me a lot about Luke over the years, and one of the things he's said is that Luke tends to be strong willed and moody and always wants his way on things." The bishop slowly shook his head. "Unless Luke has a change of heart, I fear he might never settle down and join the church."

"You think he'll decide to jump the fence and go English?"

"Could be."

Roman grunted. "Maybe it would be for the best if he did. I wouldn't want someone like Luke courting or marrying any of my daughters!"

"Grace is already married, and Ruth will be soon, so that only leaves you one daughter to worry about."

"Jah, well, I'm sure Martha would never

be interested in the likes of Luke Friesen. She's got better sense than that."

"That was sure a nice wedding, wasn't it?" Mom asked as she turned and smiled at Martha and Ruth, who sat in the back of their family's buggy.

Ruth nodded. "Sadie seemed real happy to be marrying Toby."

"They'd been courting quite awhile before they were published," Mom said. "Sadie might have been worried that Toby would never ask her to marry him."

"Oh, Toby didn't ask her; it was the other way around." Martha winced when Ruth's elbow connected with her ribs.

"You weren't supposed to say anything," Ruth protested. "I told you that in confidence."

"Sorry. It just slipped out."

"Did Sadie really propose marriage to Toby?" Mom asked.

Ruth nodded, and her face flamed. "She wanted me to do the same with Abe, and I sort of did."

"You did what?" Dad craned his neck to look back at Ruth.

Martha, fearful that their buggy might run off the road, pointed up ahead.

"Don't worry," Dad said with a shake of

his head. "Jeb won't leave the road unless I tell him to."

Mom touched Dad's shoulder. "Just the same, Roman, I'd feel more comfortable if you kept your focus straight ahead."

"Jah, okay," he mumbled, turning back around.

"Now, Ruth," Mom said, "tell us about how you sort of proposed to Abe."

The color in Ruth's cheeks deepened. "Well, Sadie had mentioned reading the story of Ruth in the Bible, and she got the bright idea that I should do something that would let Abe know I was interested in him and wanted to be his wife."

"Don't tell me you lay at Abe's feet?" Mom said with a gasp.

Ruth shook her head. "Of course not. I did, however, take a seat at the end of the sofa, and his legs were stretched out — one still in a cast."

"What happened?" Martha prompted. "Did you ask him to marry you?"

"I asked if he could think of me as an acceptable wife."

"How did Abe respond?" Mom asked.

"He reminded me that we're ten years apart and said he thought I could find a younger man." Ruth paused and sucked in her bottom lip. "I can't imagine what Abe must have thought about my boldness."

"He must have agreed to marry you, or else you wouldn't be making plans to be married in January," Martha pointed out.

"Our conversation was interrupted when Abe got the news that Willis had fallen in the pond." Ruth sighed deeply. "Some time after Willis's funeral, I found Abe in the barn, offering Gideon comfort because he blamed himself for his brother's death. It was then that Abe finally asked me to marry him."

"I'm sure it was the Lord's timing," Mom said as she turned back to the front of the buggy. "Just as all things are."

"Wasn't that Steven Bates's car I saw going in the opposite direction?" Ruth asked.

Dad grunted. "Jah, and I gave him a friendly wave, but he didn't bother to wave back."

"Maybe he didn't know it was you," Mom said.

"I'm sure he knew who I was, Judith. The man looked right at me as he went past. He never cracked a smile."

Mom said nothing more. Martha figured it was because she knew Dad would only rehash the past if the subject of Steven Bates continued.

Martha's thoughts went to Luke. A couple

of years back when Luke was still working for Dad, some cabinets Steven had ordered for his wife fell off the back of the wagon Luke had used to deliver them. Steven had blamed Dad for it, and Dad put the blame on Luke. Steven had also told Dad that he was done doing business with him. Ever since then, Steven hadn't spoken to Dad. Talking about Steven, the broken cabinets, or Luke always set Dad on edge.

Martha leaned her head against the back of the padded wooden seat. Would God see fit to bring her and Luke together, the way He had Ruth and Martin and then Ruth and Abe? It seemed doubtful, since Dad didn't care for Luke.

The buggy jostled this way and that, and Martha's eyes grew heavy.

Sometime later, the buggy lurched as Dad gave a sharp pull on the reins and guided the horse up their driveway. They drove past Dad's woodworking shop, and then their house came into view.

"Look, Roman," Mom cried. "Someone's thrown eggs all over the side of our house!"

Ruth gasped. "There's a headless scarecrow on our front porch, too!"

Dad halted the horse and jumped down from the buggy. Martha watched as he leaped onto the porch, bent over to study the scarecrow, and plucked something off the scarecrow's shirt. With a grim expression, he marched back to the buggy and waved a piece of paper in the air. "I can't believe it!"

"What is it?" Mom asked, leaning out the opening on her side of the buggy.

He handed her the paper. "This!"

Mom's voice quavered as she read the words: "IT'S NOT OVER YET. BE PREPARED FOR MORE."

CHAPTER 5

Martha sank to the edge of her bed with a moan. For the last few days, Mom had been acting jumpier than usual. Dad hadn't notified the sheriff about the latest vandalism, and he kept saying that Mom was overreacting — that pranksters could have egged the house.

The recent attack had made Martha even more determined to learn who was responsible. Last night, she'd updated the list she'd made of the previous attacks, adding the egging and headless scarecrow.

Since it was Monday and Martha didn't have to work for Irene, she'd decided to go over her list of suspects and try to figure out who might have egged the house. It had to be someone who wasn't at Toby and Sadie's wedding.

During the wedding meal, Martha had spoken to Luke's mother. Betty had mentioned that Luke hadn't come because he'd had to work for John. *Did Luke really work for John on Thursday, or could he have . . . ?*

Martha thumped the side of her head. *It couldn't have been Luke. I don't want it to be him, but I need to know for sure he didn't egg our house or leave the scarecrow on our porch with the threatening note.*

She stared at the notebook in her hand and read the list of suspects:

Luke — upset with Dad for firing him.

Gary Walker — said he would get even with Grace for breaking up with him.

Steven Bates — stopped doing business with Dad and said Dad would be sorry for ruining the cabinets that fell off the wagon and broke.

Bill Collins, the land developer who wanted to buy our land — left the area some time ago but could have hired someone to cause trouble.

Ray Larson — has been using his binoculars to watch our place from his neighboring property and once asked about buying our land.

Martha drew in a deep breath and released it quickly. As much as she didn't want to admit it, Luke *was* a suspect.

She rose from the bed. *The first thing I*

need to do after breakfast is pay a visit to John's woodworking shop and find out from Luke where he was during Toby and Sadie's wedding.

"Do you want me to stain that set of cabinets in the back room?" Luke asked John when he'd finished sanding the legs of a table.

"You'd better wait and do the cabinets after lunch. I've got some deliveries to make, and I'd like you to be near the front of the shop so you can wait on customers and answer any phone calls while I'm gone."

Luke nodded. "I can do that, but wouldn't you like me to get some work done while you're gone?"

John pushed an unruly strand of dark, curly hair off his forehead. "I guess you could finish up sanding that table you've been working on and then do the chairs that go with it. You can do that by the front of the store."

"Sure, no problem."

John clasped Luke's shoulder and gave it a squeeze. "Just want you to know that I'm glad you came to work for me. You're a hard worker, and I appreciate all that you do."

Luke smiled. "Thanks." It made him feel good to know John appreciated him.

"I plan to stop by the bakeshop while I'm in Berlin," John said. "Would you like me to bring you back something?"

"Maybe a lemon-filled doughnut."

John quirked an eyebrow. "Just one?"

Luke chuckled. "Better make that two or three."

John grinned and headed out the door.

As Luke continued sanding, he thought about John and how easy he was to work for compared to Roman. He did wonder, though, why John made most of the deliveries himself. After all, Luke had a driver's license.

Maybe John doesn't trust me as much as I thought. He does know about those cabinets that fell off Roman's wagon a few years back when I was making a delivery to Steven Bates. Maybe he's afraid something like that will happen while I'm working for him. Luke grimaced. He wondered if anyone trusted him these days.

The bell above the shop door jingled, and Luke looked up. His heart skipped a beat as Martha stepped into the room.

"Wie geht's?" he asked with a smile.

"I'm doing okay." She glanced around the room. "Where's Flo? I didn't see her outside anywhere."

"John had some deliveries to make, and

he took the dog along." Luke shook his head. "When you first sold Flo to John, I thought the poor critter would never quit howling, but it didn't take the dog long to warm up to John. Now she's his constant companion."

"As nice as John is, I'm surprised he doesn't have a wife and houseful of kids by now."

"Maybe he hasn't met the right woman yet."

"That could be." Martha moved closer to Luke. "We missed you at Sadie and Toby's wedding last Thursday."

"I had to work that day," he said with a shrug. "How'd the wedding go?"

"It went fine, but I'm sure Toby was disappointed that you weren't there."

"John has a lot of work going right now, and I didn't think I could ask him for the day off." Luke gave the table a few solid swipes. "Besides, I don't think Toby really missed me."

"Why do you say that? You and Toby have been friends since you were little."

"Lately, I've begun to think Toby has it in for me."

Martha's forehead wrinkled. "You really think that?"

Luke nodded. "You heard the way he was

goading me at the pizza place a few weeks ago. It's like he's got an axe to grind or something. Toby's always been very competitive, and whenever I've done anything better than him, he's gotten jealous."

Martha leaned against a workbench. "So you think Toby's trying to make you look bad?"

"I wouldn't put it past him. Toby's gone tattling to his daed more than once in the last few years about something I said or did that he didn't like. If nothing else, I think he's hoping I'll get in trouble with my folks." Luke dropped the sandpaper to the floor and stood. "I wouldn't be a bit surprised if Toby's connected to the attacks in some way and is trying to make it look like I'm the one responsible."

"Do you think Toby's capable of doing something so terrible?"

"I'm not sure, but I do know Toby likes to rattle me, and we can't rule anyone out until we know for sure that they're not involved."

"I agree." Martha moved away from the workbench and took a step closer to Luke. "Which is why I've made a list of suspects."

Luke's interest was piqued. "You've made a list already?"

"Jah. I started working on the list after we had pizza together." She shifted her weight from one foot to the other and stared at the floor. "I added to it after what happened on Thursday."

"What happened on Thursday?"

"You haven't heard?"

He shook his head. "Since yesterday was an off-Sunday from church, I haven't seen anyone who would have told me what's been going on."

Martha frowned. "When we got home from Sadie and Toby's wedding Thursday evening, we discovered someone had egged our house and put a headless scarecrow on the front porch with a note pinned to it."

Luke's eyebrows pulled together. "What'd the note say?"

"It said: IT'S NOT OVER YET. BE PREPARED FOR MORE." Martha's frown deepened as she slowly shook her head. "Mom's been on edge ever since. These attacks have gone on way too long. I don't know how much more any of us can take."

"I'll do whatever I can to help you find out who's responsible," Luke said.

Martha's face relaxed. "I'm relieved to know where you were last Thursday. If my daed suggests you had anything to do with last Thursday's vandalism, I can tell him you were here working for John all day."

Luke grimaced. "Is that why you came

70

here today? To check up on me and see where I was during the wedding? Did you think I'd stayed away from the wedding so I could sneak over to your place and vandalize it? Is that what you thought?"

Martha dropped her gaze to the floor. "I didn't really think that, but I needed to be sure."

He sighed. "I guess everyone's a suspect until proven otherwise, huh?"

"Jah." She reached into the black handbag draped over her shoulder and pulled out a writing tablet. "If you really want to help, how about reading my list of suspects and telling me what you think?"

Luke nodded. "I'd be happy to take a look, but if my name's on the list, I'll have to scratch it off right away!"

As Ruth moved about Abe's kitchen, trying to get breakfast on the table for his family, a feeling of weariness washed over her like a drenching rain. Although she tried to act as if nothing was bothering her when she arrived at Abe's house each morning to help get his children ready for school, she'd felt drained ever since she and her family had gotten home from Sadie and Toby's wedding last Thursday and discovered the vandalism. Each attack reminded her of the tragic event that had taken Martin's life nearly a year ago. Despite her love for Abe and his children, she wasn't sure she would ever completely get over Martin's death.

Ruth shook her head, trying to clear her thoughts. Thanksgiving was only a few days away, and despite the things that had been going on at her folks' place, she really did have a lot to be thankful for.

"Are you feeling all right, Ruth?" Abe asked as he joined her in front of the stove.

"I . . . I'm fine. Just feeling kind of drained this morning."

"Didn't you get enough sleep last night?"

"I slept okay." Ruth sighed as she stirred the eggs around in the pan.

A shadow of worry crossed his face. "Are you still fretting over what happened at your folks' place?"

Ruth nodded as her throat constricted.

Abe touched Ruth's arm, and she shivered when his warm breath tickled her neck. "I'll be glad when we're married. Then you won't have to worry about being vandalized or threatened anymore."

"That's what Martin said before I married him, and look what happened."

Abe's fingers closed gently around her arm. "There are no certainties in this life, Ruth, but we must trust the Lord."

"Jah, I know, and I'm trying to do that, but whenever another attack occurs, my faith begins to waver." Ruth glanced over her shoulder and spotted Esta and Owen staring at her. Abe's family had been through a lot in the last few years, too — first losing Alma when she was struck by lightning and then losing young Willis when he drowned in the pond. "Maybe we should talk about this later," she said, keeping her voice low.

Abe nodded. "You're right. We'll continue this discussion after the kinner have gone to school."

Ruth was tempted to remind Abe that he needed to go to work as soon as he'd finished breakfast, but she figured Ivan would probably open the harness shop if Abe wasn't there right away.

"Papa, I can't wait 'til you marry Ruth," Esta spoke up from her place at the table.

"I'm looking forward to our wedding day, too." Abe gave Ruth's arm a gentle squeeze; then he returned to his seat at the table.

"After you're married, we can all start calling Ruth *Mama,*" Esta said with an enthusiastic nod.

Josh, Owen, and even Abe's youngest child, two-and-a-half-year-old Molly, nod- ded, but Gideon, who'd just turned thirteen, sat staring at his empty plate. Was he unhappy about Ruth marrying his dad, or did the boy have something else on his mind? Ruth was on the verge of asking but changed her mind. If something was bothering Gideon, Abe would deal with it. She wasn't in any frame of mind to deal with anything right now. It had taken all her energy just to show up for work today.

How am I going to handle things once Abe and I are married? Ruth wondered. *Am I really ready to become Abe's wife and mother to his five children?* She drew in a deep breath and tried to focus on the job at hand. She wished she felt free to tell Abe how she felt, but she didn't want him to know the conflicting emotions swirling in her mind. He might not understand her doubts and take them to mean she didn't want to marry him. *I wish Aunt Rosemary were here. She's so easy to talk to and seems to understand me better than anyone.*

No one in Ruth's family had heard anything from Rosemary for the last few weeks, and Ruth had begun to worry that her aunt might not arrive in time for the wedding in January. She gripped the spatula as a feeling of trepidation crept up her spine. *If I don't get some problems resolved in my mind, I'm not sure I can go through with the wedding.*

CHAPTER 6

"Are you getting tired, Ken? I'd be happy to drive for a while if you are," Rosemary said as she leaned over the backseat in her son's minivan and touched his shoulder.

Ken shook his wavy blond head. "I'm fine, Mom." He nodded at his wife sleeping in the seat beside him. "Sharon's the one who's tired."

Rosemary smiled. Her daughter-in-law had fallen asleep soon after they'd left their hotel this morning. Five days of traveling had taken its toll on all of them. She was glad Ken and Sharon had been able to take vacation time from their jobs at the bank in Boise. It would have been a long, lonely trip to Ohio if Rosemary had made it on her own. It had been much more pleasant riding in Ken's minivan and having her own car towed behind the moving van she'd hired to move her things. She looked forward to introducing her son and his wife to her

Amish family, and she was glad they would be able to share Thanksgiving dinner together.

"We should be in Holmes County by late afternoon," Ken announced. "Do you want to go straight to the house you've bought, or do you want to see your brother and his family first?"

"Let's drop by my house to see if the moving van's arrived with my furniture and car, and then we can drive over to Roman's place."

"Sounds like a plan."

Rosemary leaned back in her seat and tried to relax as memories from the past crowded her mind. She'd only been eighteen when she'd left home to try out the English way of life. Then she'd met fun-loving, charismatic Bob, and it had been love at first sight. They'd gotten married soon after and moved to Boise, Idaho. Rosemary had written a letter to her folks, letting them know where she was, but had never gotten a response. She'd written several more letters, but there was no reply. Finally, deciding that her family wanted nothing to do with her, Rosemary had quit writing. It wasn't until shortly before Bob's death that he'd confessed to intercepting those letters and throwing them away so she would have no contact with her Amish family.

Rosemary had always known Bob was the controlling type, but she'd never dreamed he would do anything that would sever the ties with her family in Ohio. It had taken Rosemary several months after Bob's death to come to grips with what he'd done. Once she'd been able to forgive him, she'd made a trip to Ohio in the hope of being reconciled to her family.

Rosemary was anxious to see Roman and his family again and hoped nothing had changed between them while she'd been in Boise getting ready to move to Holmes County permanently. She only wished she'd been able to talk Ken and Sharon into moving there, too. But they both had good jobs at the bank in Boise and didn't want to relocate. Since children were not in their immediate plans, they'd become committed to their careers.

Rosemary leaned closer to Ken. "Are you sure you're okay with the idea of me moving to Ohio? I still feel bad about leaving you and Sharon."

"It's okay, Mom. I want you to be happy. If moving back to your birthplace does that, then you have my blessing."

Rosemary touched his shoulder. "Thank you, Ken. It means a lot to know I have your support."

"Of course," he added with a chuckle, "that doesn't mean I understand your desire to leave the modern world behind and live among the Plain people."

She rapped the back of his head lightly with her knuckles. "I'm not leaving the modern world. I just feel the need to be near my Amish family. They've gone through some rough times lately, and I can't offer my complete support if I'm living in Idaho."

"I understand, Mom." Ken remained silent for a time; then he glanced in the rearview mirror and said, "Are you thinking about becoming Amish again?"

Rosemary pursed her lips. She'd thought about it, but she'd been English too long and didn't think she would feel comfortable wearing plain clothes and driving a horse and buggy again.

"Mom? Does your silence mean you're considering joining the Amish faith?"

"Oh, I don't think so. But I do plan to live a simpler life and keep my focus on God, family, and friends, not all the fancy, modern things the world has to offer."

He shrugged. "You will come to visit us, I hope."

"Of course, and I'd like you and Sharon to come visit me whenever you can, too."

"We'll make a trip to Ohio at least once a year," he said.

Rosemary smiled. She was thankful for her son and glad he hadn't turned out like his father.

Martha had just stepped out of the barn when she saw a minivan pulling into the yard. She didn't recognize the driver, but when the back door of the van opened and Aunt Rosemary stepped out, she knew the driver must be Aunt Rosemary's son.

Martha sprinted across the yard and raced up to the car. "Aunt Rosemary! It's so good to see you!"

Aunt Rosemary held her arms out and gave Martha a hug. "It's good to see you, too, sweet girl."

"We hadn't heard from you in a while and didn't know for sure when you'd be coming."

Aunt Rosemary smiled. "We wanted to surprise you, and I thought it would be nice if we could celebrate Thanksgiving together."

"I'm glad you're here, and I know Mom and Dad will be, too." Martha gave Aunt Rosemary another hug. "Did you have a good trip?"

"Yes, and we saw lots of interesting sights

along the way, which was one of the reasons I suggested we drive rather than fly." Aunt Rosemary motioned to the young man with wavy blond hair, and the woman whose dark brown hair was pulled into a ponytail. "Martha, I'd like you to meet my son, Ken, and his wife, Sharon." Smiling at the couple, she added, "This is my niece Martha. She's Roman's youngest daughter."

Ken was the first to extend his hand. "It's nice to meet you, Martha."

"Same here." Martha shook Ken's hand then turned to his wife. "It's nice to meet you, too."

Sharon smiled, although it appeared to be forced. Her gaze traveled slowly around the yard as though she was scrutinizing everything.

Aunt Rosemary gave Martha's shoulder a gentle squeeze. "How's your kennel business doing?"

"Heidi had another batch of puppies a few weeks ago, and Polly just had a litter of seven pups."

"I always wanted a dog when I was a boy, but my dad never let me." Ken chuckled. "I'm making up for it now, though. Sharon and I own two dogs — a beautiful black Labrador retriever and a frisky cairn terrier."

Martha glanced at the minivan. "Did you bring your dogs along?"

Ken shook his head. "We thought it would be an inconvenience, so we boarded them near our home."

"I'd like to be able to board dogs someday," Martha said wistfully, "but I'm not set up for that yet."

"Are you still working for Irene Schrock, or are the dogs taking up all your time these days?" Aunt Rosemary asked.

"I work for Irene a few days a week. If I ever make enough money with the dogs, I'll probably quit that job." Martha pursed her lips. "Of course Irene would have to find someone to replace me. She's so busy with the dinners she serves tourists these days that there's too much work for her and Carolyn to do by themselves."

"I'm sure she appreciates your help." Aunt Rosemary motioned to the house. "Is the rest of the family at home? We stopped by Roman's shop on the way up the driveway and discovered it was closed."

"It's getting close to supper, so Dad's probably up at the house by now. Mom and Ruth were in the kitchen when I went out to the barn a short time ago." Martha grimaced. "I'll probably get a lecture for taking so long with the dogs and shirking my kitchen duties."

Aunt Rosemary looked at her watch. "I hadn't realized it was almost time for supper. Since we're two hours behind you in Boise, I guess my time's still off."

"No problem. I'm sure the folks will insist on you eating supper with us."

"That would be an imposition. I think we should drive back to Berlin and eat at one of the restaurants there." Sharon's dark eyes darted from Martha, to Ken, and back to Martha again. The young woman was clearly uncomfortable.

"There's no need for that," Martha said with a shake of her head. "Mom always fixes way more than the four of us can eat. Besides, we can visit while we share our meal."

"Judith is a wonderful cook," Aunt Rosemary said. "I think you and Ken will enjoy eating one of her delicious meals — not to mention getting the opportunity to know my brother and his family."

Ken reached for his wife's hand. "Let's go inside and meet everyone, shall we?"

Martha slipped her hand in the crook of Aunt Rosemary's arm. "I'll make the introductions first, and then I'll run up to Grace and Cleon's place and see if they'd like to join us for supper."

"Would you pass me the basket of biscuits, please?" Luke's stomach rumbled as the savory aroma of freshly made stew and biscuits wafted up to his nose. He'd worked hard and felt hungrier than usual.

"I noticed that you didn't get after that wood I asked you to chop this morning," Mom said as she handed him the biscuits.

"I was running late and didn't have time to do it before I left for work."

Mom's eyebrows pressed together. "Is that the truth, or are you giving me another one of your excuses for not getting things done around here?"

Luke shook his head. "It's not an excuse."

"From what I hear, you work hard enough for John Peterson, but around here you tend to slough off," Mom said.

Luke grunted. "Are you saying I'm lazy?"

She slathered a biscuit with butter. "You're not exactly lazy, but you sure don't do what I ask these days. It seems you've always got something else on your mind other than what you're supposed to be doing. You've been kind of moody lately, too. Don't you agree, Elam?"

Luke glanced across the table to gauge his

dad's reaction, but Pop just sat there, dipping a biscuit up and down in his bowl of stew as though he hadn't heard a word that had been said.

Mom leaned closer to Luke and looked him right in the eye. "I think you need to quit fooling around and make a decision about getting baptized and joining the church."

Luke grunted and reached for another biscuit. "I will when I'm ready. In the meantime, I've got a lot on my mind."

Mom squinted at him. "A lot on your mind?"

"Jah."

"What kind of things could be on your mind that would keep you from joining the church?"

"Just things, that's all."

"Maybe he's got some woman on his mind," Pop spoke up.

"A woman?" Mom nudged Pop with her elbow. "If he had a woman on his mind, he'd be more than ready to join the church." She gave a little gasp as she covered her mouth with her hand. "Ach, Luke! Please don't tell me you've found an English girlfriend and she's the reason you haven't joined the church."

Luke's mouth dropped open. " 'Course

not. I don't have any girlfriend, much less one who's English." He hoped his mother didn't press him on this, or he might end up admitting that he had more than a passing interest in Martha Hostettler.

"Whether you've got your eye on any particular woman or not, I think it's past time for you to get baptized and join the church."

Luke opened his mouth to argue the point, but Pop interceded with a raised hand. "And I think it's time we drop this subject, don't you, Betty?"

Mom gave Pop a quick nod, but Luke could see by the look on her face that she was none too happy about it. Fact was, if Pop hadn't put a halt to the conversation, Mom probably would have pestered Luke all the way through supper.

Luke reached for his glass of milk. *If the folks knew I had a truck hidden in the woods and had been hanging around with some rowdy English fellows, I'd probably be in for another lecture.*

"Are we still going to Henry and Luann's house for Thanksgiving?" Luke asked, deciding it was time for a change of subject.

Mom nodded. "Your big brother's looking forward to having us, as well as your four other brothers and their families, over that day."

"Henry's not that much older than me," Luke said with a frown. "How come you referred to him as my 'big brother'?"

"It's just a figure of speech," Pop said before Mom could reply. "Why do you have to be so nitpicky all the time?"

"I wasn't. I was just making a point."

Mom laid a gentle hand on Luke's arm. "Let's not have any more fussing tonight, okay?"

Luke nodded. Tempers had flared and harsh words had been spoken at their supper table more in the last few months than in all of Luke's twenty-two years. If only Mom and Pop would quit pestering him about joining the church. If they'd just let him live his life the way he thought best.

"Have you asked your boss about joining us for our Thanksgiving meal?" Mom asked.

Luke nodded. "I mentioned it to John this morning, but he said he'd made other plans. He'll be out of town until Saturday, so his shop won't be open again until then."

Pop's eyebrows arched upward. "He's single, with no family in the area. What other plans could he have made?"

"I don't know and didn't ask."

Pop grunted. "No wonder you don't have

an *aldi.* You never think of anyone but your-self."

Luke gritted his teeth. Was Pop trying to start another argument by bringing up the fact that he didn't have a girlfriend? "I didn't press John for details because I didn't think it was any of my business."

"Even if John doesn't have other plans for Thanksgiving, he might not feel comfortable with the idea of having dinner with people he doesn't know," Mom said.

Pop reached for his glass of water. "He knows Luke."

"That's true, but he doesn't know us that well."

Luke pushed his chair away from the table and stood. He'd had enough supper conversation.

"Where are you going?" Mom motioned to Luke's half-eaten bowl of stew. "You haven't finished your meal."

"I'm full right up to here." Luke touched his chin. "And I've got somewhere I need to go."

Pop's forehead creased. "And where might that be?"

"I'm going outside to take care of that wood Mom's been after me to chop," Luke said as he grabbed his stocking cap off the wall peg near the back door.

"That can wait until tomorrow," Mom called.

Luke rushed out the door. Even though he was in no hurry to chop wood, it would be better than sitting at the table being nagged at throughout the whole meal.

As the Hostettlers sat around the kitchen table with Aunt Rosemary, her son, and his wife, Ruth couldn't help but notice how uncomfortable Sharon appeared to be. Was she shy, or did she feel out of place sharing a table with a group of people she didn't know?

Everyone else seemed relaxed and happy, as Aunt Rosemary and Dad caught up on each other's lives, and Ken alternated between talking to Martha about her dogs and to Cleon about his bees and honey. Grace juggled the baby on her lap while keeping Anna entertained, and Mom kept trying to engage Sharon in conversation. It felt good to have the whole family together — almost as if everything in their life was normal.

But it's not normal, Ruth thought regretfully. *My family is still under attack by someone who wrote a note reminding us that it's not over yet. To make matters worse, I'm having doubts about whether I should marry*

Abe or not.

"If our Thanksgiving meal is anything like this meal, then I sure have something to look forward to," Ken said as he took another helping of chicken potpie.

"We'll be eating at Grace and Cleon's place on Thanksgiving, and Grace is a fine cook," Mom said. "I'm sure you'll enjoy every bite."

Grace smiled as her cheeks turned pink. "I won't be the only one cooking that day, Mom. You'll be furnishing the pies."

Mom nodded. "Ruth's planning to make a fruit salad, and Martha will bring some of those sweet potato biscuits Irene taught her to make."

Ken patted his stomach. "Sounds good to me." He looked over at Ruth and smiled. "I understand you'll be getting married in January."

"That's right — the second Thursday," Ruth replied.

"I'll bet you're getting excited already," Sharon spoke up.

Ruth nodded and forced a smile.

Aunt Rosemary reached over and touched Ruth's arm. "If you're like most brides, you're probably feeling a few prewedding jitters."

"She's got nothing to be nervous about,"

Dad put in from his place at the head of the table. "Ruth's marrying the finest man in these parts. I'm sure they'll have a real good marriage."

"Yes," Aunt Rosemary said before Ruth could respond, "but that doesn't mean she's not feeling a bit nervous." She leaned close to Ruth and whispered, "As soon as we've finished supper and the dishes are done, how about the two of us having a little heart-to-heart chat?"

Ruth nodded as a sense of relief flooded her soul. If anyone could help her deal with the unsettled feelings swirling around in her head, it was Aunt Rosemary.

As Rosemary stood at the kitchen sink, doing the dishes after supper, she thought about how quiet Sharon had been during the meal and wondered how she was getting along in the living room with Grace and Judith. The men and Martha had gone out to the barn, and at Ruth's suggestion, she and Rosemary had become the designated dishwashers.

"Are you ready for that talk now?" Rosemary asked Ruth. "Or would you rather wait until we're done with the dishes?"

Ruth reached for a clean plate to dry. "We can talk while we work, if you like."

"I could tell by the way you responded when Sharon asked about your upcoming wedding that things aren't quite as they should be."

"No. No, they're not."

Rosemary sloshed the dishrag along the edge of the glass and waited to see if Ruth would continue. After a few minutes, Ruth spoke again.

"I love Abe, and I want to be his wife, but I'm not sure I'm ready to get married again."

"Is it because you still love your first husband?"

Tears pooled in Ruth's eyes. "There will always be a place in my heart for Martin, but there's more to what I'm feeling than that."

"Is there a problem with Abe's children? They've all accepted you, right?"

"All but Gideon. He's been so moody and unpredictable lately. I can't be sure what he's thinking."

"He's probably struggling with the idea of someone moving into their home and taking over the role of his mother."

"But I've been working as Abe's *maad* for some time."

"Even so, a maid's not the same as a new wife for Gideon's father."

"True." Ruth's gaze dropped to the floor.

"Is there something else troubling you?"

"Jah. I'm afraid for my family. We're still being attacked, Aunt Rosemary. The last act of vandalism included a threatening note." Ruth drew in a shuddering breath. "Abe thinks I'll be safe living at his place, but even if I am, I'll still be worried about my family. What if the attacks get worse? What if —"

Rosemary lifted her hand from the soapy water. "You mustn't borrow trouble."

More tears filled Ruth's eyes. "But you know what happened to Martin and me. The attacker rammed us off the road, and —"

Rosemary shook her head. "You don't know that the person who rammed your buggy is the same one responsible for the attacks against your family."

"I — I don't know it for a fact, but I feel it in my heart."

"Worrying about your family won't solve a thing." Rosemary dried her hands on a clean towel and touched Ruth's shoulder. "Your folks wouldn't want you to set your happiness aside and continue living here just because you're worried about their safety. If something's going to happen, it will happen whether you're living here or not."

"I suppose you're right."

"Was the sheriff notified after the last attack?"

"No."

"Why not?"

"Dad didn't think it was necessary. He thinks if the sheriff really wanted to put a stop to the attacks, he would see that the area is patrolled more often."

"After I get settled into my new home, I might pay a call on Sheriff Osborn. In the meantime, I want you to commit everything to God and start counting the days until your wedding."

Ruth gave Rosemary a hug. "It's real good to have you back, Aunt Rosemary."

"Thanks. It's good to be here."

CHAPTER 7

As Luke crawled out of bed on Thanksgiving morning, a wave of nausea hit him with the force of a speeding horse. He groaned and clutched his stomach. They were supposed to have dinner at his brother Henry's home, but the thought of eating all that Thanksgiving food made him feel even worse.

Another wave of nausea came, and Luke dashed into the bathroom just in time to empty his stomach. When he stepped out several minutes later, his stomach lurched again at the smoky odor of bacon coming from the kitchen. He felt light-headed, and his legs trembled so badly he could barely stand. He inched his way down the hall to the kitchen. "Have you got a bucket I can use?" he asked his mother, who was at the stove.

"What do you need a bucket for?" she asked over her shoulder.

"I'm grank, and I don't think my shaky legs will keep taking me to the bathroom."

Mom whirled around. "Ach, Luke, you must be sick. Why, your face is paler than a bucket of goat's milk!" She quickly pulled out a chair at the table. "You'd better sit down."

He grasped the back of the chair and shook his head. "I — I just need a bucket so I can go back to my room."

"I'll get one right away." Mom opened the door to the utility closet and handed Luke the bucket she used for mopping floors. "Do you think you've got the flu?"

Luke grimaced. "Sure looks like it. Either that or I've got a bad case of food poisoning. Even the thought of food makes my stomach churn."

"I don't think it could be food poisoning," Mom said. "You ate the same thing your daed and I ate for supper last night, and neither of us feels sick."

"John and I had lunch in town yesterday," Luke said. "It could have been something I ate there."

Mom slowly shook her head. "I'm sorry you're not feeling well. Guess you won't be up to going with us to Henry's this afternoon."

"No, I just want to go back to bed."

Another wave of dizziness hit Luke, and he closed his eyes.

"Your daed's out in the barn right now." Mom slipped her arm around Luke's waist. "I'd better help you back to your room."

Luke didn't argue. He felt too weak to resist. Clinging to the bucket with one hand and holding onto Mom's arm with the other, he made his way upstairs. There would be no turkey and pumpkin pie for him today. All he wanted to do was crawl back in bed and sleep until he felt better.

"If everything looks as good as it smells, I think we're in for a real treat," Ken said as everyone gathered around Grace and Cleon's table.

"I'm glad you and Sharon could join us," Grace said with a smile. "It's always nice when family can be together for a special holiday." She glanced over at Cleon. "I wish your folks could have joined us today, too, but by the time I invited them, your mamm had already planned a big Thanksgiving dinner and invited your brothers and sisters to join them."

Cleon nodded. "I think she would have liked it if we could have been there, too, but we'd already made plans to have your family here."

Grace knew Cleon wasn't trying to make her feel guilty. He was just stating facts. She looked down the long table to where Abe sat with his children and smiled. Having them here would make the day go easier for Ruth. Last Thanksgiving, Martin had still been alive. Despite the fact that Ruth would soon be marrying Abe, Grace figured her widowed sister was probably feeling some sorrow and regret today.

"Now that everyone's seated, let us bow for silent prayer," Dad said.

All heads bowed, and Grace offered her private prayer. *Heavenly Father, bless our family this day, bless the food we're about to eat, and help us to remember to trust You as we face each new day. Amen.*

Dear Lord, Martha silently prayed, *bless this food, bless my family, and help me find out who's responsible for the attacks that have been made against my family.*

When she ended her prayer and looked at the faces around the table, a lump formed in her throat. *If only things could be as peaceful and joyous every day as they are today. If only we no longer had to worry about being under attack.*

"Martha, would you please get the potatoes going?" Mom asked when everyone had opened their eyes.

"Jah, sure." Martha reached for the bowl of mashed potatoes and passed it to Sharon, who sat to her right.

"Danki."

Martha's mouth dropped open. "I'm impressed. You've only been here a couple of days, and already you know how we say thank you."

"Rosemary taught us a few simple words on the drive here from Idaho," Sharon explained.

"I'm surprised she remembered any German-Dutch," Dad spoke up from his seat at the head of the table. "It's been so long since she spoke our language."

Aunt Rosemary's cheeks turned pink. "I may not be able to speak it as fluently as I did when I was a girl, but the language of my youth has never left me."

Martha shifted uneasily in her chair. Was Dad trying to embarrass Aunt Rosemary? If so, it made no sense; the two of them had made their peace several months ago.

As if sensing her discomfort, Dad leaned closer to Rosemary and said, "I wasn't trying to embarrass you, sister. I was just surprised, that's all."

She smiled and patted his arm. "Pleasantly, I hope."

He nodded. "You never cease to surprise me."

Martha breathed a sigh of relief. She was glad things were still okay between Dad and Aunt Rosemary.

"Gemaeschde grummbiere," Ruth said when Sharon handed the bowl of potatoes to her.

Sharon tipped her head. "What was that?"

Ruth pointed to the potatoes. "Gemaeschde grummbiere — mashed potatoes."

Abe's youngest daughter, Molly, who sat beside Ruth in a high chair, bobbed her head up and down. *"Es bescht."*

Ruth nodded. "Jah, mashed potatoes are the best."

Abe, sitting on the other side of Molly, spoke up. "If there's one thing my little girl likes, it's potatoes."

"I like 'em, too, Papa," nine-year-old Esta said. "So does Owen and Josh." She looked over at her older brother, Gideon, and frowned. "I ain't so sure 'bout him, though. Gideon don't like much of anything these days."

"It's 'I'm not' not 'I ain't,' Esta," Abe said. "And let's not get anything started between you and your *bruder* right now."

"Argumentative kids — that's one of the reasons my wife and I have decided not to have any children," Ken said with a shake of his head. "I don't think either of us has the patience for it."

"Raising children isn't just about dealing with arguments," Mom said. "It's a joy to watch your children grow up." She patted Martha's hand. "I wouldn't trade being a mother for anything."

A lump formed in Ruth's throat. She had wanted to be a mother for such a long time, but the tragic accident that had claimed Martin's life and left her unable to have any children of her own had ended those hopes. She glanced at Abe out of the corner of her eye and realized he was smiling at her. *Thank You, Lord, for bringing this kind man into my life. Thank You for giving me the chance to be a mudder to Abe's special kinner.*

As the family continued to eat their Thanksgiving meal, they talked about the beautiful fall weather they'd been having, Martha's dog venture, Cleon's bee business, Dad's woodworking shop, and Ruth's upcoming wedding.

Finally, pushing his empty plate away from him, Dad announced, "Now that we've eaten such a good meal, I think we should take turns saying what we're thankful for. I'll get things started by going first." He leaned back in his chair. "I'm thankful we're all in good health and able to be together today. God has walked by our side this past year, and I think our faith has been strengthened, despite the attacks against us." He nodded at Mom. "Judith, why don't you go next?"

Mom smiled and had just opened her mouth to speak, when — *ka-boom!* — an earth-shattering noise from outside rattled the windows.

Everyone jumped up and rushed out the door.

As they started down the driveway, Ruth saw smoke and flames shooting into the air.

"It's my shop!" Dad hollered. "It's been blown to bits!"

CHAPTER 8

Martha ran down the driveway after the men. Her heart leaped into her throat when she saw what was left of Dad's shop. Pieces of wood and burning debris lay everywhere.

"Someone, run to the phone shed and call 911!" Dad shouted as he, Cleon, Abe, and Ken raced for the two hoses connected to the water faucet near his shop.

"I'll call on my cell phone," Ken hollered.

Martha glanced around the yard, hoping to spot the person who had done this horrible deed. Except for her family and their Thanksgiving guests, who were now all gathered on Mom and Dad's front porch wearing stunned expressions, she saw no one in sight. Whoever had blown up Dad's shop had taken a chance doing it in broad daylight.

Martha's heart nearly stopped beating. No. The person responsible for this attack must have known they were having their meal at Cleon and Grace's place.

"Oh, dear Lord," Martha said, "how can this be happening to us?"

Grace and Ruth joined her on the lawn, but Mom remained on the porch with Sharon and the children.

"I . . . I can't believe this." Ruth's voice quavered, and her eyes widened with obvious fear. "Must we let these attacks keep going on until someone else is hurt?"

Martha put her arm around Ruth's waist. "Ken's called 911. I'm sure the sheriff will be here soon. Once he finds out what's happened, he'll hopefully try to find out who's responsible for blowing up Dad's shop."

Ray and Donna Larson dashed into the yard just then. "We heard an explosion and saw smoke and flames coming from your place!" Ray shouted. "I phoned the fire department right away!"

"My cousin phoned them, too, for all the good it will do," Martha said with a shake of her head. "Dad's shop is gone."

Ray turned to Donna. "You stay here with the women. I'd better go see if I can lend Roman a hand."

"I don't know what Dad's going to do without his shop," Ruth said to no one in particular. "How's he going to earn a living with no place to do his woodworking?"

"Maybe he'll decide to move," Donna spoke up. "I'd certainly encourage Ray to move if something like this happened to us."

"Dad will never move," Grace was quick to say.

Martha couldn't stand there and listen to the women's conversation any longer. She needed to see how things were going with the men. With a quick, "I'll be back," she sprinted down the driveway. Halfway to the shop, she heard sirens blaring in the distance. A few minutes later, two fire trucks pulled in, with Sheriff Osborn's car and John Peterson's rig right behind them.

The next few days went by in a blur. As upset as Roman was over losing his shop, he took comfort in knowing no one had been hurt. He'd been overwhelmed when his friends and family had rallied around, offering supplies and money so he could start up his business again. With winter around the corner, he'd decided to temporarily use one section of the barn as his shop and to rebuild in the spring. The sheriff had promised to do a thorough investigation and said he would keep a closer watch on the Hostettlers' place.

"I hope he means it this time," Roman mumbled as he headed for the barn on

Saturday morning. The sheriff had made that promise before, but had he? *No!* He'd used the excuse that he was either too busy or couldn't spare the men to patrol the area regularly. Roman had begun to think the sheriff didn't care. But when he'd shown up on Thanksgiving Day, he'd acted genuinely concerned — even said he was thankful no one had gotten hurt.

When the attacks had first begun, Roman hadn't wanted to involve the sheriff. He'd figured they'd been random acts by rowdy kids looking for a good time. But as the attacks continued, he'd become more concerned. Of course he hadn't told Judith or his daughters the way he really felt. He was trying to set an example — show them how strong his faith was and that he was trusting God to protect them. Despite Roman's resolve to remain strong, his nerves were beginning to wear, and Judith's were, as well. Since Thanksgiving, she'd had trouble sleeping. She'd also been acting jittery as a June bug. He wondered how much more she could take.

Roman glanced at the field behind their place. The cows and horses grazed peacefully, basking in the early morning sun. A few dried-up wildflowers lined the fence, and birds chirped from the trees.

If only life could be calm and undisturbed like the scene set before me, he thought regretfully. *If we could just put the past behind and forget about all the frightening things that have been done to us.* He grunted. *Guess that won't happen until this horrible nightmare ends — if it ever does.*

As Roman stepped into the barn, two pigeons that had been roosting in the hayloft swooped down and landed on the floor. His heart leaped into his throat, and he jumped back. *Get a grip,* he told himself. *You can't let every little noise set you off.*

He moved to the nearest shelf, grabbed a book of matches, and lit a lantern. *I just need to continue to pray and seek God's direction.*

As Rosemary stood in her driveway, saying good-bye to Ken and Sharon, a lump formed in her throat. Moving away from her only son was harder than she'd thought it would be. Even so, her place was here in Holmes County right now. Her Amish family needed her more than ever.

"I wish you'd forget about staying here and come home with us," Ken said with a worried expression. "I'm concerned for your safety, Mom."

"I'll be fine," she assured him. "The attacks have only been made on the Hostet-tlers, not me. Besides, I'm trusting God to protect me."

Sharon slowly shook her head. "Look where trusting God's gotten the Hostet-tlers."

Rosemary clasped her daughter-in-law's hand. "There are times when it seems as if God has abandoned us, but that's when we need to draw closer to Him."

Ken nodded as he put his arm around Rosemary. "You're right, Mom. It won't be easy not to worry about you, but if you're determined to stay here, then Sharon and I will remember to pray every day — for you and for your Amish family."

Rosemary smiled as tears clouded her vision. "I'll be praying for you and Sharon, too."

Ken looked over at Sharon. "If you're ready, I guess we'd better hit the road."

She nodded. "I'm ready."

Rosemary gave them both another hug, and as their vehicle pulled out of her drive-way, she heard a cow's mournful *moo* in the distance. A sense of unease tightened her stomach. Did she really have the faith to believe everything would be all right?

Proverbs 29:25 popped into her mind: *"The fear of man bringeth a snare: but whoso putteth his trust in the* L<small>ORD</small> *shall be safe."*

She drew in a deep breath and closed her eyes. "Help us all to trust You completely, Lord."

Luke stepped into John's woodworking shop on Saturday morning and found John on his knees, sanding the underside of an old chair. "Hard at work already, huh?"

John looked up and smiled. "Since we didn't work on Thursday or Friday, I thought I'd better get an early start today."

"Which is why I'm here fifteen minutes sooner than you told me to be. I figured you'd want to make the most of our day." Luke removed his jacket and stocking cap and hung them on the coat tree. "What would you like me to do first?"

"Why don't you get those stained?" John motioned to a set of cabinets on the other side of the room. "There's a new bed-and-breakfast opening in Sugarcreek in a few weeks, and they'd like the cabinets done by the first of next week."

"I'll get right on it," Luke said as he got out a can of walnut stain.

They worked in silence for a time; then Luke looked over at John and said, "You're doing a nice job on that chair."

"Guess it comes from years of practice."

"You're not that old. I doubt you could have been doing woodworking all that long," Luke said as he dipped his brush in the can of stain.

"I started working part-time for a carpenter out in Oregon when I was sixteen. By the time I'd turned eighteen, I was working full-time." He grunted. "Of course I didn't really have much choice, since my stepdad had died, leaving Mom and me to fend for ourselves."

"Does your mother live in Oregon?"

"She did, but she died a few years after Harold, my stepdad, did."

"What about your real dad? Is he still living?"

John shook his head. "He died when I was two. I don't even remember him." He grabbed another piece of the sandpaper and started working on the chair legs.

"Do you have any brothers or sisters?"

"Nope."

"What about grandparents, aunts, uncles, or cousins?"

John stood and arched his back. "Can we talk about something else? Family — or the lack of it — is not my favorite topic of conversation."

"Sure, no problem." Luke was surprised John had told him as much as he had. In all the time he'd been working here, John hadn't told him much more than the fact that he was single and had no family living in the area. Hearing John's story made Luke realize those in his Amish community weren't the only ones who suffered hurts and disappointments. It also made him appreciate the family he had.

"Did you hear what happened at the Hostettlers' place on Thanksgiving?" John asked.

"I spent Thursday and Friday in bed with the flu, so I haven't heard much of anything. What happened at the Hostettlers'?"

"Roman's shop was blown up."

Luke's mouth dropped open. "Are you sure about that?"

John nodded. "I saw the fire trucks speeding down the road on my way home Thanksgiving night. When they turned in at the Hostettlers', I followed to see what had happened."

"I thought you were going out of town and weren't planning to be back until Friday night."

"My plans changed, so I had Thanksgiving dinner at a restaurant in New Philadelphia and headed for home soon after that."

"And you say Roman's shop was blown up?"

"Yep. From what I heard, they'd just finished eating their Thanksgiving meal when the big bang occurred." John's forehead wrinkled. "You should have seen the mess it made. There was nothing left of Roman's shop, and he lost all his woodworking tools and everything else in that explosion."

"That's terrible. Was it an accident, or do they think it was another attack?"

"The sheriff and the fire marshal said they would conduct an investigation. From what I heard, it sounded like they think there was foul play involved."

Luke slowly shook his head. "What's Roman going to do? I mean, without his woodworking business, how's he going to support his family?"

"I asked him about that, and he said he planned to work out of his barn until he can build another shop. I'm planning to go over there later today and give Roman a few tools. I'm sure he'll get some help from some of the families in his community, too."

Luke nodded. Whenever anyone in their community had a need, everyone always rallied. He just wished he felt free to offer his help, as well. Unfortunately, any help he might offer Roman would be flatly refused.

"I can't believe the kind of luck the

Hostettlers have had," John said. "It sure seems like someone's out to get them, doesn't it?"

Luke nodded. *I may not be able to help Roman, but I can help Martha try to figure out who's responsible for blowing up her daed's shop.*

CHAPTER 9

Clutching a flashlight, Martha tiptoed out of her room. She took the steps slowly, being careful not to wake Mom, Dad, or Ruth. The last thing she needed was for one of them to see her sneaking outside to search for clues. She'd been planning to do this on Friday evening but had been so tired she'd fallen asleep and hadn't woken up until morning. This was the first chance she'd had to really look things over, and she hoped she might find one or two clues — anything to learn who had blown up Dad's shop.

When Martha reached the bottom of the steps, she grabbed her jacket from the wall peg and slipped out the back door. As she stepped into the yard, the cold night air jabbed at her skin. Winter would be here soon.

As she passed the barn, the sour, pungent aroma of horse manure wafted up to her nose. Dad would probably clean the horse stalls sometime tomorrow. Otherwise, he'd never be able to work in the barn.

The gravel under Martha's feet crunched as she headed down the driveway, using her flashlight to illuminate the way. A quiver of expectation crept up her spine. Would she find anything in the rubble left from Dad's shop that might give her some clue as to who had done this horrible thing? Maybe the sheriff and fire marshal had missed something.

As Martha approached the spot, she lifted the flashlight and rotated it from side to side, letting the light shine all around. She kicked at a charred piece of wood with the toe of her sneaker and groaned. "I'll never find anything in this mess."

"Probably not, and you shouldn't be out here alone in the dark."

Martha whirled around, her heart pounding against her rib cage. "Luke! You scared me half to death! What are you doing here, anyway?"

"Same as you. I came to look for some clues." He lifted the flashlight he had in his hands.

"I guess you heard what happened here on Thanksgiving then."

"When I got to work this morning, John

told me about your daed's shop being blown up."

She nodded. "John stopped here soon after the fire trucks arrived. He said he'd seen them racing down the street and followed them when he realized where they were headed."

"John's going to give your daed some of his extra tools. Said he couldn't believe the kind of luck your folks have been having."

"I wouldn't call it luck." Martha frowned. "I'd say it's more of a curse than anything."

"So have you found anything in this mess?" Luke asked, shining his light on the rubble.

She shook her head. "But then, I haven't been here very long."

"Was the sheriff called this time?"

"Jah. Both he and the fire marshal came over on Friday morning and checked around. They concluded that Dad's air compressor must have blown up."

"What'd your daed say about that?"

"Dad said he's sure he didn't leave the compressor running when he closed his shop the night before. He couldn't figure how the power could have been turned on. He's sure someone broke into his shop and tampered with the compressor so it would blow up."

"If the sheriff and the fire marshal didn't find anything helpful, what makes you think you will?" Luke asked.

Martha resisted the urge to scream. Didn't Luke think she was smart enough to figure anything out? "Do I look stupid?" she asked a bit too sharply.

"Sorry. I was out of line for making it sound as if I thought you were *dumm.*" He stepped closer to her. "I don't think that, Martha. I think you're one of the smartest, bravest women I know. I'm just worried about you, that's all. It's not safe for you to be out here in the middle of the night, searching for clues." He made a sweeping gesture of the debris with his flashlight. "What if whoever did this came back tonight and found you out here alone?"

Martha smiled. Luke obviously cared for her, if only as a friend, or he wouldn't seem so upset about finding her here. "I told you before that I was going to do some investigating," she said. "This was the first chance I've had to come out here and look around."

"I can't believe anyone would do this to your daed's shop." Luke slowly shook his head. "These attacks have gone on so long it's almost unreal. Seems by now someone would have caught the culprit in the act of doing at least one of these things, doesn't it?"

She nodded. "Dad thinks our faith is being tested. He said the other night that being afraid of what people might do to us is unnecessary if we trust in God."

"I don't think that means we should sit back and let these kinds of things happen without trying to put a stop to them."

"That's why I want to find out who's responsible for doing this."

"Have you looked for footprints?" Luke asked.

"No, but the sheriff did. He said since our driveway and the parking lot by Dad's shop are graveled, no prints showed."

"How does he know the attacker came up the driveway?" Luke turned toward the field closest to them — the one separating their property from the Larsons'. "Maybe we should search for clues farther away from your daed's shop. Whoever did this might have come onto your property that way and left some clues."

Martha shined her flashlight in that direction. "Do you really think so?"

"It's worth looking, don't you think?"

"I suppose it is."

"Then let's head over there and see what we can see."

■ ■ ■ ■

Luke led the way as they trudged through the field, shining their flashlights in every direction.

"This would be a whole lot easier in the light of day," he mumbled. "If there *was* any evidence, we could step right over it and not even know."

"I know, but I feel led to keep looking for a while."

Luke moved on, continuing to shine his light. Suddenly, he came to a halt.

"What is it, Luke? Why'd you stop?"

"Look here." He bent down and picked up a wrench. "I'm guessing the person who blew up your daed's shop might have used this to damage the valve on the air compressor so it wouldn't release the pressure, which would cause it to blow sky high."

"We'd better take the wrench to the sheriff so he can check for fingerprints."

A cold sweat trickled down Luke's back as he shook his head. "That's not a good idea, Martha."

"Why not?"

He shined the light on the wrench. "Now that I foolishly picked this up, my fingerprints are on it. If anyone else's prints were on the wrench, now they're all messed up."

In the soft glow of the moonlight, Luke saw Martha tremble. He took a step back, resisting the desire to pull her into his arms. "Any idea what we should do with the wrench?"

"I suppose I could hide it somewhere — at least until we've had time to do more investigating."

A sense of relief flooded his soul. "I think that's a good idea — unless you'd rather I take the wrench home with me."

She shook her head. "I'll find a place to hide it."

Luke handed the wrench over to her. "Guess I'd better get on home. My daed gets up early to milk the cows, and if he goes to my room looking for help and discovers I'm not there, he'll have a conniption."

"I need to get back up to my room, too." Martha turned toward her house but whirled back around. "You wouldn't have blown up my daed's shop, would you, Luke?"

"Of course not! I can't believe you would even ask me that question." A sense of irritation tinged his voice. "I thought by now you had figured out that I was innocent and wanted to help you find out who's behind the attacks so we can keep your family safe and clear my name."

"I'm sorry, Luke. I'm just feeling confused and a little bit scared right now."

Throwing caution to the wind, Luke stepped forward and pulled Martha into his arms. "You don't have to be scared when you're with me," he murmured against the top of her head.

Martha leaned heavily against Luke's chest, and the nearness of her was almost his undoing. He wanted to tell Martha how much he'd come to care for her. He wanted to ask if he could court her. But it was too soon for that. He needed to clear his name before he could declare his intentions.

Slowly, Martha pulled away. "I'd better go now. Good night." She hurried off before Luke could find his voice.

Boom! Boom!

Roman bolted upright in bed. *That sounds like gunfire. Is someone hunting nearby?* He had posted NO HUNTING signs on his property several weeks ago, so surely whoever was hunting couldn't be too close.

Boom! Boom! Boom! More gunfire in rapid succession.

"Roman, that sounded like gunfire!" Judith exclaimed.

"I know, and I think it's real close." Roman scrambled out of bed and slipped into his trousers.

"Where are you going?"

"Outside, to see what's up."

Judith scrambled out of bed and raced to the window. "It's not even fully light."

"It's light enough for me to see, and I'm going to check things out. If someone's hunting on our property, I'll run 'em off."

Judith clutched his arm. "But they've got a gun. What if they're not hunters at all? What if —"

He held up his hand to silence her. "I'll be okay, Judith."

She grimaced, a look of desperation on her face. "How can you be so sure?"

"There are no certainties in life, but as Christians, we're supposed to trust God to take care of us."

"That doesn't mean we should put ourselves in danger foolishly."

"There's nothing foolish about a man going out to see if someone's hunting on his property." Roman slipped into his boots then turned to face her. "I'll be back in a few minutes. While I'm gone, why don't you get breakfast started?"

"I won't be able to fix breakfast until you're back in the house and I know everything's all right."

He patted her shoulder. "I'll be fine; you'll see."

When Roman stepped outside a few minutes later, he was greeted by the chattering of squirrels eating from one of the bird feeders. He listened for more gunfire but heard none. Apparently, the shooter had either bagged a deer or moved on.

Just to be sure everything was okay, he decided to walk the fence line. He started with the fence closest to the house and moved on back. When he came to the pasture where he kept his beef cows, he halted. Five of them lay dead! That gunfire hadn't been from a hunter at all. Someone had deliberately shot his cows!

Martha groaned and rolled over in bed. She'd been dreaming about someone shooting a gun and chasing after Luke. She rubbed her forehead, trying to clear her mind. It hadn't been a dream. She'd heard a gun go off; she was sure of it.

Martha scrambled out of bed and raced over to the window. Someone stood in the pasture where Dad's beef cows were kept. She squinted against the early morning light. It looked like Dad, and he seemed to be bent over something. Alarm rose in her chest. Had someone been shot?

She slipped into her sneakers, threw on her robe, and dashed from the room. She met Mom in the hallway at the bottom of the stairs. "What's going on? I thought I heard a gun go off, and when I looked out the window, I saw Dad in the pasture."

"It was gunfire," Mom said. "Your daed thought someone might be hunting on our property. Against my wishes, he went outside to check on things."

Martha raced out the back door, tore across the yard, and headed straight for the pasture. She found Dad kneeling in front of a cow. He looked up and slowly shook his head. "It's been shot dead, along with four others."

Martha gasped then covered her mouth with her hand, horrified. It was bad enough that five of Dad's prized cows were dead. What if whoever had shot the cows had been lurking in the field last night when she and Luke had been looking for clues? If the shooter had discovered them, their lives could have been in danger.

CHAPTER 10

Martha touched her father's trembling shoulders. "Why would someone want to shoot your cows?"

"Why would they have done any of these terrible things to us?" He slowly shook his head. "Someone's got a grudge against me. The question is who?"

A shiver shot through Martha's body. She rubbed her hands briskly over her arms and drew in a deep breath. Luke had a grudge against Dad — or at least, Dad thought he did. If she told Dad about Luke being here last night and that the two of them had been looking for clues, would he believe her? Or would Dad think Luke had been skulking around, waiting to attack?

"Will you let the sheriff know about this?" Martha asked.

He grunted. "Wouldn't have to if he'd been doing his job better. After what happened to my shop on Thanksgiving, I figured he'd be keeping a close watch on our place like he said he would."

"The sheriff can't be everywhere at once."

"Maybe not, but he's got deputies working for him. You'd think with my shop being blown to bits just a couple of days ago, someone would at least have been keeping an eye on our place. Every morning when I get out of bed, I ask myself, 'What will this day bring?' And each time there's another attack, I try to keep the faith, but it's getting harder to believe the attacks will ever come to an end."

Martha cringed when she heard the anger and pain in her father's voice. Despite his resolve to remain hopeful that the attacks would stop, he was obviously feeling discouraged. If only she could say something to make him feel better. If she could just do something to solve the mystery of who was behind these horrible attacks.

"Was is letz do?" Mom asked breathlessly as she stepped up to Martha.

"I'll tell you what's wrong here — someone's shot five of my beef cows!" Deep lines etched Dad's forehead, and his clenched jaw revealed the extent of his despair.

Mom gasped as she stared at the cows lying in the pasture. "Ach! Roman, why would anyone do such a terrible thing?"

He rose to his feet. "You know why, Judith. Someone's got an axe to grind against me."

"You don't know that," she said with a shake of her head. "This might have been done by that reporter fellow. Grace still thinks he came to Holmes County in order to make her pay for breaking up with him when she was going through rumschpringe."

"I don't think so. If it was Gary Walker, and he was only after Grace, then only she would have been attacked." Dad touched Mom's arm. "Think about it. Most of the attacks have been done to our property, not hers."

"But some were done to Grace," Martha spoke up. "Don't forget about her and Cleon's house being burned."

"That's true, but most of the attacks have been done here." He motioned to the dead cows. "Guess I'd better notify the sheriff about this mess, and then I'm going to see if some of our friends and neighbors will help me cut and process these critters so I can share with others. No point in all this good meat going to waste."

Mom turned toward the house, her shoulders slumped. "I'll be in the kitchen fixing breakfast."

Martha looked at Dad. "Do you need my

help, or should I go up to the house with Mom?"

"There's not much you can do here," he replied. "You may as well help your mamm."

Martha nodded and hurried off. She stopped by the barn to check on her dogs. Finding them to be okay, she went straight to the house.

When she stepped into the kitchen, the savory aroma of sizzling bacon filled the room. Ruth was busy setting the table, and Mom stood in front of the stove.

"What can I do to help?" Martha asked.

Mom turned, and her hand trembled as she pushed a wayward strand of hair away from her face. "If you'd like to get out some eggs and scramble them in a bowl, it would be much appreciated."

Martha nodded. "Jah, sure, I can do that."

Steam rose from the whistling teakettle, and the heat of the kitchen brought a film of perspiration to Mom's flushed cheeks. She turned back to the stove and turned the bacon.

As Martha headed to the refrigerator, Ruth stepped up to her and whispered, "Mom told me what happened to Dad's cows. She's really upset about this."

"There's no need to whisper," Mom said, "and you needn't talk about me behind my back. I'm not going to fall apart, if that's what you're worried about."

Ruth looked at Martha and shrugged her shoulders. Martha gave a slow nod. She knew her sister was probably thinking the same thing she was: that despite Mom's denial, she was definitely not herself.

"You look like you could have used a few more hours sleep last night," John said when Luke entered the shop, yawning. "What'd you do — stay up all night counting sheep?"

Luke couldn't tell John he'd been over at Roman's place in the middle of the night searching for clues, so he merely shrugged and said, "Yeah, something like that."

John stretched his arms over his head and yawned. "Just looking at your bloodshot eyes and dark circles makes me feel tired."

Luke snorted as he plucked off his stocking cap. "I don't think I look all that bad."

"Well, as long as you can give me a fair day's work, I don't care what you look like." John motioned to the rocking chair he'd been working on. "Speaking of work, I'd like you to go in the back room and get some coffee going while I get back to work on this old gem."

Luke nodded and headed for the back room. He was happy working here and didn't mind when John asked him to do the grunt work. At least John didn't yell at him the way Roman used to.

Luke got the coffeemaker going and thought about the night's activities while he waited for the coffee to brew. *I wonder what Martha did with that wrench we found. It was sure stupid of me to pick it up. I wonder if Martha will keep her promise and not tell anyone about the wrench.*

As Martha entered the barn to get her horse ready to go to Irene's that afternoon, she looked up at the hayloft and thought about the wrench she'd hidden there. Had she been right to agree not to tell anyone about it? The wrench did have Luke's fingerprints on it.

Could Luke have tampered with Dad's compressor and dropped the wrench in the field as he was fleeing? Was that why he'd picked it up and made such an issue of his fingerprints being on it?

Martha remembered the expression on Luke's face when she'd asked if he would have blown up Dad's shop. He'd looked at her as if she'd asked if he would consider lighting his own house on fire.

She grimaced. What was there about Luke that made her emotions so unstable? Trust one minute, confusion and mistrust the next. She had to make up her mind whether she trusted him or not. She couldn't keep changing her mind like this.

"I trust Luke," she murmured as she led Gid out of the barn. "I *have* to trust him."

Martha had just finished hitching her horse to the buggy when Aunt Rosemary's car pulled into the yard. "Where's your dad?" Aunt Rosemary called to Martha as she stepped out of her vehicle. "I have something for him."

"He's in the barn with Cleon. They're taking the hide off a couple of his cows."

Aunt Rosemary quirked an eyebrow. "He's butchering cows? I figured he'd be busy trying to set up his shop in the barn. That is where he plans to do his woodworking until he can build a new shop, right?"

Martha nodded. "Five of Dad's beef cows were shot and killed early this morning." She motioned to the pasture out back. "Abe Wengerd and Cleon's brother, Ivan, are out there loading the rest of the cows on one of our wagons."

"What?" Aunt Rosemary's jaw dropped.

"It's true. We heard shots while we were still in bed, and then Dad discovered the cows lying dead in the pasture."

"I can't believe this." Aunt Rosemary

shook her head. "First your dad's shop, and now his cows? How much more can your family take?"

"I don't know. I just don't know."

Aunt Rosemary opened her purse and removed her cell phone.

"What are you doing?"

"I'm calling the sheriff; that's what I'm doing."

Martha shook her head. "You don't need to do that. Dad called Sheriff Osborn from our phone shed earlier this morning, and the sheriff came out right away."

"I'm glad to hear that. It's about time my brother decided to notify the sheriff right after one of these attacks has occurred."

"Dad had the sheriff called when the shop blew up. Finding some of his cows dead this morning only magnified his feelings of frustration."

"He has good reason to be frustrated." Aunt Rosemary started for the barn. "Maybe when he sees what I brought him, he'll feel a little better about things."

When Rosemary entered the barn, she spotted Roman and Cleon removing the hide from one of the cows hanging from the rafters.

"I just talked to Martha," she said, stepping close to Roman. "I'm sorry about your cows."

He shrugged. "At least the meat won't go to waste."

"Martha says the sheriff came out this morning."

"Jah."

"What'd he have to say?"

"Said he'd double his patrol time around our place."

"He's said that before," Cleon put in, "but the attacks haven't stopped, have they?"

"Maybe the sheriff will catch the guilty party this time." Rosemary hoped her voice sounded more optimistic than she felt. After speaking to the sheriff herself a couple of times, she didn't feel he cared that much about the things that had happened at her brother's place. She wondered if he might be prejudiced against Roman because he was Amish. She'd even wondered if —

"What brings you over today?" Roman asked, breaking into Rosemary's disconcerting thoughts.

She reached into her purse and pulled out a check. "I came to give you this. It's to help rebuild your woodworking business."

Roman took the check, and as he studied it, an awkward silence filled the space between them. Finally, he spoke. "I can't take this."

"Why not?"

"It's for five thousand dollars. That's way too much."

"No, it's not. I love you and your family, Roman. I want to help out." Rosemary touched his arm. "Christmas is just a few weeks away, you know."

"So?"

"I'm sure you can use some money to buy your family a few presents, not to mention all the supplies you'll need to purchase to replace what was lost when your shop was destroyed."

A muscle on the side of his face quivered. "I'm touched by your generosity, sister," he said in a near whisper. "Especially after the way I acted when you first came back home."

She smiled as tears clouded her vision. "That's in the past. It's over and forgiven. It's the *now* that counts."

"Your sister's right," Cleon said. "It does no good to dwell on the past."

Roman nodded as he offered Rosemary a smile. "Danki, sister." He held up the check. "Danki for this and for moving back to Holmes County."

CHAPTER 11

As Grace entered the schoolhouse, where Anna and the other schoolchildren would be putting on their Christmas program, weariness settled over her like a heavy fog. The past few weeks had been stressful for everyone. Not only had Dad's shop been blown up and his cows killed, but also two days ago, Dad and Mom had come down with a bad case of stomach flu, which meant they wouldn't be able to attend Anna's program tonight. Grace hoped no one else in the family came down with the flu.

At least there have been no attacks in the last two weeks, she thought as she took a seat behind Anna's desk. Anna had scurried behind the curtain at the front of the room, and Cleon stood near the back, holding Daniel.

She glanced around the room and spotted Abe standing at the back near Cleon. Cleon's brother Ivan was there, too, along with his girlfriend, Amanda. Grace figured it was just a matter of time before Ivan and Amanda became engaged. Soon Cleon's folks would only have Carolyn living at home.

Children grow up too quickly, she thought as she spotted Abe's daughter Esta slip behind the curtain, along with her brothers Josh, who'd recently turned eleven, and Gideon, the oldest. Ruth sat at a desk with Abe's youngest boy, five-year-old Owen, beside her, while she held little Molly in her lap.

Grace smiled when Ruth nuzzled the top of Molly's blond head. *My sister will make a good mudder to Abe's kinner. I'm glad she's found love again.*

"How are your folks feeling?" Aunt Rosemary asked as she took a seat across the aisle from Grace. "I hear they've both got the flu."

Grace nodded. "They're still pretty sick. Martha stayed home to see to their needs so Ruth could be here to watch the program."

Aunt Rosemary's eyebrows puckered. "Does that mean they're going to miss Christmas?"

"It looks that way. You're still invited to our house on Christmas Eve, and we're planning to come to your place on Christmas Day. If no one else gets sick, that is," Grace quickly added.

"We'll have to pray they don't."

"Jah."

Grace turned toward the front of the room as the children's teacher stepped in front of the curtain. "Welcome to our Christmas program," she said. "We'll begin with some recitations and poems by our first and second graders."

The first graders gave their recitations first, and then it was Anna's turn. She glanced at Grace and smiled. "A long time ago, a sweet baby was born. God's Son, Jesus, came to earth that special morn."

Grace smiled and gave Anna a nod to let her know she'd done a good job reciting the poem.

As the program continued, Grace thought about what Christmas meant to her. It was a joyful, peaceful time of the year, when family and friends gathered to celebrate the birth of Jesus and thank God for His many blessings. She thought about the sacrifice God had made to send His Son to earth to die for the sins of the world and how Jesus had suffered so those who believed in Him might have eternal life.

Nothing we've had to go through can com-

pare with the suffering Jesus endured, Grace thought. *Even what Mary and Joseph went through as they searched for a place where Mary could give birth had to have been stressful.*

She watched Esta, dressed as Mary, enter carrying a baby doll in her arms. Grace thought about how God had told Joseph to take Mary and Jesus and flee to Egypt because Jesus' life was in danger. Trials and suffering would always be part of life, she realized, but it was how people chose to get through those trials that made the difference. They could either cry about their troubles and live in fear, or they could trust God and rely on Him to see them through. Tragedies either drove people away from God or drew them closer to Him. Grace hoped everyone in her family would draw closer to God during this Christmas season and keep their focus on Him, not the unpleasant circumstances that had been brought into their lives.

Martha pulled the heavy quilt on her bed aside and sank onto the crisp, white sheets. She'd spent all day waiting on Mom and Dad and was exhausted. She rolled onto her back, watching the evening shadows dance across the ceiling and trying to relax.

As tired as she felt, sleep refused to come.

Ping! Ping! Ping!

Martha bolted upright in bed and turned on the battery-operated lamp by her bed. It sounded like someone was throwing something against her window. She jumped up and raced over to the window, pulling the curtain aside. A man wearing Amish clothes, bathed in the light of the full, bright moon, appeared to be staring up at her room.

She opened the window and stuck her head out, hoping to see who it was.

"*Psst.* Martha! Can you come down?"

The man looking up at her was Luke. Martha willed her heart to stop throbbing.

"I'll be right there!" She closed the window and slipped out of her nightgown and into a dress and sneakers. She quickly did up her hair, set her kapp in place, and tiptoed out of the room. When she reached the bottom of the stairs, she stopped and listened, hoping Mom and Dad weren't awake. Except for the soft snores coming from their room, all was quiet. She grabbed her jacket from the wall peg and slipped out the back door.

The smile Martha gave Luke when she stepped up to him took his breath away. "Luke, what are you doing here?" she asked.

"Came to see you."

She glanced around. "I don't see your horse and buggy. I hope you didn't walk all the way over here in the cold."

He shook his head. "I drove over in my truck, parked it down the road a piece, and came the rest of the way on foot. Didn't want to take the chance of anyone hearing me come in." He leaned casually against the trunk of a tree and reached into his jacket pockct, hoping she wouldn't know how nervous he felt. "I wanted to give you this," he said as he pulled out a paper sack.

"What is it?"

"Just a little something for Christmas."

"Ach, Luke, I wish you hadn't done that."

"Why not?"

She dropped her gaze to the ground. "Because I have nothing for you."

"That's okay. I didn't expect anything." Luke pushed the paper sack at her, and she lifted her gaze. "It's not much, but I thought you might like it."

With another smile that warmed Luke's heart, Martha took the sack and peered inside.

"It's a book on grooming and boarding dogs. I figured since you've had some trouble breeding dogs, you might like to try something different for a change."

Martha removed the book from the sack and stood staring at it.

"If you don't like it, I can take it back. I bought it at a bookstore in New Philly, so it won't be hard for me to return."

Martha shook her head. "No, no. I like the book. Danki, Luke."

"You're welcome."

"I've actually thought about boarding dogs, but the notion of grooming dogs has never occurred to me. It's something to consider for the future."

"If you got into boarding and grooming dogs, would you continue to breed them, too?"

"Probably so."

"At least the dogs you raise are well cared for, and you always make sure they get good homes."

"Jah. John Peterson is taking good care of Flo, and the same holds true for the Larsons and Esta Wengerd." Martha's forehead wrinkled. "Unfortunately, I won't be able to keep in close contact with everyone who buys my dogs."

"Most folks who spend the money to buy a purebred dog will see that it's cared for, don't you think?"

"I hope that's always the case."

Luke glanced up at the house. "I didn't

wake your folks when I threw pebbles at your window, I hope."

She shook her head. "Mom and Dad have been down with the flu. I'm sure they're asleep."

"What about Ruth?"

"She went to the Christmas program at the schoolhouse with the Wengerds, and she's not back yet."

Luke blew out his breath, wishing he could say all that was on his mind.

Martha pulled her jacket tighter around her neck and shivered. "It's sure cold out here. I wish I could invite you in for some hot chocolate, but —"

He held up his hand. "It's okay; I understand. If your daed knew you were out here talking to me, that would be bad enough. If he found me sitting in your kitchen sipping hot chocolate and eating cookies, he'd probably have a heart attack."

She playfully poked his arm. "Who said anything about cookies?"

He snickered. "Guess my stomach was doing some wishful thinking."

"I don't know when or how it's going to happen, Luke, but I feel confident that one day Dad will finally realize you're a good man."

"And that I'm not the one responsible for

the attacks against your family," he added.

"That, too." Martha groaned. "I'm sure you heard about some of my daed's cows being shot a few weeks ago."

He nodded and was about to express his concerns, when he heard the distinctive *clippety-clop* of a horse's hooves on the road out front.

"That might be Abe bringing Ruth home," Martha said.

"I'd better go in case it is." Luke started to walk away but turned back. "Would it be all right if I come over to see you at Irene's place sometime? I'd like to talk some more about the attacks and who I think might be responsible."

"I'd like that, too, but I don't think it's a good idea for us to talk in front of Irene or Carolyn. Maybe we can meet somewhere in town."

"Okay. When and where do you want to meet?"

She shrugged. "The next few weeks will be busy with Ruth and Abe's wedding coming up, so I probably won't have much chance to meet with you until that's behind us."

"I understand. If we have a minute to talk after the wedding, maybe we can decide on a time and place then."

The sound of the horse drew closer. Luke turned and saw the silhouette of a horse and buggy starting up the driveway. He had to go. "Have a Merry Christmas, Martha," he called before racing around the side of the house and into the field.

CHAPTER 12

As Ruth stood in front of the stove, stirring a pot of chicken soup, she thought about last Christmas Eve and how her whole world had been turned upside down. When they'd climbed into Martin's buggy that night, Ruth had never imagined it would be the first and last Christmas Eve she would spend with her husband.

"Are you sure you don't want me to stay here with Mom and Dad so you can join Grace and her family this evening?" Martha asked, halting Ruth's thoughts.

Ruth turned and forced a smile. "You stayed home last night so I could go to the Christmas program at the schoolhouse. It's your turn for an evening out."

"I wouldn't mind staying home again."

"I'll be fine here with Mom and Dad," Ruth said. "Besides, if they're feeling up to it, we'll all be going to Aunt Rosemary's for dinner tomorrow afternoon."

Martha nodded. "I checked on them a few minutes ago, and they said they felt well enough to eat some of this delicious soup they've smelled."

"If they're getting their appetites back, it's a good indication that they're feeling better."

Martha slipped into her coat and picked up the pan of frosted brownies she'd made. "I still feel guilty about leaving you here."

Ruth waved a hand. "Well, don't. You can't always be the one making sacrifices. You deserve to have some fun."

"Jah, okay. I'll see you later then." Martha slipped out the back door.

A few minutes later, Mom and Dad entered the room. Dad ambled over to the stove and peered at the soup. "Ah, there's nothing better than a pot of homemade chicken soup," he said.

"Especially after a body's been without food for a couple of days." Mom moved over to the stove. "What can I do to help?"

Ruth shook her head. "Not a single thing. You and Dad have a seat at the table, and I'll bring you some soup and crackers."

Mom looked like she might argue the point, but Dad nudged her and said, "Just do as your daughter says, Judith. You're still weak and shaky; you ought to rest."

"You're right. I am a bit unsteady on my feet." Mom pulled out a chair and sat down. Dad took his chair at the head of the table.

Ruth ladled soup into three bowls and brought them over to the table, along with a basket of saltine crackers. "Would either of you like anything else?" she asked as she took her seat.

"Soup and crackers will be plenty for me," Mom said.

Dad nodded in agreement. "Shall we offer our thanks now?"

All heads bowed, and when the silent prayer was over, Ruth handed the crackers to her mother. "When I went out to the chicken coop awhile ago, the air felt like it could snow. I wonder if we'll have a white Christmas."

"It would be nice to have snow for Christmas," Mom said. "As long as it doesn't snow heavy and cause the roads to be icy, the way it did last year." She covered her mouth and gave a muffled gasp. "Ach, Ruth, I'm sorry for bringing that up."

"It happened, Mom. Not talking about it won't change a thing." Ruth blew on her soup and took a tentative taste.

"Even so, it's Christmas Eve, and I think we should focus on positive things," Mom said. "It always amazes me the way God can take a bad situation and turn it into something good."

"Are you referring to anything specific?" Dad asked.

"Jah. I was thinking that even though both Ruth and Abe lost their mates, God brought them together. Why, in just a few weeks, Abe will have a new fraa and a mudder for his kinner." Mom looked over at Ruth and smiled. "And you have been given the opportunity to raise Abe's kinner."

Ruth swallowed around the lump that had formed in her throat. "I'm not marrying Abe just so I can be a mother, you know."

Mom reached over and patted Ruth's arm. "No, of course not. I know you love Abe, as well."

Thump! Thump! Thump!

Ruth jumped at what sounded like boots clomping up the back stairs. A loud knock sounded on the door.

"I wonder who that could be," Mom said.

"Well, there's only one way to find out." Dad started to push away from the table.

Ruth jumped to her feet. "I'll get it, Dad. Why don't you stay here with Mom and finish your soup?"

He nodded.

Ruth hurried out of the room and opened the back door. Sheriff Osborn stood on the porch, holding a small box in his hand.

"Good evening, Ruth," he said. "I just dropped by to see how you folks are doing and also to bring you this." He handed the box to Ruth. "It's a fruitcake from the bakeshop in Berlin."

"That's very nice. Thank you." Ruth smiled. "Mom and Dad are in the kitchen, eating some soup. They're just getting over a bout with the flu; otherwise, I'd invite you in."

"That's okay," the sheriff said. "I need to be on my way home. Don't like to keep the wife and kids waiting on Christmas Eve." He started to walk away but turned back. "Oh, would you give your dad a message?"

"Of course."

"Tell him I still have no leads on who shot his cows or blew up his shop, but I have requested that one of my deputies patrol your area throughout the holidays. Hopefully, that will keep the one responsible from doing anything else." He popped a piece of gum in his mouth. "Have a Merry Christmas."

"You, too, Sheriff Osborn."

Ruth returned to the kitchen with an uneasy feeling in the pit of her stomach. Even if one of the sheriff's men patrolled the area, that didn't guarantee the attacks would end.

Martha watched Grace and Cleon, as they interacted with their children at the supper table. A pang of jealousy stabbed her heart. *Unless someone takes an interest in me, I may never marry and have children.* She toyed with the napkin beside her plate. *Luke's the only man I want, but that seems impossible.*

She thought about Luke throwing pebbles at her window. She'd been so surprised when he'd given her a Christmas present. *I wish I'd have had something to give him. He probably thinks I don't appreciate him helping me find out who's been attacking our family.*

"How are Mom and Dad feeling tonight?" Grace asked.

"Better. When I left the house, they were getting ready to join Ruth for a bowl of soup."

"Do you think they'll be up to eating supper at my house tomorrow?" Aunt Rosemary asked.

"I hope so." Martha smiled. "If Dad doesn't come, I'll eat his share of pie."

"I'll be sure to send some pie home with you in case they don't come." Aunt Rosemary sighed. "I wish Ken and Sharon could have come to Ohio for Christmas, but they

149

used the last of their vacation time helping me move."

"Had you considered going back to Idaho for Christmas?" Cleon asked.

She nodded. "With everything that's gone on with Roman lately, I didn't feel good about leaving. I'm needed here more than ever."

"We appreciate having you here, too," Grace said with a smile. "It means a lot to Dad to have you living in Holmes County again."

Anna looked over at Martha. "I wish you could have been at the Christmas program last night. It was lots of fun, and Esta got to be Mary."

"I'm sorry I missed it," Martha said, "but I needed to be at home taking care of your grandpa and grandma."

"Anna said a real nice poem." Grace gave her daughter's arm a little squeeze. "Why don't you recite your poem so Aunt Martha can hear it?"

Anna looked over at Martha.

Martha nodded. "I'd like to hear the poem, Anna."

"Okay." Anna sat up straight, and in a clear, sweet voice, she said, "A long time ago, a sweet baby was born. God's Son, Jesus, came to earth that special morn."

"That was very nice, Anna," Martha said with a nod. "You said your lines perfectly."

Anna beamed. "Maybe next year, when I'm older, I'll get to be an angel in the Christmas program."

"Maybe you will."

"Or maybe you'll get to play the part of Mary," Aunt Rosemary put in.

Anna's eyes widened. "You think so?"

Aunt Rosemary nodded. "As well as you said that poem, I'm sure your teacher will consider you for a really good part."

Anna's smile stretched ear to ear as she reached for a biscuit and slathered it with butter.

Martha smiled, too. Aunt Rosemary had a special way with everyone in the family. It was a good thing she'd come back to Holmes County.

"Grace, why don't you let Martha and me do the dishes?" Rosemary suggested when dinner was over and the women had begun to clear the table. "You worked hard preparing the meal, so I think you should go in the living room and enjoy being with your family before it's time to put the children to bed."

Grace hesitated but finally nodded. "If

you're sure you don't mind, that does sound nice."

"I don't mind, do you?" Rosemary asked looking at Martha.

Martha shook her head. "Don't mind at all."

"Okay, danki." Grace cleared the rest of the glasses from the table and headed for the living room.

Martha followed Rosemary over to the sink. "Can I ask your opinion on something?"

"Of course."

"I've been wondering if I should give up on the idea of raising dogs and do something else."

Rosemary smiled. "Are you thinking about getting married and raising a family instead of dogs?"

Martha's face turned bright pink. "I'd need to find a man who was interested in marrying me first."

"I wouldn't think that would be a problem for someone as smart and pretty as you."

Martha dropped the sponge into the pan of soapy water, and tiny bubbles rose to the ceiling. "I've never thought of myself as smart or pretty."

"Then you're not taking a close enough look." Rosemary gave Martha's shoulder a gentle squeeze. "Is there something you'd rather do than raise dogs?"

Martha shrugged. "I've thought about boarding dogs, but Dad hasn't given his approval on that idea yet." The color in her face deepened. "I've also considered grooming dogs, and the book Luke gave me says —" She clamped her hand over her mouth. "I mean —"

"Luke gave you a book on dog grooming?"

"Jah."

"When was this?"

"Last night." Martha's voice lowered to a whisper. "He came over to our place after the folks were in bed and said he had something he wanted to give me for Christmas."

"The book on dog grooming?"

Martha nodded as she sucked in her bottom lip. "Dad doesn't want Luke to come around our place anymore, so he came over when he thought Mom and Dad would be asleep.

"I see." Feeling the need to put Martha's mind at ease, Rosemary said, "Your folks won't hear about Luke's visit from me."

"Danki."

"You know," Rosemary said, "dog grooming might actually be something for you to consider."

"Jah, I'm going to give it some serious thought, but I probably won't do anything like that for some time. It would take awhile to learn everything, and it might take even longer to line up some customers."

Rosemary picked up a dish towel and reached for the first plate, when a wave of nausea hit her. "Oh no," she groaned.

"What's wrong?"

"I think I might be coming down with the flu." She raced out of the kitchen and headed straight for the bathroom.

Christmas Day dawned with snow lightly sprinkled on the ground and clinging to the trees like a dusting of powdered sugar.

Martha had just returned from Grace and Cleon's place, where she'd gone to pick up her aunt. Since Aunt Rosemary had been so ill last night, Grace had insisted she sleep in their guest room. Thankfully, Aunt Rosemary was feeling a bit better, although she was still weak and shaky. Since Cleon's parents were expecting Grace, Cleon, and the children for Christmas dinner, Martha had suggested she bring Aunt Rosemary home with her. Now she was upstairs resting in Grace's old room. It wasn't the Christmas they had planned, with dinner at

Rosemary's house, but at least none of them would have to be alone on Christmas Day.

As Martha scurried around the kitchen getting breakfast, she thought about Luke and the gift he'd given her. Since she didn't want Mom and Dad to know he'd been here or that he'd given her a gift, she'd hidden the book in the bottom drawer of her dresser.

I hate sneaking around like this, she thought ruefully. *I wish I felt free to tell Mom, Dad, and the rest of the family how much I care for Luke and that the two of us are working together to figure out who's been attacking us.*

"Do you need any help in here?" Ruth asked.

Martha whirled around. "Ach, Ruth, you scared me."

"Didn't you hear my slippers scuffling down the hall?"

"No, I was deep in thought."

"What were you thinking about?"

"Nothing much — just Christmas and such."

Ruth sighed and took a seat at the table. "With Dad and Mom just getting over the flu, and now Aunt Rosemary coming down with it, this isn't much of a Christmas, is it?"

"It's not the worst Christmas we've ever had."

Ruth slowly shook her head. "No, it's not. Last Christmas was the worst."

When Martha saw the sorrowful look on her sister's face, she wished she could take back what she'd said. She hurried across the room and took a seat beside Ruth. "I'm sorry, Ruth. My words were not the best choice, and —"

Ruth held up her hand. "No need to apologize. I can't expect everyone to walk on eggshells because of me. I'm just a bit oversensitive right now."

Martha gave Ruth's shoulder a gentle squeeze. "I understand. It's not easy to lose someone you love, and when their death occurs on a holiday, every time that holiday comes around, it's a painful reminder of what you lost."

Ruth leaned over and gave Martha a hug. "When did my little *schweschder* get to be so *schmaert?*"

Martha patted Ruth's back and said, "I think maybe being around my two big sisters so much is what's made me smart."

When Ruth pulled back, tears clung to her eyelashes. "I think maybe being around Aunt Rosemary has made us all a little smarter, don't you?"

"She does have some pretty good advice." Martha glanced at the door leading to the hallway. "Not that Mom's not schmaert; she's taught us plenty of things. It's just that Mom tends to be kind of emotional about certain things. I think maybe it clouds her judgment sometimes."

Ruth tipped her head. "Are you thinking of anything in particular?"

"Not really. It's just that whenever I try to talk to her about anything, she never sees things my way and starts getting all emotional."

"You mean the way she gets when she thinks you spend too much time with your dogs?"

Martha nodded. "I don't think either Mom or Dad understands why I keep trying to get my kennel business going, in spite of the setbacks I've had."

"I would think Dad should understand. Look at the setbacks he's had with his woodworking business, yet he keeps on going."

"Speaking of going . . ." Martha rose from her chair. "We need to get breakfast going so you can get ready to spend Christmas Day at Abe's."

Ruth smiled. "I am looking forward to that. Thanks to Aunt Rosemary's good counsel, I'm also looking forward to my wedding day in a few weeks."

CHAPTER 13

As Martha sat on a wooden bench inside Grace and Cleon's house, watching Ruth and Abe say their vows, she was filled with mixed feelings. The look of contentment she saw on Ruth's and Abe's faces made her happy, but she couldn't keep her jealousy at bay. *Will I ever know the kind of love my sisters share with their husbands?*

Martha glanced across the room to where the men and boys sat. She spotted Luke sitting beside his cousin Raymond. At least he hadn't missed Ruth's wedding because of work. Although if Luke was going to miss any wedding, Ruth's would be the one, since he and Ruth had dated for a while.

Martha watched Luke's expression for any sign of jealousy over Ruth marrying Abe but couldn't detect anything. Luke stared straight ahead with a placid look on his face.

At one time, Ruth had thought Luke might be the one attacking their family.

She'd even believed it was Luke's truck that had rammed their buggy last Christmas Eve. After Ruth had learned that, except for a quick trip to borrow something from a neighbor earlier in the day, Luke had been home that evening, she'd seemed to accept that he couldn't have been responsible for Martin's death. Ruth's close relationship with Aunt Rosemary and falling in love with Abe had helped heal her broken heart and given her a sense of peace and purpose in life.

Martha glanced over her shoulder. Aunt Rosemary sat beside Cleon's mother, Irene. Martha was glad Aunt Rosemary felt well enough to be here today. She'd come down with a bad cold after her bout with the flu.

Aunt Rosemary gave her a smile and a nod. Martha smiled in return. Having Aunt Rosemary living nearby had not only been good for Ruth but also for everyone in the family. Dad seemed mellower when Aunt Rosemary was in the same room. Mom and Grace related well to her, too. Martha had discovered that she and her aunt had one important thing in common — they both wanted to find out who was behind the attacks that had been done to her family.

Rosemary was about to head for Roman's

place, where the wedding meal would be served, when someone tapped her on the shoulder. She turned.

A tall Amish man with faded blond hair and piercing blue eyes gave her a slanted grin. "Well, if it isn't my little sister who 'yanked over.' Roman said you'd come home."

Rosemary had heard that the Amish who lived in Geauga County referred to Englishers as *Yankees* and that when an Amish person left the faith, it was said that he or she had *yanked over.* Her mouth went dry. The man who stood before her was none other than her brother who lived in Geauga County. "Walt? Is . . . is it really you?"

He nodded. "Came down for Ruth's wedding."

Rosemary wanted so badly to give her brother a hug, but she thought it might not be appreciated. So she smiled and said, "It's good to see you again, Walt."

He gave a quick nod. Wasn't he glad to see her? Did he harbor ill feelings toward her because she'd left the Amish faith?

As if sensing Rosemary's discomfort, Walt reached out and touched her arm. "Roman says you've decided to move here permanently."

She nodded. "That's right. My son and

his wife helped me move. I wish you could have met them."

He glanced around. "They're not here now?"

She shook her head. "They used their vacation time to help me move. They both work at a bank in Boise, Idaho."

"It's too bad they couldn't be here today. It would've been nice to meet them," Walt said with a genuine smile. Maybe he wasn't angry with her, after all.

"Where's your family?" she asked. "Are they all here today?"

He shook his head. "Just me and Mary came down. Our two sons live in Wisconsin, and our four daughters have settled in Pennsylvania."

Rosemary smiled. "I'd like to meet Mary. Where is she?"

"She's still in the house talking to Judith and Grace. Let's head in there now, and I'll introduce you."

Rosemary smiled. It really was good to be home again.

As Luke headed down the driveway toward the Hostettlers', he thought about Martha and how pensive she'd looked throughout most of her sister's wedding. Had she been thinking about Ruth and wondering if things would go better for her being married to Abe than they had when she'd been married to Martin?

Luke was almost to the house, when someone tapped him on the shoulder. Toby was walking beside Sadie. The two of them had only been married a few months, but already Toby had a good beard.

"I'm surprised to see you here," Toby said with a scowl. "Since you had to work the day Sadie and I got married, I figured you'd be working again today."

Luke shook his head. "We're getting caught up at work, so John said I could have the day off."

"I see." Toby nudged Sadie's arm. "Why don't you go on into the house?"

"Aren't you coming?"

"I want to talk to Luke for a few minutes, but I'll be in soon."

Sadie shrugged and headed for the back porch.

"What'd you want to talk to me about, Toby?" Luke hoped they weren't going to have another one of their disagreements.

Toby folded his arms and stared hard at Luke. "There was an article in the paper yesterday morning about some windows that were broken at the schoolhouse in Charm."

"That's too bad."

"The article said someone who lives near the school saw a black truck cruising around the area the night before."

"What's that got to do with me?"

"Duh! You own a black truck."

Luke stiffened. "I hope you're not suggesting that I had anything to do with those broken windows."

Toby shrugged. "I'm not accusing; just wondering is all."

"Wondering if I broke the windows?"

"Jah."

Luke gave a small rock a hefty kick. "I had nothing to do with those windows being broken, and I wasn't out driving my truck in the middle of the night."

"Can you prove it?"

Luke leaned closer to Toby. "I don't need to prove it. Especially not to you."

Toby scowled at Luke. "You think you can do whatever you want and get away with it, don't you? It's just like when we were kinner, and the two of us got caught doing something we weren't supposed to do. You always got off easy, while I was punished."

Luke sucked in his breath. So that was the problem. How immature to be carrying a grudge around all these years. Truth be told, Toby probably wished he had owned a truck during his running-around years. But since Toby's dad was the bishop, he probably hadn't dared make waves. Luke was tempted to defend himself and try to make Toby see reason. But what was the use? He'd never been able to make Toby see things as they were in the past, so why try now? Luke turned on his heel and stalked off toward the Hostettlers' barn.

When Martha saw Toby enter the house with a red face, she knew something was up. She glanced around but didn't see any sign of Luke.

"I'll be back in a few minutes," she whispered to Ruth, who sat beside her new groom.

"Where are you going? We'll be eating soon."

"I need to go outside and check on something."

Ruth released an exasperated sigh. "You're not going to check on those puppies again, I hope."

"Well, I —"

"You checked on them before the wedding, and they were fine."

"I know, but —"

"It's all right," Abe put in. "If Martha checks on her hundlin, then she'll come back to the house and enjoy the rest of the day." He looked up at Martha and smiled. "Isn't that so?"

"Jah." Martha gave her sister's shoulder a gentle squeeze then scooted out of the room.

When she entered the barn, she spotted Luke inside one of the stalls, petting a beautiful black gelding. "When I didn't see you inside, I wondered if you might have come out here," she said, stepping up to him.

He nodded.

"Are you okay? Are you upset about something?"

"I'm upset all right. Upset and irritated with my so-called friend, Toby."

"What did Toby do?"

Luke grunted. "He as much as accused me of breaking out some windows in the Charm schoolhouse."

"What?" Martha's mouth dropped open. "When did that happen?"

"Toby said he read about it in yesterday's paper. I guess it happened the night before."

"What makes him think you had anything to do with it?"

"Someone saw a black truck cruising around the area."

Martha's throat constricted. What if Luke

had been driving his truck near the school-house that night? What if —

Luke grabbed her arm. "I didn't have anything to do with those broken windows, Martha. You believe me, don't you?"

She swallowed around the lump in her throat. She wanted to believe him; she really did. But if a black truck had been seen —

"It wasn't my truck," Luke said.

His grip tightened on her arm, and she winced. "You're hurting me."

Luke let go of her arm and stepped back. "I'm sorry. I sure didn't mean to hurt you, Martha."

Tears pricked the backs of her eyes. "I'm okay."

"My truck's still parked in the woods, and I haven't driven it in over a week. Not since the last time I went to the mall in New Philadelphia with Tim and Rod."

"Are they some of the English fellows you've been hanging around?"

He nodded.

"If I ask you a question, will you be honest with me?"

"Jah, sure."

"How come you've become friends with those English fellows who everyone knows are rowdy?"

Luke shifted his weight from one foot to

the other and stared at the straw-covered floor. "I . . . uh . . . can't really say."

"Can't or won't?"

He lifted his gaze to meet hers. "If I tell you what I've been up to, do I have your word that you won't repeat it to anyone?"

Martha nodded. She hoped Luke wasn't about to tell her that he'd decided to jump the fence and go English.

Luke cleared his throat. "When I first started hanging around Tim and Rod and some of their friends, it was to have a good time. But then when I got wind that they'd pulled some pranks in the area, I decided to stick around them and try and find out if they might be the ones responsible for the attacks on your family."

"Really?"

He nodded. "At first, it was only because I wanted to clear my name with your daed. But then, when things got really bad, I realized you — all of you — could be in danger. So I've been trying to figure out who's been doing the attacks, and I figured if I gained Tim's and Rod's trust, sooner or later, one of them would spill the beans."

"Have they?"

He shook his head. "Not yet."

"Maybe they aren't the ones responsible."

"That could be, but they have pulled some

pranks around the area."

"Like what?"

"They admitted that they'd toilet-papered a few places, turned over some schoolhouse outhouses, and tipped some cows." Luke grunted. "I wouldn't be surprised if they aren't the ones who broke the windows at the school in Charm — which is why I need to keep hanging around them so I can find out."

"Does either of them own a black truck?"

He shrugged. "Not that I know of, but just because a truck was seen cruising the area the night before the windows were broken doesn't mean the driver of the truck's the one who broke 'em."

Martha nodded. "Good point." Hearing Luke's reasons for hanging around the English fellows gave her hope that Luke really was innocent.

"In case you haven't figured it out, one of the reasons I haven't joined the church yet is so I'd be free to investigate the attacks."

Martha nodded slowly. She knew if her father found out she was trying to investigate the attacks, she'd be in for a lecture.

"So when I said I'd be willing to help you find out who's been trying to hurt your family, I meant it," Luke added.

"I appreciate that, because I need all the

help I can get. You know that wrench you found in my daed's field?"

He nodded.

Martha motioned to the hayloft. "Well, I hid it up there, and when I was looking for the right spot to put it, I discovered some initials engraved on the handle."

Luke's eyebrows lifted. "What were the initials?"

"H. C." Martha pursed her lips. "I don't know anyone with those initials, do you?"

"I sure don't." His forehead creased. "Let's get together to talk about this some more, okay?"

Martha opened her mouth to reply when Grace stepped into the barn. "I figured I'd find you out here. Were you checking on your dogs?"

"Uh . . . jah, I was planning to."

"Well, Ruth's looking for you, so I hope you'll check on the dogs and get back to the house soon." Grace glanced over at Luke.

He shuffled his feet nervously, gave Martha a nod, and said, "Guess I'd better get back inside, too. If I don't show up soon, my mamm will probably come looking for me."

Ruth smiled at Aunt Rosemary and said,

"I'm glad you could be here for our wedding."

Aunt Rosemary looked over at Abe and smiled. "You take good care of my niece, you hear?"

He nodded. "Of course I will."

"I'll leave you two to enjoy your meal, but before I go, I was wondering if I could ask a favor."

"What's that?" Abe asked.

"Would it be all right if I take a few pictures of your children so I can send them to Ken and Sharon? Since they couldn't be here for the wedding, I'm sure they'd enjoy seeing how cute the little ones looked today."

Abe glanced at Ruth, as though seeking her approval.

"They're your children," she said.

He touched her arm. "Now that you're my wife, the kinner belong to both of us."

"If you have no objections to Aunt Rosemary taking the kinner's pictures, then I'm in agreement with it," she said, smiling at Abe.

"All right then." Abe rose from his chair. "I'd better gather up our brood, because they're scattered all around the room."

As Abe and Aunt Rosemary left, Martha took a seat next to Ruth. She smiled and placed a small package on the table.

"Is this a wedding present?"

Martha nodded. "I know it's not customary for the bride and groom to receive gifts if they've both been married before, but I wanted to give you something anyway."

Ruth tore the wrapping off the package and withdrew a lovely sampler. Her and Abe's names had been embroidered on it, as well as the names of his five surviving children — her children now.

She thought about the sampler Martha had given her when she'd married Martin. After his death, she'd packed the sampler away because it had hurt too much to look at it and be reminded of her loss. But now that Abe and his children were in Ruth's life, she felt as if she was being offered a second chance, and for that she was grateful.

"The sampler is beautiful," she said, tears clogging her throat. "Danki, Martha."

"You're welcome."

Just then, Abe's daughter Esta stepped up to the table and handed Ruth a small box wrapped in white tissue paper. "This is for you. Papa helped me pick it out, and I paid for it with some money I earned cleanin' the floor in Papa's harness shop."

Ruth smiled and took the gift from the

child. "It was sweet of you to think of me."

Esta's eyes twinkled as she wiggled around. "Aren't you gonna open it?"

"Jah, of course." Ruth tore the paper off the box and lifted the lid. Inside lay a delicate hanky with white lace around the edges. She gave Esta a hug. "Danki, it's beautiful."

"I'm glad you like it —" The child hesitated then leaned close to Ruth's ear. "Is it all right if I call you Mama now?"

Ruth nodded and swallowed around the lump in her throat. "I'd like that very much. I hope your *brieder* and little schweschder will call me Mama, too."

"I'm sure my sister will. After all, Molly's been callin' you *mammi* ever since you came to work for Papa." Esta frowned. "I'm not sure about the brothers, though — at least not Gideon. He's such an old sourpuss these days. He might refuse to call you Mama just 'cause he's so stubborn."

Ruth glanced around. "Where are Molly and your brothers?" she asked, making no comment about Gideon's recent behavior. Today was a special day, and she didn't want to think about anything negative. "Did your daed gather all of you together so my aunt Rosemary could take your picture?" she asked, patting Esta's arm.

Esta's head bobbed up and down. "After the picture takin' was done, Molly started to fuss, so —"

"Grace took our little girl over to her house," Abe said, stepping up beside Esta.

"See you later, Mama." Esta gave Ruth a quick hug and darted away.

Abe reclaimed his seat and leaned close to Ruth. His warm breath against her neck caused her to shiver. "Grace and Cleon volunteered to keep our brood until tomorrow morning, so it'll just be you and me staying here with your folks tonight."

Ruth's cheeks warmed at the thought of spending the night with Abe sleeping next to her. Would he find her desirable even though she could never give him a baby? Would he be tender and loving, the way Martin had been?

As if sensing Ruth's reservations, Abe reached under the table and gave her fingers a gentle squeeze. "Tomorrow, after we've helped clean things up here, we'll take our kinner home to our place and begin a new life together."

Ruth smiled and squeezed Abe's fingers in response. "I'm looking forward to that."

CHAPTER 14

Ruth was getting ready to put a pot roast in the oven for supper, when Gideon stepped into the kitchen. "Are you just getting home from school?" she asked, glancing at the battery-operated clock above the refrigerator. "The others have been here for nearly an hour already."

Gideon scrunched up his nose. "Teacher kept me after school. Didn't Esta tell you I was gonna be late?"

Ruth's forehead wrinkled. "No, she just said you hadn't walked with them. I figured you'd walked by yourself through the woods or had decided to walk with some of your friends."

"I ain't got no friends," he said, shaking snow off his stocking cap.

"Don't have any," she corrected. "And what makes you think you don't have any friends?"

Gideon hung his coat and hat on a wall

peg and flopped into a chair at the kitchen table. " 'Cause nobody wants to be around me, that's what!"

Ruth put the roast into the oven and took a seat in the chair opposite him. "Does this have something to do with you having to stay after school?"

He shrugged.

"Gideon, I need to know what's going on. I can't help if you don't talk about it."

"I don't wanna talk about it, and you ain't my mamm, so I don't need your help, Ruth!" Gideon pushed his chair away from the table and rushed out the door as the chair toppled over with a crash.

Ruth sighed. All of Abe's children except Gideon had begun calling her *Mama*. She had a hunch he hadn't because he resented her marriage to his dad. Could that resentment be the cause of Gideon's problems at school?

As Martha directed her buggy horse toward Irene's house, a feeling of despair settled over her like a drenching rain. She was thankful for this job but wished she could become self-supporting through her kennel business.

Without telling her folks about the book Luke had given her, she'd mentioned the possibility of dog grooming to them the other night. Dad had said he thought it would be too much work because Martha had enough to do right now with her job at Irene's and raising puppies. Mom's only comment was that she thought Martha should give up working with dogs altogether and find a husband.

Thinking about marriage made Martha's thoughts turn to Luke. She'd only seen him once since Ruth and Abe's wedding — at their biweekly preaching service, which had been held at his folks' house. After the service, Luke had disappeared, so she hadn't been able to say hello, much less ask if he'd had any success finding out who was behind the attacks.

Of course I haven't learned anything yet, either, she thought ruefully. Preparations for Ruth's wedding had kept Martha busy for weeks. She'd also had her dogs and her job at Irene's. During the holidays, they'd been busier than ever, serving dinners to the employees of several local businesses that had decided to host their Christmas parties at an Amish sit-down dinner.

Tonight, they would be cooking for people who worked at the newspaper in Millersburg. Since they'd been too busy to accommodate the group before Christmas, it would be an after-the-holidays gathering.

Having taken care of her horse and buggy, Martha stepped into the kitchen and found Irene and Carolyn scurrying around, faces glistening with perspiration. Even on a chilly winter day, the kitchen was hot. Martha figured by the time their guests arrived they would all be sweating.

Irene turned from cutting up chicken and smiled. "Ready for another big dinner?"

"Ready as I'll ever be," Martha replied. "What do you need me to do?"

Irene motioned to another chicken lying on the cutting board. "You can begin by cutting that, and then there are ingredients for a tossed green salad in the refrigerator."

Martha slipped into her work apron and set right to work. She kept so busy that she barely took notice when the group of Englishers arrived and took their seats at the table. It wasn't until a deep male voice said something to Irene that Martha glanced that way. Gary Walker, the reporter who'd dated Grace during her rumschpringe days, stood near the door that separated the kitchen from the dining room.

She leaned casually against the counter and listened to his conversation with Irene.

"I'm hoping to write another article about your business here," Gary said. "The last one I did generated a lot of reader response, which made my boss happy."

Irene smiled. "Soon after the article was printed, several more people made reservations for a meal."

"That's good to hear, Mrs. Schrock," Gary said in his usual, charming voice. He glanced over at Martha and winked. "Maybe after this article comes out, you'll have to hire a few more lovely women to help with your dinners."

Martha averted her gaze and busied herself filling water glasses that had been set by each plate.

For the remainder of the evening, she stayed busy in the kitchen, returning to the dining room only when necessary. The sight of Gary flirting with the dark-haired woman beside him was enough to make Martha's stomach churn. She couldn't figure out what Grace had ever seen in that arrogant man.

When the meal was over and the guests began to file out of the house, Martha breathed a sigh of relief. Maybe now she could focus on something other than the irritating man in the other room.

She'd just gone outside to deposit a bag of trash in the garbage can, when Gary stepped onto the porch and leaned against the railing. "Nice night, isn't it?"

She shivered and knew it wasn't from the chilly night air. "I thought everyone had gone home."

"Everyone but me." He moved to stand beside her. "I decided to stick around awhile so I could talk to you."

"What about?"

"I have a few questions I'd like to ask about your dog business."

"My dog business?"

"Yeah. I'd like to know if I can come by your place tomorrow and take a look at your kennels."

"Are you interested in buying a dog?"

He grunted. "Hardly! I hate dogs. Have ever since one bit me on the nose when I was a kid."

Martha dropped the sack into the trash can and started walking back to the house.

Gary followed. "I'm interested in writing a story about your kennel business for the newspaper."

"Why would you want to write a story about me? I only have a few dogs. I don't think there's much about my struggling business that would be worthy of a write-up in the newspaper."

He eyed her curiously. "It's struggling, huh?"

"I've been trying to get it going for some time, but either my dogs aren't able to get pregnant, or something happens to one of the pups." Martha felt like biting her tongue. She had no idea why she'd answered any of Gary's questions, and she certainly wasn't going to allow him to come to her house and nose around. Grace would be upset if Gary came anywhere near their place. Besides, Martha didn't trust the man as far as she could toss one of Dad's buggy horses.

Her thoughts went to the article that had been in the paper several weeks ago, accusing some Amish of running puppy mills and abusing their dogs. If Martha gave Gary an interview, he might write something that would make her look bad.

"I'm not interested in having an article written about me or my dogs," she mumbled.

"Why not? If your business is struggling, a newspaper article might be just the thing that would bring in more customers."

She shook her head.

Gary followed her onto the porch. "What are you afraid of?"

"I'm not afraid of anything."

He shrugged. "You must have something to hide if you won't let me do a story about your dogs."

A brigade of shivers ran up Martha's spine. What was Gary trying to prove? Was he hoping to find something at her kennels to make her look bad? "I have nothing to hide," she said.

"That's good to hear. For a minute there, I thought you might be running one of those puppy mills and didn't want me to know about it."

Martha's anger outweighed her fear. "I am not running a puppy mill! I take good care of my dogs, and I have a kennel license!"

Gary tipped back his head and roared.

Her defenses rose. "What's so funny?"

His laughter slowed to a few chuckles and then stopped. "You remind me of Grace in many ways, only you're prettier."

"I have nothing more to say, so if you'll excuse me, I have work to do." Martha tromped across the porch, jerked open the door, and stepped into the house. She wished Gary Walker would leave Holmes County for good!

CHAPTER 15

As Martha sat around the breakfast table with her folks a week later, she was shocked to discover an article in the newspaper written by Gary Walker. It was about Amish puppy mills again, only this time he mentioned her as a breeder who had refused an interview. *"Could Ms. Hostettler be running a puppy mill?"* the article read. *"Is that why she wouldn't allow this reporter to see her kennels or ask any pertinent questions?"*

Martha slammed the paper down so hard it jiggled her mother's cup, spilling some of the coffee.

"Ach! Martha, watch what you're doing!" Mom grabbed a napkin and mopped up the spill.

"What's wrong with you this morning?" Dad asked crossly. "You shouldn't be reading the paper while we're trying to eat."

"This is what's wrong!" Martha pointed to the newspaper. "There's an article by

Gary Walker. He insinuates that I might be running a puppy mill!"

Mom's mouth dropped open. "Where would he get such a notion?"

Dad snatched up the paper. He studied it a few seconds then slapped it down hard, jostling his own cup of coffee. "That man has some nerve saying those things!"

"What'd he say, Roman?" Mom asked. "Did he accuse Martha of running a puppy mill?"

"Not in so many words, but he said Martha's a dog breeder and that she refused an interview with him. It also says he suspects she might be running a puppy mill." Dad looked over at Martha and frowned. "Any idea where he got such a notion?"

Martha reached for her glass of orange juice and took a drink, hoping to buy some time. Dad was upset enough; she didn't want to say anything that might rile him even more.

Dad leaned closer to Martha and tapped his finger against the newspaper. "Have you talked to that nosy reporter recently?"

Martha nodded. "He came to Irene's last week with some others who work at the newspaper. After everyone else had left, Gary cornered me and started asking a bunch of questions."

"What'd you tell him?" Mom asked.

"I just said my business was struggling, and when he asked if he could come by our place to take a look at my dogs and interview me, I turned him down."

"Ah, I see how it is." Dad frowned deeply. "You got Mr. Walker riled when you refused to let him interview you, so he's trying to get even by writing things that aren't true."

"Well, I —"

"If an Englisher raises more than one breed of dog and doesn't have a license, it's considered 'enterprising.' If an Amish person raises more than one breed and has a license, it's called 'running a puppy mill.' "

"Some Amish and Englishers probably don't take good care of their dogs," Martha said. "But I'm not one of them."

"Of course you're not," Mom said. Her hand shook a bit as she patted Martha's arm.

Dad gave the newspaper another good rap and grunted. "If that man comes around here asking a bunch of nosy questions, I'll give him a piece of my mind. Fact is, I've got half a notion to go over to that newspaper office and have a little talk with Gary's boss. He ought to know one of his reporters is writing things that aren't true."

Martha figured if her father hadn't gone

to the sheriff when most of the attacks had occurred, he wasn't likely to go to the newspaper office and file a complaint.

"Calm down, Roman. You're getting too upset about this," Mom said. "I'm sure anyone reading that article will know it's not true." She added more coffee to her cup. "Would . . . would you like more coffee, Roman, or another piece of toast?"

Dad shook his head and pushed away from the table. "I've lost my appetite, so I think I'll head out to the barn and get busy on that new set of cabinets the bishop ordered the other day. Nothing gets me calmed down better than work."

Dad grabbed his stocking cap from the wall peg and slipped into his jacket. He turned and looked right at Martha. "If you ever see that reporter again, don't say a word to him. Is that clear?"

"Jah, Dad," she mumbled. She hoped she hadn't made a promise she might not be able to keep, because if she ran into Gary again, she'd probably give him a piece of her mind.

As Luke headed home from work that afternoon, he spotted Toby's rig pulling out of his folks' driveway. *I wonder what he was doing at our place.* Luke lifted his hand in a wave, but Toby looked the other way and kept on going.

When Luke entered the house, he found his mother sitting at the kitchen table massaging her forehead. His dad sat across from her wearing a frown. Something must be wrong.

"What's going on?" Luke asked. "Why was Toby here?"

Pop glared at him. "You don't know?"

"I have no idea."

"He came about that stupid truck of yours."

"My . . . my what?"

"Don't play dumm with me, Luke." Pop's voice raised an octave, and a muscle on the side of his neck quivered. "Toby told us you have a truck you keep hidden in the woods so we won't know about it. Is it true?" He leveled Luke with a piercing stare. "Well, is it?"

Luke dropped his gaze to the floor. "Jah, it's true."

Pop slammed his fist on the table, sending the napkin holder sailing across the room. "I might have known you'd go behind my back and do something like that!"

"Now, Elam, please calm down." Mom's voice was pleading, and Luke figured she was close to tears. She had never approved of yelling in the house.

Apparently, Mom's cocker spaniel, Cindy, didn't care for Pop's yelling, either, for the shaggy little dog left her place by the wood-stove and ducked under the table.

"I won't calm down!" Pop shouted. "Not until our son gets rid of that truck!"

"I've not joined the church yet, so I have every right to own a motorized vehicle." Luke's defenses rose. "What all did Toby say that's got you so riled and demanding that I sell my truck?" he asked.

"He said a black truck matching the description of yours was seen cruising around the schoolhouse near Farmerstown last night."

"I wasn't riding around in my truck last night."

"Jah, well, Toby says the fellow driving the truck was wearing a baseball cap like you sometimes wear." Dad grunted. "You oughta be wearin' an Amish man's hat, not what the Englishers wear."

"So someone was driving a truck that looks like mine, and he was wearing a baseball cap," Luke said, making no reference to what he should or shouldn't be wearing. "What does that prove?"

"It proves that whoever egged the school-house during the night could have been the same one driving the truck."

Luke's eyebrows lifted high on his forehead. "The schoolhouse was egged?"

Pop nodded. "The public school in Charm had some windows broken out awhile back, and now the Amish schoolhouse in Farmerstown's been singled out."

"I hope you don't think I egged the schoolhouse or broke those windows in Charm."

"I'm not saying you did either of those things," Pop replied, "but Toby believes you did because he saw your truck in the area."

"So it was Toby who supposedly saw me, huh? A minute ago you said Toby told you someone else had seen my truck." Luke clenched his fists. "That *someone* was Toby, wasn't it?"

Pop nodded slowly.

"Well, he's lying! I wasn't driving my truck last night, and I didn't egg the schoolhouse."

"We believe you, Luke," Mom said. "But we don't want folks making accusations."

"If the bishop's son is the one making those accusations, then people are likely to listen," Pop added.

Luke folded his arms. "I don't care what other people think. I didn't vandalize either of those schools, and I'm not the one responsible for any of the attacks against the Hostettlers."

Mom shot out of her chair. "Now where'd you come up with that? Your daed never accused you of —"

"He didn't have to," Luke interrupted. "I already know Roman thinks I'm the one responsible for the things that have been done at their place." He rocked back and forth on his heels. "I don't know why, but it seems as if Toby's trying to make me look bad, even to my own parents."

"You don't look bad," Mom said with a shake of her head. "It's just that we want you to —"

"Get rid of that truck!" Dad said. "That way if anybody sees someone driving a black truck and wearing a baseball cap, they won't accuse you."

Luke shook his head. "I'm not selling my truck because Toby's likes to *blabbermaul.*"

"He may like to blabber, but if he can convince others that you're responsible —"

"I don't want to sell my truck. At least not now."

"If you don't, then you'll likely be blamed for everything that happens in this area." A vein on the side of Pop's neck bulged, and Luke knew he was walking on thin ice.

"I'll have a talk with Toby if you like," Luke said. "Maybe I can talk some sense into him — make him realize it wasn't me who did all those things."

Pop shook his head. "Forget talking to Toby. I want you to sell that truck!"

"And if I don't?"

"Then you'll have to move out."

Luke turned sharply toward the door. "Fine then, I'll move out!"

"Please, don't do that!" Mom grabbed the sleeve of Luke's jacket. "Where would you go?"

"Guess I'll head for the woods and sleep in my truck."

"It's too cold to be sleeping in your truck." Mom turned pleading eyes on Pop. "Please say something to convince Luke he shouldn't move out."

Pop shrugged his shoulders. "Betty, there's not much I can say if the boy wants to live in his precious truck."

Luke moved toward the door, but Mom positioned herself in front of it. "I won't sleep a wink tonight if I have to lie in bed thinking about you freezing to death. Please, don't go, Luke. Stay here and we'll work things out."

"There's not much to work out unless he agrees to sell his truck," Pop said, shooting a piercing glance at Luke.

Luke drew in a deep breath and released

it with a huff. He didn't like seeing his mother so upset. Truth was, he really didn't want to sleep in his truck — especially in the dead of winter. "I'll tell you what," he said, reaching into his pocket and withdrawing his truck keys. "How about I leave these with you for two weeks? During that time, if any attacks occur where a black truck is seen, then you'll know I wasn't driving the truck or doing the dirty deed."

Pop held out his hand and accepted the offered keys. "All right then. It's agreed."

CHAPTER 16

When Martha went out to the barn to feed her dogs the following morning, she discovered Fritz, her male sheltie, lying in the corncrib on a pile of dried corn. Her heart gave a lurch. Had someone come into the barn and let the dog out? No, that was impossible; the barn door had been locked. She was just being paranoid.

"How did you get out of your kennel, boy?" Martha murmured, reaching out to pat Fritz's head. "And what are you doing here in the corncrib?"

The dog lifted his head and responded with a lethargic grunt. He was obviously quite comfortable.

Martha was sure she had latched all the cage doors securely last night. She glanced around, wondering if any of the other dogs had gotten out. To her relief, there was no sign of them.

"Come on, Fritz. You can't stay here all

day." Grasping the dog's collar, Martha led him back to his kennel. The door to his cage was hanging open, although the latch didn't appear to be broken. Could Fritz have figured out some way to open the gate? If that were the case, she would have to rig something up so he couldn't get out. Martha put Fritz back in his cage and inspected the rest of the cages. Everything was just as it should be.

Smiling, she leaned against the wire fence that enclosed the dog run and watched Heidi's growing puppies scamper around, yipping and nipping at one another in play. She glanced at her beagle Polly and was pleased to see that her pups were nursing. The little scamps were sure growing. Maybe she would run an ad in the *Bargain Hunter* and sell some of the puppies for Valentine's Day.

I hope that article by Gary Walker won't hurt my sales.

Pushing her disconcerting thoughts aside, Martha hurried to get the dogs fed and watered. She didn't have to work for Irene today, so after breakfast, she planned to head to Berlin to do some shopping for Mom.

Should I lock the door? Martha wondered as she left the barn a few minutes later. *No, everything will be fine. I'm just feeling anxious for nothing.* Martha closed the barn door and headed for the house to help Mom with breakfast.

"I can't get over that article Gary Walker wrote in yesterday's newspaper," Grace said.

Cleon nodded as he scooped his lunch pail off the counter. "The man ought to get his facts straight before he writes a story like that."

"I think he wrote those things about Martha on purpose, just to make our family look bad."

Cleon grunted. "You don't still think he's trying to get even with you for breaking up with him when you were a teenager, do you?"

"I don't know. He's denied it several times, but I don't trust him." Grace sighed. "After the way he treated me when we were dating and the upsetting things he's said to me since he came to Holmes County, I wouldn't put anything past him."

Cleon glanced at the kitchen table where eight-year-old Anna sat eating her oatmeal. Daniel was seated in his high chair next to her. "We shouldn't be talking about things like this in front of the kinner," he said, lowering his voice. "I don't want them to live in fear that something bad's going to happen."

"Daniel's not old enough to know what's going on," Grace said. "Anna's another story. She's already been through a lot, so I'll try to be more careful what I say in front of her."

Cleon gave Grace a hug. "There haven't been any more attacks for a while, so try not to worry."

As Grace stood in the doorway, watching Cleon walk down the driveway toward her father's barn, she whispered a prayer. "Dear Lord, please put an end to these attacks."

As Martha left the hardware store, where she'd purchased some new feeding dishes for her dogs, she spotted Luke coming out of the market with a disposable camera in his hands.

Luke waved.

She waved back, wondering if he would make his way across the parking lot to say hello. To her delight, he did.

"What are you doing in town in the middle of the day?" she asked as he stepped up to her. "I figured you'd be working."

He nodded. "I am. John sent me to town to pick up a few things he needed, so I decided to make a stop of my own."

"For that?" she asked motioning to the camera in his hand.

"Jah."

"Why do you need a camera?"

"To take pictures, of course."

"Of what?"

Luke's voice lowered to a whisper. "Since I'm trying to help you figure out who's behind the attacks, I figured I might get some pictures."

She tipped her head in question.

"If another attack occurs, I'll come out with my camera and take pictures of the damage and any evidence that might be there."

Martha lifted her gaze to the sky. "Like my daed's going to let you do that."

"He doesn't have to know. I'll do it when he's not around."

Martha shook her head. "I don't think that's a good idea, Luke."

"Why not?"

"Even if you did get some pictures without my daed seeing you, what good would the pictures do?"

"If the pictures show anything helpful, I guess I could take 'em to the sheriff." Luke shrugged. " 'Course, I'm not sure how much good that would do, since he hasn't done much to stop the attacks. Makes me wonder . . ."

"Did you see that article in yesterday's paper written by Gary Walker?" Martha asked.

"Nope. I haven't even read yesterday's paper. What was it about?"

"It had to do with the rumors that some Amish in the area are running puppy mills." Martha shook her head. "Gary insinuated that I might be running a puppy mill."

Luke's mouth dropped open. "You're kidding."

She shook her head. "He attended dinner at Irene's a few weeks ago, and before he left, he cornered me, asking if he could come to our place and interview me about my dogs."

"What'd you tell him?"

"I said I wasn't interested in being interviewed for the newspaper." Martha rubbed a sore spot on the side of her head, knowing she was on the verge of a full-blown headache. "I figure he probably wrote that article to get back at me for refusing to let him do a story about my kennel business."

Luke grunted. "Gary Walker is not a nice man. In fact, he's near the top of my list of suspects."

Martha nodded. "Mine, too."

"You know what I think we should do?"

"What's that?"

"I think we should plan to meet somewhere again and go over our lists. I have a few ideas I'd like to talk to you about."

"When did you want to meet, and where?"

"What are you doing this Saturday?"

"I'm not working that day, and I have no special plans."

"How about we meet at Keim Lumber? It's always crowded there on Saturdays, and we'll probably go unnoticed."

"You want to sit in the parking lot in our buggies and talk about the attacks?"

Luke shook his head. "I figured we could meet there and then drive somewhere out of the area in my pickup where we're not likely to be seen by anyone we know."

Martha's heart began to race. She'd only seen Luke's truck when it was parked in the woods, and she certainly never expected to take a ride in it. What if someone she knew saw her getting into his truck? Would they tell Dad? Would they think she and Luke were courting?

Before she could formulate a response, Luke snapped his fingers and said, "Rats! I almost forgot."

"What?"

"I can't go anywhere in my truck because my daed has the keys."

"You gave him the keys to your truck?"

He nodded.

"I didn't think your folks knew you had a truck."

"Thanks to that blabbermouth Toby, my folks found out." Luke grimaced. "Toby told Pop he saw a truck like mine cruising around the schoolhouse in Farmerstown the night it was egged. Pop thinks once the word gets out that I've got a truck and someone spotted a truck like mine near the schoolhouse, I'll be blamed for the vandalism. He was so upset about all this that he demanded I get rid of the truck."

"What'd you say?"

"I refused. Then he said I'd have to move out." Luke tugged his earlobe. "When I said I would leave, Mom got real upset. The next thing I knew, I'd opened my mouth and suggested that I leave my truck keys with my daed for the next couple of weeks. Then I said if a truck was seen anywhere near a place that had been vandalized, Pop would know I hadn't done the dirty deed."

Martha stood, too dumfounded to speak. If Toby had been so brazen as to tell Luke's folks about his truck and that he thought Luke might be involved in the schoolhouse vandalism, what else was Toby saying about Luke, and to whom was he saying it?

Luke touched Martha's arm, and the strange tingle she felt made her wish even more that they were a courting couple.

"The uncertain expression on your face makes me wonder if you believe I'm responsible for those acts of vandalism."

"No, I —"

"I didn't do it, Martha. You've got to believe me."

"I do believe you."

"Then you'll still meet me on Saturday?"

She nodded. "If the roads aren't too bad, maybe we could take separate buggies and meet somewhere other than Keim Lumber. That way, if someone should see us, it won't look like we're together."

Luke groaned. "I hate sneaking around all the time. I ought to have the right to see you without having to hide it."

"Well, if you'd just —"

Luke snapped his fingers. "Why don't we meet in Mt. Hope at Mrs. Yoder's restaurant? It's not likely we'll see anyone we know up there."

"That's true, but even if we do see someone we know, they'll probably think we came there separately and are sharing a table."

"I'll see you at Mrs. Yoder's on Saturday then. In the meantime, I'd better get back to work before John comes looking for me."

Martha smiled. "It was good seeing you, Luke."

"Same here."

As Luke sprinted toward his buggy, Martha smiled. She could hardly wait until Saturday.

CHAPTER 17

As Martha took a seat at a table near the window in Mrs. Yoder's restaurant, her heart started to pound. She could hardly wait to see Luke. The more time she spent with him, the more she realized that she'd foolishly allowed herself to fall in love with him.

She stared out the window, watching a slow-moving truck follow a horse and buggy up the road, but her thoughts remained on Luke. Was he telling the truth about giving his truck keys to his father? Was she absolutely sure Luke could be trusted? Did he really want to help her learn the identity of the person who'd done the attacks?

If Dad knew I'd fallen in love with Luke and that I've been seeing him on the sly, he'd be furious. Martha gripped the edge of the table until her knuckles turned white. *If Luke knew how much I cared, what would he think?*

"A nickel for your thoughts."

Martha jerked at the sound of Luke's voice. "Oh, I didn't know you were here."

"I just arrived and saw you sitting here by yourself so figured I might join you."

"Jah, please do." Martha smiled and glanced around. If anyone they knew saw them together, Luke was doing a good job of making it look like they'd accidentally met and had decided to share a table. She hated to be sneaking like this, but she didn't know any other way they could meet and talk about the attacks.

"How are things with you?" Luke asked as he took a seat across from her.

"Okay. And you?"

He shrugged. "Things are kind of tense at home, but at work, things are fine and dandy."

"You enjoy working with wood, don't you?"

He nodded, and a sparkle of light danced in his dark eyes. "I'd like to have my own shop someday, but I guess that's not likely to happen."

"What makes you say that?"

He leaned both elbows on the table. "Think about it. Your daed owns one wood-working shop in our area, and John owns the other. I don't think there's a need for three, do you?"

"Probably not." Martha felt sorry for Luke. It seemed like nothing was going right for him these days. Of course things weren't going all that well for her, either. She'd spent the last couple of years putting most of her time and money into raising dogs, and she wasn't much further along now than when she'd first started.

"Maybe John would consider making you his partner," she suggested.

Luke shook his head. "I rather doubt that. He seems to like being the boss. Besides, I don't have enough money saved up to buy half his business."

"I can relate to that. I'd like to buy several more breeds of dogs to raise, but that takes money, and until I sell enough dogs —"

"Have you two decided on what you'd like to order?" their young Mennonite waitress asked, stepping up to the table.

"I'll have the salad bar," Martha replied.

Luke nodded. "I'll have that, too."

Martha tipped her head. "Is that really all you're having?"

"Jah." He patted his stomach. "I had a very big breakfast this morning."

"Would you like anything to drink other than water?"

Luke shook his head, and Martha did the same.

"Help yourself to the salad bar then."

Martha pushed away from the table and smiled at Luke as he walked beside her. This almost felt like a real date.

As Luke sat at the table eating his salad and watching Martha eat hers, a deep sense of longing filled his soul. If things weren't so mixed up right now, and if he knew he could gain Roman's approval, he would probably ask to court Martha.

"You look kind of *verwart,*" Martha said, breaking into Luke's thoughts. "Is something wrong?"

Luke took a drink of water before he spoke. "I . . . uh . . . This whole thing with the attacks is enough to make anyone feel perplexed."

She nodded. "If only we could find out who's been attacking us and make him stop, things would be back to normal."

"Have you come up with any new ideas on how we're going to do that?"

"Not really. I thought I'd make a trip to see the sheriff."

"What for?"

"To tell him that I plan to do some investigating on my own and say that I'd like his help."

Luke shook his head vigorously. "I don't

think that's a good idea, Martha."

"Why not?"

He leaned forward and lowered his voice. "I've been mulling things over the last few days, and I've put the sheriff on my list of suspects."

"What?" Martha's mouth dropped open. "Why would you think Sheriff Osborn had anything to do with the attacks?"

"Think about it. The attacks have been going on since before Grace married Cleon. Wouldn't you think by now the sheriff would at least have some leads?"

"Maybe he'd have some leads if my daed had told him about the attacks sooner."

"But he knows now, and nothing's been done."

"He's been keeping an eye on our place ever since Dad's shop was blown up."

"How long do you think he'll keep doing that?"

She shrugged. "I don't know."

"Doesn't it seem strange that a man who's sworn to uphold the law and do all he can to keep people safe hasn't done much more than drop by your place and make your daed a few promises to keep an eye on things?"

"That could be Dad's fault. By the time Sheriff Osborn has found out about most of the attacks, the perpetrator's trail's grown cold."

Luke nearly choked on the water he'd just put in his mouth. "Perpetrator? What have you been reading lately — Nancy Drew mystery novels?"

Martha's face flamed, and she blinked a couple of times. "Are you making fun of me?"

"Sorry," he mumbled.

"I'll admit I have read a few mystery stories. I know for a fact that if too much time passes after a crime is committed, it's that much harder to determine who did the crime." Martha folded her arms. "I've also thought about questioning some of the suspects on my list during my free time."

Luke shook his head. "That's not a good idea, either."

"Why not?"

"If the person you're questioning turns out to be the one responsible for the attacks, you could be in danger."

"I'm not afraid."

"Well, you should be. Look what happened to Ruth and Martin. If the person who rammed their buggy is the same one who did all the other things to your family, then he — or she — won't think twice about harming you."

Martha's face paled. "You really think I could be in danger?"

"It's possible." Luke reached across the table and touched her arm. "Promise you won't do anything foolish?"

"I promise."

CHAPTER 18

When Martha returned home from her meeting with Luke, she was filled with a sense of hope. Not only did he want to help her find the person responsible for the attacks, but also he was concerned for her safety. She saw it as a sign that he might care for her — hopefully as more than a friend. She wondered if Luke might decide he wanted to court her once they found out who was behind the attacks.

"That's probably wishful thinking," Martha murmured as she stepped into the barn to put her horse away.

"What's wishful thinking?"

Martha whirled around. "Dad, I didn't know you were in here."

He stepped out of the shadows near the back of the barn. "Came in to get a roll of wire. One of our fences in the back pasture has been cut. If I don't get it fixed right away, the horses will all be out."

"Not another attack," she said with a moan. "I was hoping now that the sheriff has been watching our place more, the attacks would end."

Dad reached out to stroke her horse's ear. "Someone's obviously trying to get even with me for something."

"Or maybe they want our land."

He huffed. "I won't be run off this place, and I won't spend my days living in fear."

"Would you mind if I go with you to fix the fence?" Martha asked. Maybe she would discover some clue as to who had cut the wire.

He shrugged. "If you've got nothing better to do, you're welcome to come along."

"I'm free for the rest of the day." Martha glanced toward the barn door. "Should I run up to the house first and tell Mom where we'll be so she won't worry in case she comes looking for you?"

He shook his head. "Your mamm's not home. She went over to Abe and Ruth's place to see how things are going with them. I doubt she'll be back until it's time to start supper."

"Okay. I'll put my horse away, and then I'll be ready to head out."

When Luke stepped onto the back porch of

his home, he heard voices coming from the kitchen. One he recognized as his mother's; the other he was sure belonged to Judith Hostettler.

As Luke opened the door, he heard Judith say, "This afternoon, Roman discovered someone had cut the fence in our back pasture." She groaned. "I'm getting so tired of these attacks."

"I hope Roman doesn't think Luke had anything to do with it. I know he's accused him of doing some of the other things."

Luke's spine went rigid as he halted. He could see the back of his mother's head through the doorway to the kitchen on the other side of the utility room.

"I think my husband was wrong when he accused your son," Judith replied. "I know Luke's going through rumschpringe and all, but I can't imagine he would do any of the horrible things that have been done to us."

Mom nodded. "Luke tends to be impulsive and stubborn at times, but he's a good boy. We've raised him to respect other people's property."

"Our Martha's the same way — stubborn and impulsive but always polite and respectful."

Luke edged closer to the back door. Should he make himself known, keep on listening, or turn around and head back outside?

"What's Roman going to do about the fence?" Mom asked Judith.

"He was planning to fix it right away."

"I meant, what's he planning to do about the vandalism that keeps happening at your place?"

"There's not much he can do."

"He could notify the sheriff."

Judith sighed. "The sheriff's supposedly been watching our place, but obviously it hasn't kept the attacker from thinking up more things to do."

"How do you feel about all this?"

Judith gave another long sigh. "Each attack makes me feel more nervous, but I'm asking God to calm my fears, and I'm praying that eventually the one who's been doing these things will either be caught or will decide to quit tormenting us on their own."

Luke pressed his weight against the wall. *I wonder what Mom and Judith would say if they knew Martha and I were trying to find out who's responsible?*

Judith's chair squeaked as she pushed away from the table. "Well, I'd best be on my way. I told Roman I was going over to see Ruth, and if I don't get there soon, it'll be time to turn around and head home again so I can start supper."

Luke knew if he didn't do something soon, his presence would be known. He quietly opened the back door and slipped outside. Maybe he would head over to the Hostettlers' place and check on the fence that had been cut. By the time he got there, Roman should be finished with his repairs. This would be a good chance to take a few pictures and look for some evidence.

Ruth settled into the rocking chair with Molly in her lap, leaned her head back, and closed her eyes. She'd had another disagreement with Gideon this morning, and it had left her feeling drained and more discouraged than ever. If only there was something she could say or do to make the boy happy and compliant. If she could just think of a way to get through to him — make him understand that she cared about him and needed his acceptance. Ruth felt that Gideon needed her, too; he just didn't realize it.

She thought about Abe — the steady, gentle man she'd married. She felt blessed to be his wife and hoped she could make him happy.

As Ruth rocked the bundle of sweetness in her lap, she sang an old song her mother used to sing when she and her sisters were young. *"Well, I don't care if the birds don't sing; I don't care if the bells don't chime; just as long as you love me. I don't care if the world don't turn; I don't care if the fire don't burn; just as long as you love me."*

Ruth was close to drifting off when the back door creaked open. She turned her head. Thinking it might be Abe, she was surprised to see Mom enter the room.

Ruth nodded at the sleeping child in her lap. "Let me put her on the sofa, and then we can go to the kitchen for a cup of tea."

Mom smiled. "She's awfully *schee,* isn't she?"

"Jah, she's a very pretty child." Ruth stood and placed Molly on the sofa; then she quietly followed her mother into the next room.

It wasn't until they were seated at the table and had cups of tea in their hands that she noticed her mother's furrowed brows and grim expression.

"Is something wrong, Mom? You look upset."

Mom sighed deeply. "I am upset. Someone cut your daed's fence near the back pasture."

"Did any of his cows or horses get out?"

Mom shook her head. "Luckily, your daed

215

found the cut before that happened."

Ruth reached over and took her mother's hand. "Oh, Mom, are these attacks ever going to end?"

Mom stared into her cup and slowly shook her head. "I don't know. I just don't know." She lifted the cup with a shaky hand and took a sip of tea. "Your daed seemed pretty calm about the whole thing. He told me earlier that he's still trusting God to put an end to all this. In the meantime, he plans to keep a closer eye on things."

Ruth released a heavy sigh as she leaned heavily against her chair. "Why does everything have to be so unsettled? Why can't things be safe and peaceful?"

"I'm afraid we'll never know complete peace until we're face-to-face with our heavenly Father."

"I realize that. I just wish —"

"You look troubled, too, Ruth," Mom said. "Are things okay between you and Abe?"

"Everything's fine. It's my relationship with Gideon I'm worried about."

"What seems to be the problem?"

"Gideon's so defensive whenever I say anything to him. He won't join any family games or contribute much to our conversations. He just wants to be off by himself.

Abe has an awful time getting the boy to even do his chores."

"Do you think Gideon's still mourning his mudder's death?"

"Jah, I do. I also think he resents me being his daed's new fraa."

"Give him more time, Ruth. I'm sure the boy will come around eventually."

"I hope so, because it's getting harder to deal with, especially when Abe's other four kinner are sweet and compliant."

Mom took another sip of tea. "God has blessed you by bringing Abe and his kinner into your life. I think you should keep your focus on that right now."

Ruth nodded and reached for her cup. "You're right, Mom. We all need to focus on the positive things."

"Danki for helping me fix the fence," Dad said, smiling at Martha. "Since I have no sons, it's nice to have a daughter who's not afraid to get her hands dirty."

"Jah, that's me — Martha the tomboy."

"So, how was your morning, and where all did you go?" Dad asked, as they moved away from the fence.

"My morning was fine. Since most of the snow has melted, the roads were good. I did a little shopping, and then I went out to lunch." Martha was careful not to mention who she'd had lunch with.

"I'm glad you were able to get away for a while. You spend too much time around here with those hundlin of yours."

"I like spending time with my dogs."

"I know, but you're a young woman and need to be thinking of finding a suitable mate so you can marry and raise a family. Don't you agree?"

Martha shrugged. There was no way she could tell her father that she'd already found someone she'd like to marry. Dad would ask who, and if she told him it was Luke, she was certain he would become angry and forbid her to see Luke again. Of course she wasn't really seeing Luke in a boyfriend-girlfriend sort of way. They were just friends trying to solve a mystery together.

"Guess I'd better get going," Dad said, pulling Martha out of her musings. "Ray Larson's driving me to Millersburg right after lunch so I can get some supplies I need. I'd better get back to the barn and lay some things out for Cleon to do while I'm gone." He turned and started walking away. "Are you coming?"

"It's not as cold today as it has been. I think I'll go for a walk, but I'll head for the house soon."

"Jah, okay," he said with a wave.

Martha was glad Dad had given no objection to her taking a walk. She wanted to snoop around a bit and see if she could find anything that might give some clue as to who had cut the fence.

She walked along slowly, checking the stubble of grass sticking through the clumps of melting snow. Several feet from the fence, in a cluster of bushes, she spotted a worn-looking glove.

"Hmm, what have we here?" She bent to pick up the glove.

"What's that you're holding?"

Startled by the deep voice behind her, Martha jumped up and whirled around. There stood Luke, holding his camera. "You . . . you scared me."

"Sorry about that." Luke glanced around with an anxious expression. "Your daed's not anywhere nearby, I hope."

She shook her head. "He was here a few minutes ago — fixing our fence that someone cut."

"I heard about it."

"Who told you?"

Luke's face colored. "I'd just gotten home from having lunch with you, and when I stepped into the house, I heard your mamm and my mamm talking in the kitchen. When your mamm said your fence had been cut, I decided to hightail it over here and do a little investigating." He gazed at the fence. "Which part was cut?"

"Right here." Martha moved over to stand by the fence and pointed to the spot her father had fixed.

Luke lifted his camera and took a picture; then he turned to Martha and said, "Did you find that glove somewhere nearby?"

She nodded. "Found it in the bushes right before you showed up."

"Mind if I have a look-see?"

She handed him the glove.

"Looks like a work glove to me. I'm guessing whoever cut the fence must have dropped the glove when they were running away."

"That's what I figured, too," Martha said with a nod. "Do you think we should keep the glove or tell the sheriff about it?"

He shook his head. "Like I said at lunch, I'm not sure he can be trusted. Besides, we have no definite evidence as to who the attacker might be, so I think it's best that we keep all the evidence we find to ourselves. Don't you?"

"I suppose. If we get more evidence and decide the sheriff doesn't have anything to do with the attacks, we can turn everything we've found over to him."

Luke nodded, handed the glove back to her, and snapped another picture.

"Do you really think that's going to do any good?"

Luke shrugged. "You never know. The other glove might show up somewhere. If it does, I'll know who it belongs to."

"But if we keep the glove, we won't need a picture of it."

"Good point." He grinned. "Guess I'm not real good at this detective thing yet. Maybe the camera was a dumb idea."

"It was a good thought," Martha was quick to say, "but I really don't think taking pictures will help that much." She tucked the glove under the band of her apron. "Guess I'd better keep this in a safe place for now."

"Did you check for footprints?"

She shook her head. "I haven't gotten that far yet."

"Then let's do it now."

Martha and Luke spent the next several minutes scrutinizing the area around the part of the fence that had been cut. "There's the print of my sneaker," Martha said, pointing to the footprints her shoes had made. "And there are some boot prints, but

I can't be sure whether they were made by the person who cut the fence or by my daed." She grunted and slapped the side of her head. "Guess I should have thought to look for footprints before Dad and I started working on the fence."

"Where are you gonna put the glove?" Luke asked.

"Probably in the hayloft where I hid the wrench."

"Are you sure no one will find it there?"

She nodded. "It's in a box under a mound of hay where the cats like to sleep. Dad keeps all the hay he needs for feeding the horses in one side of the barn, so he really has no reason to go into the hayloft for anything right now."

"Okay. I'd better go. Can we meet somewhere soon to discuss things more?" Luke asked.

Martha's heartbeat picked up speed, the way it always did whenever she thought about spending time with Luke. "I have next Saturday off."

"Where do you want to meet?"

"How about Heini's Cheese? That's a public place, and if someone sees us, they'll figure we just met there accidentally and are talking. Would two o'clock work for you?"

Luke smiled and nodded. "I'll see you at Heini's then."

As Roman and Ray drove through Millersburg in Ray's station wagon that afternoon, they passed the newspaper office. It made Roman think about Gary Walker and the article he'd written. He had threatened to have a talk with Gary about the things he'd written that weren't true. Maybe this was the time to make good on his threat.

He turned to Ray and said, "Would you mind dropping me off at the newspaper office?"

Ray blinked. "I thought you wanted to go to the Wal-Mart store."

"I do, but if you don't mind, I'd like to run into the newspaper office first. I have something I need to take care of there."

"Sure, no problem." Ray pulled over to the curb. "This a no-parking zone, so I'll drive around the block a few times, and when I see you standing out front, I'll pick you up. How's that sound?"

"Sounds good to me." Roman stepped out of the car and closed the door. Then he hurried up the steps and entered the building. He spotted a young woman sitting at a desk just inside the front door. "Excuse me, but is Gary Walker in his office today?"

The woman shook her curly blond head. "Gary Walker doesn't work here anymore."

"He — he doesn't?"

"No. Gary took a job at a newspaper in Redding, California. He's been gone for over a week."

Roman heaved a sigh of relief. If Gary had been attacking them, the attacks would finally be over. If he wasn't responsible, then it had to be someone else on his list of suspects.

CHAPTER 19

As Martha headed for the barn, a biting wind stung her cheeks, and huge flakes of snow landed on her woolen jacket.

When she stepped into the barn, she brushed the snow off her jacket and started for the kennels.

Woof! Woof! Fritz bounded up to Martha, planting both paws on her knees.

"Fritz! What are you doing out of your cage again?" Martha gently pushed the dog to the floor.

The sheltie responded with another loud bark and a couple of wags of his tail.

"Come on, boy. Let's get you back to your cage." Martha headed in the direction of the kennels with Fritz at her side. When she arrived at his cage, she halted. The door hung wide open.

"I can't believe this," she groaned. "How are you managing to get that latch undone?"

Fritz stared up at her with sorrowful

brown eyes and released a pathetic whimper. Was it possible that he'd figured out a way to open the door to his cage, or could someone have let the dog out on purpose? But if that were so, then why only Fritz and not the rest of her dogs?

Martha put Fritz back in his cage, closed the door, and waited to see what he would do. Fritz gave a friendly wag of his tail and scurried off to his doghouse.

"Of course you're not going to do anything while I'm standing here." Anxious to finish her chores in the barn so she could speak to her father, Martha hurried through the feeding process. When that was done, she returned to the house.

"You're right on time," Mom said as Martha stepped into the kitchen. "I just started putting breakfast on the table. Since it's so cold and snowy this morning, I fixed a big pot of oatmeal."

Martha removed her coat and hung it on a wall peg near the back door. "That's good to hear. I'm hungry and more than ready to eat." She hurried across the room and washed her hands at the sink.

Dad looked up from where he sat, reading the morning newspaper. "How'd it go in the barn? Did you get the dogs all fed and watered?"

"The feeding went okay, but I found Fritz out of his cage again." Martha flopped into the chair opposite him. "It makes no sense how he keeps getting out."

"Did you close and latch the cage doors last night?" Mom asked.

"Jah, of course. I even checked them twice to be sure."

"Maybe Fritz has figured out a way to unlatch his door." Dad folded his paper and set it aside. "Some animals, even the smaller breeds, can be real clever when it comes to things like that."

"Fritz may be clever, but he's never gotten out of his cage until recently."

"Here's the oatmeal," Mom announced.

As soon as Mom was seated at the table and their silent prayer was done, Martha said, "I'm thinking of sleeping in the barn for a couple of nights."

"Why would you want to do that?" Mom asked.

"So I can keep an eye on things — see how Fritz is getting out of his cage."

"That's just plain *narrisch*. It's too cold to be sleeping in the barn," Dad said with furrowed brows.

"Your daed's right; sleeping in the barn in the dead of winter would be a foolish thing to do," Mom agreed.

"But I've got to find out if Fritz is escaping on his own or if someone is sneaking into our barn during the night and letting him out."

Mom blinked a couple of times. "You think someone's doing it on purpose?"

"Don't be *lecherich*," Dad said. "I've been locking the barn at night, so there's no way someone could be sneaking in. Besides, I've got a hunch we don't have to worry about being under attack anymore."

"What makes you think that?" Martha asked.

"When Ray and I were in Millersburg yesterday, I had him drop me off at the newspaper so I could talk to Gary Walker about that article he wrote about you and your kennel business."

"You spoke with that reporter fellow?" Mom's eyes were huge.

He shook his head. "Never got the chance. The young woman at the front desk gave me some very good news."

"What?" Martha asked.

"Said Gary had taken a job at some newspaper in Redding, California." Dad took a drink from his coffee mug. "Guess he's been gone a week already."

"I'm glad to hear Gary's left Holmes County again, and I'm sure Grace will be, too," Martha said. "But isn't it possible that someone else is responsible and that they've been getting into the barn through the hayloft?"

Mom's mouth dropped open, and Dad's forehead wrinkled. "You think someone's climbing a ladder and coming in the small window leading from the outside to the barn?"

Martha nodded. "I think it's a possibility."

He shook his head and grunted. "No way! It would take a tall ladder to reach that window, and I keep all my ladders inside the barn."

"Maybe whoever's doing it brings his own ladder."

"Now that is lecherich," Dad said with a snicker. "What reason would anyone have for sneaking into our barn through the hayloft in the middle of a cold, snowy night and releasing one of your dogs?"

"I don't know, but Fritz getting out of his cage has me worried, and I won't rest until I know how he's been getting out."

"Well, you're not sleeping in the barn," Dad asserted. "So if you're done talking about this, I need to get out to my temporary shop and get some work done."

"Speaking of your shop," Mom said. "I was wondering when you think you'll build a new one."

"In the spring, after the snow's all gone." He grunted. "I'll be glad to get out of that smelly barn. I get tired of hearing Martha's dogs yapping from their kennels."

"I can understand that, and —"

Martha tuned out her parents' conversation as she continued to mull over her problem with Fritz. If she couldn't sleep in the barn, she'd have to come up with some other way to find out how he'd been getting out of his kennel.

Luke had just stepped away from the checkout stand inside the hardware store in Berlin when he spotted Toby entering the store.

"What are you doing here?" Toby asked as Luke approached. "Shouldn't you be at John's place by now?"

Before Luke could reply, Toby added, "Or did you get fired from that job, too?"

Luke clenched his fingers. Why did Toby find it necessary to say cutting things every time they saw each other? "For your information, I'm still working for John." He lifted the paper sack in his hands. "And I came here to get a few things he needed before I head to work. What are *you* doing here so early? Shouldn't you be at Keim Lumber by now?"

"I don't have to be to work until ten today," Toby said. "I came to town to buy a new pair of work gloves."

"Did your old ones wear out from lifting all that heavy lumber at work?"

"Nope. I lost 'em, that's what."

Luke stared at his used-to-be friend. "You lost your work gloves and came all the way to Berlin to get a new pair?"

"Uh-huh."

"Don't they provide you with gloves at the lumber store?"

"Jah, sure, but this is the second pair I've lost in the last month, and my boss said if I lost another, I'd have to buy my own."

"I see."

"First I lost both gloves when I left 'em lying on a stack of lumber." Toby squinted. "Then the other day, one of my new gloves came up missing."

"It did, huh?"

"That's right." Toby snickered. "Sadie says she never realized how forgetful I was until we got married. Maybe it's 'cause I've got a lot more on my mind now that I have a wife to provide for."

Luke nodded. Was it possible that Toby had cut Roman's fence? Could that have been *his* glove Martha found near the fence? He was tempted to say something but changed his mind. No point in alerting his used-to-be friend that he was on to him. Not until he had some clear-cut evidence.

Roman had just lit the gas lamps in his shop, when the door opened and clicked shut. Figuring it was probably Cleon, he called over his shoulder, "*Guder mariye.* You can begin sanding that chair my sister ordered if you want."

"I don't know anything about a chair your sister ordered, but I'd like to have a word with you," a deep male voice said.

Roman whirled around. Just inside the door stood the pushy land developer who'd come around a few years back, asking to buy Roman's property.

"Remember me?" the man asked. "My name's Bill Collins, and I —"

"I know who you are. I thought you'd left Holmes County for good."

"I was gone for a time, but now I'm back, looking to purchase more land in this area."

Roman grimaced. In the area . . . out of the area. What was up with this man, anyway? For that matter, Gary Walker had been in and out of Holmes County a few times in the last couple of years, too. Didn't anyone stay put anymore?

"What do you want with me, Mr. Collins?" he asked.

"I was hoping you had changed your mind about selling and were ready to reconsider my offer to buy your property."

Roman folded his arms as he shook his head. "I wasn't interested when you came around before, and I'm not interested now."

Bill raked his fingers through the sides of his salt-and-pepper hair and plastered a smile on his face. "I heard while I was gone that there was some trouble around here."

A muscle on the side of Roman's face began to pulsate, but he made no comment.

"Heard you were the victim of some vandalism and other attacks." Bill took a step forward. "Guess some of them were pretty bad, too."

Roman grunted. Was this pushy man trying to intimidate him? Did Bill Collins think he could just show up out of the blue and talk him into selling his land?

"Here's the set of figures I offered you before," Bill said, reaching into his pocket and pulling out a slip of paper. "I'm prepared to offer you even more now."

"Forget it!" Roman took a seat behind his desk. "I told you then, and I'm telling you now: I'm not interested in selling."

Bill tapped the toe of his boot. "You strike me as a man who loves his family and wants to protect them. Am I right about that?"

"Of course."

"It seems to me if someone's out to get you, the best thing you could do for the sake of your family is to sell out and move far away from here. Go someplace where you won't be bothered."

Roman's face heated up. "Are you threatening me, Mr. Collins?"

"Not at all. I just thought I'd bring it to your attention that if you sold your land you'd be protecting your family from further harm." Bill placed both hands on the desk and leaned so close to Roman that he could smell the spicy aroma of the man's aftershave. "I think you'd do well to give my offer some serious consideration, Mr. Hostettler."

"I won't run from the problem. My family and I are trusting God to take care of this in His time, and I'm not selling out: plain and simple."

Bill snickered. "That's the dumbest thing I've ever heard. If God was going to protect you, then why didn't He stop all those terrible things from happening to you?"

"How'd you know about the attacks anyway?" Roman asked, ignoring the man's ridiculous question.

Bill leveled him with a piercing gaze. "I

234

have friends in the area. I also subscribe to the local newspaper, so I keep well-informed."

Roman cringed. *Could this man be responsible for the things that have been done to us? Did Bill Collins hire someone to do them so I'd knuckle under and agree to sell him my land? I can't let him know I'm scared, and I'm not going to be bullied into moving from here.*

He stood. "I'd appreciate it if you'd leave right now, Mr. Collins. And please, don't come back again."

Bill looked at Roman as if he didn't quite believe him. Then, with a lift of his shoulders and a muffled grunt, he sauntered out of the shop, slamming the door behind him.

Roman moved back to his chair and sank into it with a moan. "Oh, Lord, what am I going to do?"

CHAPTER 20

On Friday night as Martha prepared for bed, she made a decision. She'd found Fritz out of his cage two more times this week and wanted some answers. Since Dad wouldn't allow her to sleep in the barn, she'd decided to sit in a chair by her upstairs window and watch the barn with the binoculars she'd gotten for Christmas. From her upstairs room, she had the perfect view of the small outside window that led to the hayloft.

After only a short time of sitting in front of the window, staring through the binoculars, Martha's eyes became heavy and her arms started to ache. She flopped onto her bed with a groan. This wasn't working as well as she'd hoped. Besides, it had started snowing again, obscuring her vision.

Sometime later, she awoke with a start. She glanced at the clock on the table by her bed. It was almost four o'clock.

She dressed quickly. Grabbing the flashlight she kept by her bed, she slipped quietly out of the room and tiptoed down the stairs. When she reached the bottom step, she halted, listening for any sounds coming from her parents' bedroom. All she could hear was the steady *tick, tick, tick* of the living room clock mingling with Dad's muffled snores.

Martha hurried to the utility porch, slipped into her jacket and boots, and tied a woolen scarf around her head. Then she removed the key to the barn from the nail where it hung and stepped outside into the chilly night air. The snow swirled around her in clustered flakes, and she pulled her jacket tighter around her neck as she trudged through the snow toward the barn.

A few minutes later, with fingers stiff from the cold, she undid the padlock and entered the barn. It was dark, and her teeth began to chatter. Even so, she knew it wasn't a good idea to light a lantern. If Dad woke up and looked out the window, he'd probably notice the light in the barn and come to investigate.

With trembling fingers, Martha lifted the flashlight and shined a quick beam of light around the barn. Everything seemed fine — just as it should be. Drawing in a deep breath, she made her way toward the kennels in the back of the barn. She was relieved to see that all the cage doors were shut and the dogs were sleeping in their beds.

"Now I need to find a comfortable place to sit." She spotted a bale of hay inside one of the empty horse stalls and decided that would have to do. It was close enough to watch the kennels, but far enough away that she could stay out of sight should someone come into the barn.

Martha shivered as she plunked down on the hay. *I should have brought an old quilt from the house.* She shined the light around the stall and spotted a well-used horse blanket. It smelled like horse sweat but would help dispel the cold, and she couldn't afford to be choosy.

She clicked off the flashlight so she wouldn't run the battery down and leaned against the wall behind her, wrapping the smelly blanket around her shoulders. If someone opened one of the cage doors, she was bound to hear them.

What will I do if someone does come into the barn? I can't very well knock them to the floor and make them tell me why they've been letting my dog out of his cage or ask if they've been vandalizing our place.

A feeling of guilt coursed through Martha. She had not only disobeyed Dad by coming to the barn in the wee hours of the morning, but she'd been sneaking around seeing Luke without Dad's knowledge. *Maybe I shouldn't meet Luke at Heini's tomorrow. Maybe I should . . .*

Click . . . click . . . clang!

Martha bolted upright.

Squeeeak.

Someone must have opened one of the cage doors.

She held her breath and listened.

Woof! Woof! She recognized Fritz's deep bark. *Woof! Woof! Woof!* The other dogs chimed in.

Martha clicked on the flashlight and shined the light on the kennels. Sure enough, Fritz was out, and his cage door hung wide open. She sent a beam of light around the area. No one was in sight. If someone had come into the barn and opened Fritz's door, she would have heard them moving about. Besides, why would they open only Fritz's cage door?

Martha stepped out of the stall, and Fritz bounded up to her, wagging his tail. "You little stinker," she said, bending to pat his head. "I don't know how you're doing it, but you've figured out some way to get your cage door open, haven't you?"

Fritz gave a couple of barks, and Heidi, the female sheltie, followed suit. Soon Polly and Beau and both sets of puppies woke up and started barking, yapping, and running around their kennels.

"*Shh* . . . you'll wake up Mom and Dad." Martha grabbed Fritz's collar and led him back to his kennel. Fritz looked up at her and gave a pathetic whimper.

"You're not getting out so you can run all over the barn," she said with a shake of her head.

Using the flashlight to guide her steps, Martha hurried to the other side of the barn where some tools and supplies were kept. She returned to the kennels a few minutes later with a piece of sturdy wire, which she tied around the latch on Fritz's cage door. "That ought to hold you."

She shined the flashlight around the kennels one last time then hurried out of the barn. Mom would probably be up soon, and they'd need to start breakfast.

Luke's heart kept time to the rhythm of the horse's hooves as he headed to Berlin in his buggy. Since it had snowed again and the roads were a bit slippery, he wasn't sure if Martha would meet him at Heini's or not.

He'd been tempted to stop at her place and ask, but that wasn't a good idea.

Luke grimaced as he gripped the reins tighter. *If Roman knew Martha and I had plans to go anywhere together, he'd probably pitch a fit.*

A black truck whizzed by, honking its horn and splattering wet slush across the buggy window. The horse reared up then took off on a run.

"Whoa! Steady, boy," Luke said as he fought to keep his gelding under control.

The buggy wheels slipped on the snowy pavement, causing the buggy to slide first to one side and then the other. Just when Luke was sure his rig was going to tip over, the horse calmed down and started moving at a slower pace.

Luke wished he could have driven his truck today. It would have been safer than being out on the snowy road in a buggy with a skittish horse. He only had a few days left until his dad gave the truck keys back. He was glad there'd been no more episodes at the Hostettlers' place since the fence had been cut. To Luke's knowledge, his dad didn't know about that event, but even if he did find out, Luke had an alibi — he'd been home in bed. Since his dad had the truck keys, he couldn't accuse Luke of driving his

truck or being anywhere near the Hostettlers' place.

"I need to get to the bottom of these attacks," Luke muttered under his breath.
Maybe when he told Martha about Toby's
missing glove and said he thought Toby
might be responsible for the attacks, they'd
be able to come up with a way to catch Toby
in the act.

As Rosemary placed her breakfast dishes in
the sink, she decided it might be a good
time to pay a call on Sheriff Osborn. She'd
gone there a few weeks ago, but he hadn't
been in his office. Since then, her brother's
fence had been cut, and she was determined
to see the sheriff.

She glanced out the window and noticed
that it had finally quit snowing. Hopefully,
the roads had been cleared enough so she
could make the trip to town without any
problems. *Maybe I'll stop by and see Ruth on
my way,* she decided. It had been awhile
since they'd had a good visit, and she
wanted to see how Ruth was getting along
with her new family.

Half an hour later, Rosemary pulled her
car into the Wengerds' driveway and headed
for the back door. Ruth answered her knock,
red-faced and teary-eyed.

"Ruth, what's wrong? Have you been crying?"

Ruth nodded and hiccupped on a sob. "I'm afraid I'll never be a good stepmother."

Rosemary stepped into the house and shut the door. Then she put her arm around Ruth's waist and led her to the kitchen. "What's troubling you?" she asked, guiding Ruth into a chair.

Ruth took a napkin and wiped her nose. "I . . . I had another run-in with Gideon this morning."

"What happened?"

"I asked him to take out the garbage, and when he didn't do it right away, I asked him again." Ruth dabbed at the tears running down her cheeks. "Then he reminded me that I'm not his mudder and said I shouldn't be telling him what to do."

Rosemary's forehead wrinkled. "What did Abe have to say about his son speaking to you that way?"

"He'd already gone out to his harness shop, so he didn't hear Gideon's belligerent tone." Ruth drew in a shaky breath. "I'm trying so hard to get through to Gideon, but he just won't respond to me."

Rosemary gave Ruth's shoulder a gentle squeeze. "I know this is a difficult situation, but don't give up. Keep reaching out to the boy."

"I've been trying to, but he's not making it easy."

"Mammi." Little Molly toddled into the room.

"Come here, sweet girl," Ruth said, holding her arms out to the child.

"Mammi," the little girl said again as Ruth lifted her onto her lap. She smiled at Rosemary. "Would you like a cup of coffee or some tea?"

Rosemary nodded. "I could use something hot to drink before I head out again. It's pretty nippy this morning."

Martha's nose twitched when she stepped into Heini's Cheese Store and smelled the tangy aroma of smoked sausage and Swiss cheese. She glanced around the room, and her breath caught in her throat when she spotted Luke standing in front of one of the cheese counters.

Luke looked up as she approached and offered her a wide smile. "I'm glad to see you made it. With the weather turning snowy, I wasn't sure you'd be able to come."

"I used one of our easygoing horses and took my time coming in, so everything was fine."

"Wish I could say the same for my trip to town."

"What do you mean?"

"Some goofy driver in a pickup splashed slush all over my front window, and then my horse spooked and nearly ran away with my buggy." Luke poked another piece of cheese with a toothpick and popped it into his mouth. "My buggy swayed so much I thought it was gonna topple over." He reached for another toothpick. "Would you like a hunk of cheddar cheese?"

"No thanks." She tipped her head and studied him. "You look pretty calm. I take it you got things under control with your horse and buggy?"

He gave her a smug little grin. "Sure did."

She smiled. "There's a bench out in the entryway. Should we sit there and talk?"

"Sure." Luke headed that way, and Martha followed.

Once they were seated, she told him what had happened with Fritz and how she'd discovered that the dog had been opening his own cage door.

Luke chuckled. "That dog must have wanted freedom really bad to have figured out a way to escape."

She nodded. "Jah, but I solved the problem by wiring the door shut."

"That's good thinking."

"Another problem's been solved this week, too."

"What's that?"

"Gary Walker isn't working for the Millersburg news paper anymore. Dad found out that Gary took a job at a newspaper in California." Martha smiled. "So that's one name we can delete from our list of suspects."

"That's good to hear." Luke's voice lowered as he leaned closer to Martha. "I've got some information I think you should know about, too."

"What is it?"

"You know that work glove you found near the fence?"

She nodded.

"I think I know who it belongs to."

"Who?"

"Toby King."

Martha's eyebrows shot up. "What makes you think the glove belongs to Toby?"

"I ran into him the other day at the hardware store, and he mentioned that he'd lost a pair of gloves." Luke sucked in his lower lip. "He was buying a new pair."

"That doesn't prove he was anywhere near our place when he lost his glove."

"Doesn't prove he wasn't, either."

"What reason would Toby have for cutting our fence?"

Luke shrugged. "Maybe to get even with me."

"How would cutting our fence get even with you?"

"I told you before . . . Toby's got a grudge against me. I think he might be trying to make it look like I'm responsible for the attacks."

Martha drew in a quick breath. "I can't believe our bishop's son would be involved in anything so mean or destructive." She shook her head. "*Nee,* I can't conceive of it at all."

"Well, someone's been doing those things."

"Seems like our list of suspects keeps growing," she said.

He nodded. "Now all we have to do is figure out who it is."

CHAPTER 21

As Rosemary entered Sheriff Osborn's office, a whiff of smoke filled her nostrils. She was allergic to cigarette smoke; it gave her a headache. She would state her business and get out of the sheriff's stuffy office as quickly as possible.

The sheriff plunked his elbows on his desk and leaned slightly forward. "I heard you'd come back to the area. What can I do for you, Mrs. Cole?"

Rosemary took a seat. "I'm here about the attacks that are still being made against my brother and his family."

Sheriff Osborn's eyebrows shot up. "There has been another attack?"

She nodded slowly. "It was over a week ago."

"What happened this time, and why wasn't I informed?"

"The fence on Roman's back pasture was cut, and the reason you weren't informed is probably because Roman felt it wasn't serious." Rosemary grimaced. "At least not compared to some of the other things that have happened."

The sheriff grabbed a tablet and pen. "You'd better give me the details."

Rosemary spent the next few minutes telling the sheriff what had happened and that something needed to be done to protect her family before another attack occurred.

"I can hardly prevent things from happening when I'm usually the last one to know." He grunted. "I'm doing the best I can, but I don't have enough manpower to patrol the Hostettlers' place every minute of the day."

"I realize that, but —"

"If you want my opinion, the best thing Roman could do to protect his family is to move somewhere else."

Rosemary's skin prickled. When she'd first come to Holmes County to see Roman and his family, Judith had mentioned something about a land developer wanting to buy their land. She'd also heard one of Roman's neighbors had offered to buy his property.

"I don't think my brother has any plans to move," she said. "And I don't believe anyone should be allowed to get away with attacking him and his family in order to make him knuckle under and sell out."

The sheriff leveled her with a piercing gaze. "What makes you think the person doing the attacks is after Roman's land?"

"Isn't that what you were insinuating when you suggested he move?"

The sheriff shrugged.

"So there's nothing more you can do to stop these attacks?"

He shook his head. "I'm doing the best I can with whatever information I've been given."

Rosemary stood. She'd obviously made a mistake in coming here. It didn't appear as if Sheriff Osborn cared that much about the things that had been done to her brother and his family.

"Thank you for taking time out of your busy day to speak with me, Sheriff." She turned and marched out of the room, her snow boots clomping against the wooden floor.

Once outside, Rosemary drew a couple of deep breaths, relieved to be breathing fresh air again. *I think I'll stop over at Heini's Cheese Store for a little snack, and then I'm going over to Roman's place and have a talk with him.*

As Luke continued to talk with Martha

about Toby, her thoughts swirled like a windmill going at full speed. "I know Toby has something against you," she said. "That's obvious by the way he acts whenever the two of you are together."

Luke nodded.

She pursed her lips. "I don't see how he could have done all the attacks, though — especially when he was someplace else when most of them happened."

"Huh?"

"Take that day when our house was egged and we found a headless scarecrow in our yard. We'd been at Toby and Sadie's wedding, and the attack had to have occurred while we were there."

"So?"

"So, if Toby was at the wedding, which he obviously was, then he couldn't have been at our house throwing eggs or cutting off that old scarecrow's head."

Luke tapped his finger against his clean-shaven chin. "Maybe he had someone else do it for him."

"Who?"

"Beats me. All I know is Toby's no longer my friend, and I don't trust him as far as I can throw a mule."

"Some of the attacks might have been done by pranksters — maybe those English fellows you've been hanging around with."

He gave a quick nod. "Which is why —"

"Well, hello there, Martha. I didn't expect to see you here today."

Martha's head snapped around. "Aunt Rosemary! I didn't think I'd be seeing you here, either."

Aunt Rosemary smiled, first at Martha and then at Luke. "Hello, Luke. I'm surprised to see you here, as well."

His face colored, and he reached up to swipe at the sweat on his forehead. "I was just . . . uh . . . tasting some cheese, and Martha showed up, so —"

"So we came out here to talk awhile," Martha said, finishing Luke's sentence.

"I see." Aunt Rosemary took a seat beside Martha and patted her arm. "It's always good to see you."

"Same here."

Luke cleared his throat a couple of times. Martha could tell he was uncomfortable about having been seen with her. Truth was she felt a little apprehensive about it, too. At least it was Aunt Rosemary and not Dad who'd seen her sitting beside Luke.

"I'd better go," Luke said, rising to his feet. "I've got some errands to run, and then my daed needs my help this afternoon." He glanced over at Martha and gave her a half smile. "I'll be seeing you around."

She smiled and nodded in return.

Luke cast a quick smile in Aunt Rosemary's direction then hurried away.

"Luke seems like a nice enough fellow," Aunt Rosemary said, "but he acted kind of nervous, don't you think?"

Martha shrugged then leaned closer to her aunt and whispered, "I hope you won't say anything to my folks about seeing me and Luke together. Dad wouldn't like it."

"Why not?"

"He thinks Luke might be responsible for the attacks against us."

"Is that what you think, Martha?"

"I don't believe he is. In fact —" Martha halted her words. Should she tell Aunt Martha that she and Luke were trying to find out who was responsible for the attacks, or should she just say she'd been trying to find out on her own?

"Is there something troubling you, Martha? Something more than me seeing you with Luke?"

Martha nodded. "I'm concerned about the terrible things that have been done to my family, and I've decided to try and find out who's behind the attacks."

"You, too?"

Alarm rose in Martha's chest. Did Aunt

Rosemary already know Luke was doing some investigating of his own? "What do you mean?"

Aunt Rosemary glanced around as though she was worried someone might hear their conversation, but no one was within earshot, as far as Martha could tell.

"I've just come from Sheriff Osborn's office," Aunt Rosemary whispered. "I went there to see if he's come up with any leads and to let him know about your dad's fence being cut."

"Did the sheriff have anything helpful to say?"

"I'm afraid not. He thinks he could help more if he was told right away whenever something happens." Aunt Rosemary released a lingering sigh. "To tell you the truth, I don't think the sheriff cares all that much what happens to your family, and I . . ." Her voice trailed off.

"You what?" Martha prompted.

Aunt Rosemary glanced around once more. "I'd rather not discuss this with you here. Is there a time you can come by my house so we can visit privately?"

"I work for Irene all next week, but I'm free on Monday of the following week."

"Why don't you come over around eleven thirty? We can talk while we have lunch together." Aunt Rosemary gave Martha's arm a gentle pat. "You'll be the first lunch guest in my new house."

"You've had others over to eat in that house."

"That's true, but I was only renting the place then. Now that the home is mine, I'm starting fresh with my entertainment list."

Martha chuckled. She always felt relaxed when she was with Aunt Rosemary.

Aunt Rosemary stood. "I think I'll buy a couple packages of cheese and some trail bologna, and then I'll be on my way."

Martha smiled. "I'll see you next Monday for lunch."

"I'm done with those cabinets you wanted me to stain," Cleon said. "Did you want me to make those deliveries for you now?"

"Jah, sure," Roman answered with a nod.

"While I'm in Berlin, I'd like to stop by a couple of the shops that sell my honey and see if their supply's running low."

"No problem. Take your time."

Cleon smiled. "I appreciate you letting me continue with my honey business while working for you. I enjoy working with my bees, and it would be hard to give it up."

"Everyone in the family enjoys the honey your bees provide."

Cleon nodded. "I'd best get those chairs loaded up and head out. I should be back shortly after noon."

"No problem. Take your time."

The barn door clicked shut behind Cleon, and Roman resumed his work on some rusty hinges.

Some time later, the door opened, and Rosemary stepped into the barn.

"This is a surprise," Roman said, moving over to the door to greet his sister. "What brings you out on this cold winter day?"

"I came to see you, of course." Rosemary gave him a hug.

"I'm glad you did. How are things going? Are you all settled in?"

She nodded. "Now that all the unpacking is done, I need something else to keep me busy."

He chuckled. "I'm sure you'll find something to do. Even when you were a *maedel,* you always had to be busy."

"That's true," she admitted. "Most of the girls I knew were happy playing with their dolls, but not me. I felt I should be doing something more constructive."

"Are you thinking of finding a job?" he asked.

She shook her head. "Between the money from my husband's insurance policy and the sale of our home, I should be fine."

"But if you need to keep busy, a part-time job might be what you need."

"Maybe later. Right now, I've got something else I want to do."

He nodded toward the metal desk he'd set up in his temporary shop. "Why don't you have a seat and tell me about it?"

"Are you sure you have the time?"

"Jah, sure. I can take a little break."

Rosemary sat down, and he pulled a wooden stool over and joined her.

"So what's this 'something else' you're wanting to do?" he asked.

"I'd like to investigate the attacks that have been made against you."

His eyebrows shot up. "It's not your place to do any investigating; that's the sheriff's job."

"It should be," she said with a nod. "However, I don't think he's doing a very good job, or else we would know who's behind the attacks by now, and the culprit would be behind bars."

Roman grunted. "The sheriff blames me for that. He thinks I should call him right away whenever we've had an attack."

"Why haven't you called him every time, Roman?"

"I feel that it shows a lack of faith on my

part if I go running to the law every time someone pulls a prank on us."

"I'll admit, some of the things that have been done to you have seemed like simple pranks, but other things, like Martin's death, were obviously not."

Roman massaged the back of his neck. "We don't know for sure that the person who's done vandalism here is the one who rammed Ruth and Martin's buggy off the road. That could have been a hit-and-run driver who'd had too much to drink on Christmas Eve or was speeding and lost control of his vehicle in the snow."

Rosemary slowly shook her head. "You don't really believe that, do you?"

Roman shrugged. "I don't know what to believe anymore. These attacks have gone on longer than I thought they would. Now that irritating land developer's back in the area, asking to buy my land." He grimaced. "When the attacks first began, I was convinced Luke was doing them."

"And now?"

"Now I'm not so sure. It's possible that the land developer hired someone to do the attacks so he could scare me into selling my land."

"I've been thinking that, too."

"I haven't ruled out the possibility that

Luke's somehow involved," Roman said. "That fellow seems sneaky, and I know he hasn't liked me since I fired him for being late to work too many times."

"Do you have any other suspects?"

"At first I thought it might be Steven Bates, who got mad at me after the set of cabinets Luke delivered fell off the wagon. But then after Luke started acting so weird about things, I figured it was probably him." Roman crossed his arms. "At least we know it's not that reporter fellow, since he's moved out of the area again."

"We can speculate until the sheep are all sheared, but we won't know anything for sure until this mystery is solved."

He clutched her arm and shook his head. "I don't want you playing detective; you could get hurt."

She laughed. "I'm not a little girl anymore. I don't need my big brother watching out for me."

"You may not be a little girl, but you're a woman whose curiosity could get her in trouble if this person gets wind that you're trying to catch him."

She patted his hand in a motherly fashion. "I appreciate your concern, but I'll be fine, Roman. Just keep the faith and put your trust in God."

He drew in a deep breath and offered up a silent prayer. *I do trust You, God. I just don't trust my nosy sister to keep out of trouble.*

CHAPTER 22

As Martha headed for the barn on Monday morning, a week later, she spotted Ray Larson standing near the fence that divided their property. He held a pair of binoculars and seemed to be looking at something in their yard.

I wonder what he could be looking at, and what's he doing up so early on such a cold winter day?

This wasn't the first time Martha had seen Ray with his binoculars trained on their place. *Maybe I should ask what he's doing.*

She shook her head. *I'm being paranoid again. I need to feed my dogs and get back in the house so I can help Mom with breakfast. Then I've got to clean my room and do a few other chores before I leave for Aunt Rosemary's.*

Martha unlocked the barn door. The familiar odor of sweet-smelling hay and horseflesh greeted her. She lit a gas lamp and carried it to the back of the barn where her kennels were located. All the cage doors were shut, including Fritz's, which she'd been securing with a piece of wire every night. Since Fritz wasn't getting out anymore, she knew for certain it hadn't been foul play.

She smiled when Heidi's pups bounded up to the door of their cage. They were old enough to sell now, so she would run an ad in the paper later this week. Polly's pups would be ready soon after that. With any luck, Martha would soon have some money in her bank account.

As she got out the sack of dog food and began the feeding process, she thought about the article Gary Walker had written about her kennel business several weeks ago. Gary might be gone now, but the article he'd written could still influence someone's decision about whether to buy one of her puppies or not.

I'm glad that irritating reporter took a job in California, Martha thought as she put the bag of dog food away. *At least we know now that he wasn't responsible for the attacks.*

Rosemary had just set a kettle of soup on the stove to heat when she heard a horse and buggy pull into the yard. She looked out the kitchen window and saw Martha climb down from her buggy.

A few minutes later, Martha entered the house through the back door. "Something sure smells good," she said as she stepped into the kitchen.

"It's cheddar chowder." Rosemary motioned to the stove. "I took the recipe from one of my favorite Amish cookbooks, and I got the cheddar cheese at Heini's the other day."

"I'm sure it'll taste as good as it smells." Martha hung her coat over the back of a chair. "Is there anything I can do to help?"

Rosemary shook her head. "The table's set, and I've got some rolls warming in the oven. So if you'd like to have a seat, we can visit while we wait for the soup to finish heating."

"Okay." Martha plunked down in the chair where she'd draped her coat.

"How were the roads? Has the snow melted any?"

Martha nodded. "There was just a bit piled along the side of the road from the snowplows."

"Winter will be over soon. Hopefully we won't see much more snow before spring comes."

"Uh-huh."

Rosemary knew she was sharing idle chatter, but she wasn't quite ready to talk about what was really on her mind. Should she tell Martha what had been said when she'd visited with Roman last week, or would it be better to begin by asking Martha some questions — find out how much she knew about the attacks?

"Last week at Heini's," Martha said, "you started to tell me something, and then you stopped and said you'd tell me later, when we were alone. I've been wondering what you wanted to say."

Rosemary turned down the burner on the stove and took a seat across from Martha. "Since the sheriff hasn't done anything about the attacks, and since your dad isn't making any effort on his own to find out who's behind them, I've decided to do some investigating of my own." She paused. "And since you said the other day that you were trying to find out who's responsible for the attacks, I was wondering if you had made a list of suspects."

Martha nodded.

"Me, too, and I plan to question everyone on the list."

"Do you think that's a good idea, Aunt Rosemary? It could be dangerous for you to go poking around."

"That's what your dad said, too."

"You've spoken to Dad about this?"

Rosemary nodded. "I stopped by his temporary shop after I left Berlin last Saturday. I asked who he thought might be responsible for the attacks."

Martha's cheeks turned pink. "He still thinks it's Luke, doesn't he?"

"Maybe. But he's beginning to suspect that land developer Bill Collins — I think that's his name."

"If Dad thinks it could be the land developer, then maybe he won't care if —" Martha stopped speaking and stared at the table.

"Won't care if what?" Rosemary prompted. "Does this have anything to do with Luke?"

"Yes."

"Are you in love with Luke?"

Martha's head moved slowly up and down, and the color in her face deepened. "For all the good it'll do me."

"You mean because Luke's not one of your dad's favorite people?"

"That, and I'm also afraid I'm going to say or do something stupid when I'm with Luke."

"Like what?"

"Like blurt out to Luke the way I feel about him."

"Maybe he already knows. Maybe he feels the same way about you as you do him."

"What makes you say that?"

"I saw the way he looked at you when we were at Heini's." Rosemary chuckled. "I've seen that look on a man's face before, and it's called love, dear heart."

Martha's face lit up like a full moon. "You really think so?"

"I do." Rosemary sniffed the air. "I also think my soup's done, so we'd better eat." She stood and moved back to the stove. "We can talk more while we have our lunch."

For the next hour, Rosemary and Martha ate their meal and talked about the attacks. They worked on a timeline and wrote down the sequence of the attacks, as well as any clues, motives, and possible suspects. They talked about Luke and why Martha was convinced he was innocent. Then Martha told Rosemary that Luke was watching for clues, too.

Rosemary's mouth dropped open. "He is?"

Martha nodded. "According to Luke, he's been investigating for some time, but now we're working together on this."

"Has he gathered any evidence that would point to anyone in particular?"

Martha opened her mouth but then closed

it again.

"What were you going to say?"

"Well, I — I promised Luke I wouldn't tell anyone who he thinks did it. Since he's not really sure at this point, it wouldn't be fair to speculate."

"I guess you're right. What we need is some cold, hard evidence."

"Will you promise not to tell anyone that Luke and I are working together on this?" Martha asked.

Rosemary nodded. "Unless I see some reason to tell, it will be our little secret."

As Martha headed down the road toward home, she thought about stopping to see Ruth but realized there wasn't time. She needed to be at work for Irene by three o'clock, and she'd stayed at Aunt Rosemary's longer than planned.

But the discussion we had was good, she thought as she gave her horse the freedom to trot. *Knowing Aunt Rosemary's also investigating gives me more hope of finding out who's behind the attacks.*

A horn tooted from behind, and a truck came alongside Martha's rig. Her heart skipped a beat when she realized Luke was in the driver's seat.

He motioned her to pull over, and then

he pulled up ahead and stopped his vehicle along the shoulder of the road.

Martha guided her horse to the right and pulled her buggy in behind him. Luke hopped out of the truck, skirted around to the side of Martha's buggy, and opened her door.

"I'm surprised to see you driving your truck," she said.

"My daed returned my keys." Luke smiled. "I'm heading to New Philadelphia right now to meet a couple of my English friends."

Martha's heart took a nosedive. Wouldn't Luke ever give up his running-around days and settle down?

"There's no reason to look so upset," he said, shaking his head. "It's not what you think."

"How is it then?"

"My daed read in the newspaper this morning that a couple of outhouses at Amish schoolhouses were tipped over last night. I aim to find out if any of the English fellows I know did it."

"What makes you think that they might have tipped over the outhouses?"

"They've done it before — told me so, plain and simple."

"It seems that every time there's another

prank pulled somewhere, our place gets hit next." Martha swallowed a couple of times. "I really have to wonder if those English fellows might be the ones making the attacks."

"At first I thought they were, too, since I know for a fact that they've pulled some ugly pranks around the area." He lifted the edge of his stocking cap and rubbed the side of his head. "But that was before I started suspecting Toby."

"You don't really think Toby's been out late at night tipping over outhouses, do you?"

"I didn't mean the outhouses. I'm sure those were done by the Englishers I know. What I'm worried about are the attacks that have been made against your family." Luke reached for Martha's hand. Even through her woolen glove, she could feel the warmth of his touch. "I wouldn't want anything to happen to you, Martha." He rubbed his thumb over her knuckles. "I care for you, and I — I wish I could court you."

Martha bit her lip to keep from breaking into tears. It seemed like she'd waited a lifetime to hear those words. If only she and Luke were free to court.

"Your silence makes me wonder if I've spoken out of turn. I was hoping you might have feelings for me, too, but I guess I was wrong."

"You're not wrong." Martha lowered her gaze. "I realized some time ago that I had feelings for you, but I never thought you'd return those feelings."

Luke lifted her chin with his thumb, and the look of tenderness Martha saw on his face let her know he really did care for her.

They gazed into each other's eyes, until a passing car broke the spell. With an embarrassed giggle, Martha said, "I wish I could stay and visit longer, but I'll be late getting to work if I don't leave now."

"I understand." Luke smiled, and there was a twinkle in his eye. "I'll see you soon, Martha."

As Martha guided her horse onto the road again, she said a prayer for Luke — that he would quit hanging around his English buddies and join the church.

CHAPTER 23

"Where's my backpack?" Gideon fussed as he rummaged around the living room on a Friday morning in late February. Ruth sat holding Molly, who had run into a chair after being chased by Owen.

"Where did you put it last night?" Ruth shouted above Molly's screams. "You had it out when you did your homework."

Gideon pointed to the sofa. "Had it right here, but somebody must've took it." He glared at Josh. "I'll bet you hid it, didn't you?"

"Did not." Josh grabbed his own backpack that sat near the front door and wrinkled his nose. "We're gonna be late for school if you keep foolin' around."

"I ain't foolin' around," Gideon shot back. "If you'd help me find my backpack instead of standin' there lookin' so smug, we might be on our way to school already." He stomped across the room, bumping into the rocking chair where Ruth sat with Molly.

The little girl let out another piercing scream, and Ruth gritted her teeth to keep from screaming herself. With Molly hollering in her ear, she could barely think, much less try to resolve Gideon's problem.

Esta's sheltie darted into the room, with Esta right behind him. "Come back here, Winkie," she yelled. "Your paws are muddy and you're not supposed to be in the living room with dirty feet!"

Ruth opened her mouth to scold Esta for letting the dog in the house, when Owen, who'd been cowering in one corner of the room since he'd bumped into Molly, jumped up and started chasing the dog.

"I'll get him for you, sister!" he shouted.

Esta and Owen darted for Winkie, and their heads collided.

"Ouch!" Esta rubbed her forehead and glared at Owen. "You oughta watch where you're going."

"I was only tryin' to help." His chin trembled, and tears welled in his eyes.

"Aw, don't start bawlin' now," Gideon grumbled. "It's bad enough we have to listen to Molly screaming all the time."

Esta shook her finger at Gideon. "Don't be talkin' about our little sister that way. She's got every right to cry if she wants to."

"All right, that's enough!" Ruth lifted Molly from her lap and was about to stand, when Winkie leaped over her foot. She bent down and grabbed the dog's collar. "Get your dog, Esta." Then she turned to Owen and said, "I want you to take Molly out to the kitchen and find something to keep her entertained." She looked back at Esta. "After you've put Winkie away in the dog run, you and Josh had better head out to school."

"What about Gideon?" Esta questioned.

"He can catch up to you after he finds his backpack."

Owen grabbed Molly's hand and led her to the kitchen, while Josh and Esta rushed out the back door. Gideon stood facing Ruth with his arms folded. "Don't see why I have to look for my backpack. Can't I go to school without it?"

She shook her head. "Your homework is in the backpack, and so are your school-books. You need to think about where you put it last night before you went upstairs to bed."

"Put it right there." Gideon pointed to the floor near the door.

"Well, it's not there now, so I suggest you think of some other places to look."

He stared at Ruth as though daring her to

make him move.

She tapped her foot impatiently. "Do I need to go out to the harness shop and get your daed?"

Gideon's face turned red, and he shuffled his feet a few times. Finally, with a disgruntled grunt, he turned and stomped up the stairs.

Ruth debated about going up to his room to help search for the backpack but decided he might not appreciate it. Instead, she went to the kitchen to see what the younger children were up to. She found Molly sitting on the floor playing with two empty kettles and a wooden spoon. Owen sat at the table coloring a picture.

When Owen spotted Ruth, he hopped off his chair. "Is it okay if I go upstairs and color in my room?"

"Don't you want to sit here in the kitchen where it's warm and cozy?" she asked.

He shook his head. "Molly keeps makin' noise with those pots she's bangin'."

"Okay."

Owen had just left the room, when Gideon showed up carrying his backpack. "Found it," he announced.

"Where was it?"

"Under my bed." He sauntered out the back door before Ruth could comment.

Ruth poured herself a cup of tea and headed back to the living room. She needed a few minutes of solitude.

She set her cup on the coffee table, took a seat in the rocking chair, and closed her eyes. *I don't know how much more of this I can take. Maybe I made a mistake marrying a man with five children. Maybe I'm not cut out to be a mother.*

Ruth's eyes snapped open when she heard a pathetic whimper coming from the kitchen.

Thinking something must be wrong with Molly, she sprang from her chair and rushed to the kitchen. She found the child sitting on the floor, this time with a kettle on her head.

With tears streaming down her cheeks, Molly pointed at the kettle. *"Fascht."*

"I know you're stuck." Ruth lifted the kettle off Molly's head and sank to the floor beside her. As she held the little girl in her lap, she started to laugh. With all the serious stuff that had gone on in this house lately, she'd almost forgotten how to look for humor.

"Hungerich," Molly said, tugging on Ruth's sleeve.

"Well, then, if you're hungry, I think the two of us should have a little snack." Ruth clambered to her feet, grabbed a box of crackers from the cupboard, and placed them on the table. Then she set Molly in a chair and spread several crackers on the table in front of her.

As Ruth joined Molly at the table, she realized she'd been taking things too seriously lately. What she should be doing was asking God to help her with Gideon, not arguing with the boy or trying to solve things on her own.

She glanced over at Molly and smiled. *And I definitely need to laugh and smile a lot more.*

Thump-thump-thump! Martha jumped when she heard someone knocking at the front door. None of their friends or relatives ever used that door.

"I'll get it," Mom said as she placed her kitchen towel on the counter. She hurried from the room and returned shortly with a smile on her face. "There's someone here to look at the hundlin you have for sale."

Martha dried her hands on the towel and hurried from the kitchen. Apparently, someone had read the ad she'd put in the newspaper. Either that, or they'd seen the sign posted out front by the driveway advertising sheltie and beagle puppies.

When Martha went to the door, she discovered a middle-aged English couple on the porch. "My mother says you're interested in seeing some of my dogs?"

"Oh yes," the dark-haired woman said with a nod. "We read your ad in the *Bargain Hunter,* and we're interested in seeing the sheltie puppies." She smiled at the balding man who stood beside her. "I've wanted a sheltie for some time. Isn't that right, Philip?"

He nodded. "Can we take a look at the pups now?"

"Yes, of course. I'll just get my jacket, and then I'll take you out to the kennels." Martha hurried to the utility room where her jacket hung and then rushed back out to the porch where the couple waited. "Follow me," she said, leading the way across the yard toward the barn.

She found the barn door unlocked but figured Dad had already been out there this morning before he and Cleon had left for Sugarcreek to deliver some cabinets. What she hadn't figured on was the sight that greeted her when she stepped inside the barn and lit the nearest gas lantern. Heidi and Polly were both running free, and so were their puppies. Had the dogs figured out how to get their cage doors open now, too?

"Oh, my! What's that awful smell?" the woman asked, sniffing the air. "It smells like fresh —"

"Horse manure," the man said, finishing her sentence. "And there's the reason we smell it." He pointed to one of the beagle pups. "That dog's hair is covered with manure."

"Eww!" The woman wrinkled her nose. "That's really disgusting!"

Yip! Yip! Yip!

Martha gasped when she spotted a puppy tail sticking through a thin opening in a nearby wooden crate. Its mother, Polly, let out an ear-piercing howl and jumped up, planting both paws on the woman's jean-clad knees.

"Get down!" the woman shrieked, pushing the dog away. She looked over at Martha and frowned. "What kind of business are you running here anyway?"

"I assure you —"

"She's running a puppy mill, that's what." The man made a sweeping gesture with one hand. "No one running a respectable kennel would allow their dogs to run all over the place, rolling in horse manure, getting stuck in wooden crates, and who knows what else!"

The woman turned toward the door.

"Let's go, Philip. I would never buy a puppy from anyone who neglects their dogs in such a way!"

"I don't neglect my dogs," Martha mumbled as the couple left the barn. She glanced down at Heidi, who was looking up at her with sorrowful brown eyes. "I would never mistreat any of my dogs."

A sudden realization came to Martha. Someone must have sneaked into the barn and let the dogs out. Someone wanted to make it look like she wasn't taking good care of her dogs.

"Where do you think you're going?"

Luke halted at the bottom of the stairs and turned to face his father. "I'm heading to work."

"Without breakfast?" his mother asked, as she stepped out of the kitchen and into the hall.

"I slept later than I should have. If I don't leave now, I'm going to be late."

Pop grimaced and shook his head. "You got in late last night, didn't you?"

Luke nodded.

"I heard your truck rumble in, and when I looked at the clock, it was after midnight." Pop grunted. "Where'd you park that truck, anyway? Not on our property, I hope."

Luke shook his head. "I parked it behind some bushes along the side of the road, not far from our driveway."

Pop grunted again.

"Where were you at such a late hour, Luke?" Mom asked.

"I was in New Philly most of the evening, and then I drove around for a while."

"Drove around, huh? Don't you know we were worried?" Pop's voice rose, and a vein on the side of his neck bulged.

Luke massaged the back of his head. He'd woken with a headache — no doubt from lack of sleep. "I'm sorry if I made you worry, but as you can see, I'm fine and dandy."

Pop planted both hands on his hips. "You're fine and dandy all right — out all hours on a weeknight, driving around in that fancy truck of yours, doing who knows what." He stared at Luke. "I want to know exactly where you were and what you were doing."

Luke's jaw dropped. "I'm not a little buwe, Pop. I don't think I should have to account for every minute I'm away from the house."

Pop clapped his hands, and Mom jumped.

"Really, Elam, do you have to shout at our son like that?"

Pop scowled at her. "I do when he's being disrespectful, not to mention rebellious and defiant." He shook his finger at Luke. "I don't think you'd have been out so late last night if you'd been driving a horse and buggy, now would you?"

"Probably not, but —"

"It's that fancy truck that's causing you problems. I demand that you put it up for sale, and you'd better do it today!"

Luke shook his head. "I need my truck, Pop."

"What do you need it for?" Mom spoke softly, and Luke could see by the strained look on her face that she was struggling not to cry.

"I can't say why I need it."

"Can't or won't?" Dad hollered.

Luke shifted from one foot to the other, wondering how much he dared say to his folks without telling them the real reason he felt he needed to own a truck right now. "I'm still going through my rumschpringe, you know."

"Like we needed that reminder." Pop slowly shook his head. "You've been going through your running-around years long enough. It's time to settle down and make a commitment to God and to our church."

"I'm not ready."

Pop moved closer to Luke, until they were nose to nose. "I'm tired of all this, boy. If you won't sell that truck, then you'll have to move out of my house."

Mom gasped. "Ach, not this again! You can't mean it, Elam!"

He nodded soberly. "I do mean it."

Mom stepped forward and placed her hand on Luke's arm. "I'm begging you. Please do as your daed asks."

Luke swallowed hard. He didn't want to disappoint his mother, but he wasn't ready to make a decision about joining the church yet.

Pop nudged Luke's back with his elbow. "What's it gonna be, son?"

Luke turned and grabbed his jacket off the wall peg by the door. "I'm not willing to sell my truck at this time, and I'm not ready to join the church yet. If you're opposed to me living here under those conditions, then I guess it is time for me to move out." Before either of his folks could respond, Luke jerked open the back door. "I'll be back after work to get my things!"

CHAPTER 24

As Luke sped out of his parents' driveway, his emotions dipped like a roller coaster. Why wouldn't Pop believe him? Why hadn't he been able to find out who was responsible for the attacks against the Hostettlers? Should he give up looking for clues? Should he sell his truck and join the church? Would it be better for all if he forgot about being Amish and became English?

He gripped the steering wheel until his fingers started to throb. *If I jump the fence and go English, I'll have no chance with Martha.*

By the time Luke arrived at John's shop, he'd made a decision. He needed to continue trying to find out who was behind the Hostettler attacks, which would clear his name with Roman. Then, and only then, would he make the commitment to join the church.

When Luke entered the shop, John looked

up from the paperwork he was doing and pointed to the clock sitting on his desk. "You're half an hour late, Luke. Did another buggy wheel fall off?"

"Not this time. I drove my truck this morning."

"Did it break down on the way here or what?"

"No. I had a disagreement with my folks." Luke yanked the stocking cap off his head and tossed it on the closest workbench. "It was mostly with my dad, I guess."

"That made you late to work?"

Luke nodded. "My dad wants me to sell my truck and join the Amish church. He said if I didn't, I'd have to move out. So I left."

John's eyebrows lifted high on his forehead. "You mean you moved out of your folks' house?"

"That's right." Luke released a gusty sigh. "Guess I'll have to sleep in my truck until I can find some place to live."

John scrubbed a hand over his clean-shaven chin. "I suppose I could set up a cot for you in the back room. The sink and toilet would give you the basic necessities. I've also got a small microwave and a hot plate I could let you use."

"You'd really do that for me?"

"You need somewhere to stay. I can't have my best employee living out of his truck, now can I?"

"What do you mean, John? I'm your *only* employee."

John chuckled. "That's right, and since we've got a lot of work to do today, I think we'd better quit chewin' the fat and get busy, don't you?"

Luke nodded and grabbed a leather work apron from the nail near his workbench. "Thanks, John. Thanks for everything."

As Martha headed for the barn, she spotted Ray Larson looking over at their place with his binoculars again. She had plenty of time this morning, so maybe she should find out what their neighbor found so interesting.

She hurried across the pasture separating their place from the Larsons', and when she reached the other side, Ray trained his binoculars on her. " 'Morning, Martha. What brings you over to our place?" he asked with a smile.

"I was heading to the barn to feed my dogs when I noticed you leaning over the fence with your binoculars. I wondered what you were looking at."

He lowered the binoculars. "I was studying an unusual bird that flew toward your place. Haven't seen one like it around here before, and I wanted to get a better look."

"What did the bird look like?"

"It had an orange head and a black body." Ray scratched the side of his head. "No, I think its head was more of a yellow color."

Martha opened her mouth to comment, but Ray rushed on.

"I checked my bird identification book, and the closest I've been able to come to what I saw is the yellow-headed blackbird. But those birds are usually found in marshy areas, and I've never seen one around here." He looked right at Martha. "You didn't happen to see it, did you?"

She shook her head. "I wasn't looking for birds this morning. I was focused on getting my dogs fed."

"Speaking of your dogs, how's the kennel business doing these days?"

"Not so well. I placed an ad in the paper, and there's a sign out by the road, but so far, I haven't sold any of Heidi's or Polly's puppies." Martha thought about telling Ray about the incident with the English couple who'd come to look at puppies but decided it was best left unsaid. No point in giving Ray, who had a tendency toward gossip, something to spread around the neighborhood.

"That's too bad," Ray said with a shake of his head. "We've been real happy with the dog we bought from you. I would think anyone buying one of your pups would be satisfied, too."

Martha sighed. "Guess I'll have to keep trying."

He smiled. "That's right. I never did like a quitter."

Martha turned toward home. "I'd better get to the barn and feed those dogs, or they'll be yapping up a storm."

"Tell your folks I said hello," Ray called.

"I will," Martha said with a farewell wave.

Sometime later, with the dogs fed and watered, Martha stepped out of the barn, relieved that she'd found no messes this morning and that all the dogs had been in their cages. She was about to head for the house, when a dark blue car came up the driveway. She didn't recognize the vehicle or the middle-aged man with thinning brown hair who got out of the car. She walked up to him and was about to ask if he was looking for her father's woodworking shop, when he spoke first.

"I'm here to see my granddaughter. Is she at home?"

Martha squinted. *Granddaughter?* She figured the man must be lost. "What's your granddaughter's name? If she lives around here, I probably know her and can give you directions to her house."

"Her name's Anna, and she lives with her mother, Grace."

Martha's mouth fell open. "Are . . . are you Carl Davis?"

He nodded.

Martha knew Carl Davis was the father of Grace's deceased English husband. He was the one who'd brought Anna to live with Grace almost two years ago. Martha hadn't been home at the time, so she'd never met the man in person; Grace had told her and the rest of the family how Carl's wife had died and that he'd been having health problems and had decided Anna would be better off with her mother.

"Is Anna here or not?"

Martha shook her head. "She's in school today."

"What time will she be home?"

"Later this afternoon."

"What about Grace? Is she at home?"

Martha's heart began to pound. Except for a few letters and some gifts Carl had sent to Anna, he'd never made any other contact or come to visit the child. Martha knew from what Grace had said that she was glad he hadn't come around. It would have probably confused Anna, or maybe made her want to go back to live with the man she called "Poppy." Grace had lost Anna once, after her husband's death when his parents had taken Anna to live with them. Martha knew it would break her sister's heart if she lost Anna a second time.

She shifted uneasily, not knowing how to respond to Carl's question. It wouldn't be right to lie, but if she told Carl where Grace lived and he went over there demanding to take Anna away, Grace would be devastated.

"Did you hear what I said? I'd like to see Grace," Carl persisted.

Martha pointed to the driveway leading to Grace and Cleon's house. "Grace and her husband live up there now."

A look of relief spread over Carl's face. "Thanks. I'll leave my car parked here and walk up."

Martha wished there was some way she could warn Grace that Carl was coming. Maybe she should walk with him to Grace's house. At least that way, she'd be there to offer Grace some support.

"I think I'll walk along," she said as Carl started up the driveway.

He shrugged. "Suit yourself."

Grace had just diapered Daniel and put him

down for a nap when she heard the back door open and close. She knew it couldn't be Anna, because she was at school. It wasn't likely to be Cleon, either, since he and Dad had a backlog of orders right now and were hard at work in Dad's shop in the barn. *It must be Mom or Martha.*

"It's me, Grace," Martha called up the stairs. "Are you up there?"

"Jah, just putting Daniel down for his morning nap."

A few minutes later, Martha entered the baby's bedroom. A worried-looking frown creased her forehead.

"What's the matter? You look upset." Grace rushed to Martha's side. "Please don't tell me there's been another attack."

"No, but there's someone downstairs, and I don't think you'll be too happy to see him."

Grace's mouth went dry and her palms grew sweaty. "Is it Gary Walker? Has he come back to Holmes County?"

Martha shook her head. "It's Anna's grandfather."

Grace squinted. "Dad?"

"The other grandfather."

"Carl Davis?"

"Jah. He pulled into our driveway as I was

coming out of the barn, and he asked to see Anna."

Grace's legs wobbled, and she sank to the edge of her bed. "What did you tell him?"

"I said Anna wasn't here, that she was in school." Martha took a seat beside Grace. "Then he asked to see you, so I brought him up here." She reached for Grace's hand and gave it a gentle squeeze. "He's in the living room, waiting to speak with you."

Fear gripped Grace like a vise, and she clutched her sister's hand. "What does he want, Martha? Why, after all these months, has Carl come to Holmes County?"

"I don't know. He said he wanted to speak with you."

Grace took a couple of deep breaths and tried to think. "What if he wants Anna back? What if he's come to make trouble?" Tears welled in her eyes, blurring her vision. "I couldn't bear to lose my little girl again."

Martha shook her head. "You're not going to lose her. You need to go down there, listen to what the man has to say, and if it's what you fear, then tell him in no uncertain terms that your daughter is staying with you."

"When Carl first brought Anna back to me, I told him I would never give her up again."

"Of course you won't. You love Anna, and she's happy here with you and Cleon." Martha patted Grace's arm. "Anna loves you. I'm sure she wouldn't want to leave, even if Carl wanted her to."

Grace drew in one more deep breath and rose to her feet. "I'd better see what he wants."

"Do you want me to go with you or wait here with Daniel?" Martha asked.

"Daniel will be okay in his crib." Grace managed a weak smile. "I'd like to have you with me for moral support."

Martha nodded. "You've got it."

When they entered the living room, Grace spotted Carl sitting on the sofa. He jumped up as soon he saw Grace and moved quickly across the room. "It's nice to see you again," he said, extending his hand.

Grace didn't want to be rude, but it was all she could do to shake Carl's hand. She motioned to the sofa. "Please, have a seat."

He sat down, and Grace and Martha took seats in the chairs across from him.

"I'm surprised to see you." Grace moistened her lips with the tip of her tongue. "I — I had no idea you were coming."

"I wrote you a letter saying I was planning to come."

Grace shook her head. "I've received no

such letter."

He shrugged. "It must have gotten lost in the mail."

"How's your health?" she asked, for want of anything better to say. "Are you feeling better than the last time you were here?"

He nodded. "My doctor discovered that I had a yeast overgrowth throughout much of my body."

"What was that caused from?" Martha asked, leaning slightly forward.

"I've had trouble with sinus infections most of my life," Carl said. "Consequently, I've taken numerous courses of antibiotics, which not only killed the bad bacteria in my body but the good ones, as well. That's how the yeast overgrowth began. But with proper diet and the right supplements, it's under control. I'm feeling much better now."

Grace was glad Carl's health had improved, but she felt concern over why he'd come. "What are you doing in Holmes County?" she asked.

"I came to see Anna. I've missed my little girl something awful."

"I missed her, too, when she was living with you and your wife and I had no idea how to find her." Grace couldn't keep the bitterness out of her voice, and she blinked several times against stinging tears.

"As I told you before, I'm sorry about that. It wasn't right for us to keep Anna from you, but all that's in the past, and it can't be undone."

"I'm sure you've missed Anna," Grace said, keeping her voice steady and low, "but I don't want my daughter seeing you and getting confused about things."

"Why would she be confused?"

"She might think you've come to take her away, and if you did —"

Carl held up his hand. "I did not come here to take Anna away."

Grace hoped Carl was telling the truth, but she couldn't be sure. "I'm sorry you came all this way, because as my sister's already told you, Anna's at school."

Carl stood. "I've checked into a hotel just outside of Sugarcreek, so I'll head there now, but I'll be back this evening to see Anna."

"This evening won't work."

"Why not?"

"I . . . uh . . . need time to prepare Anna for seeing you." Grace paused and swiped her tongue over her bottom lip. "It took her some time to adjust to living here, and —"

"Are you afraid if she sees me again, she won't want me to go or might want to go with me?"

Grace nodded, as tears stung the back of her eyes.

He took a step forward. "As I said, I haven't come to take Anna away. But I did come to see her, and I'm not leaving until I know how she's doing. So if I can't see Anna this evening, then how about tomorrow evening or Saturday?"

"You can come by on Saturday morning," Grace finally agreed.

CHAPTER 25

"I'm going home to get some of my clothes and a few other things," Luke told John after they'd finished work for the day.

"No problem," John said. "You've got a key to the shop, so when you get back, let yourself in and you can settle into the back room."

Luke smiled. "I sure appreciate this, John."

John thumped Luke on the back. "Not a problem. I'm heading over to my place now to get a few more things you might need. If I don't see you when you get back with your clothes, I'll see you in the morning."

"Thanks." Luke headed for his truck. He hoped Pop wasn't home from work yet. The last thing he needed was another confrontation, which would probably lead to a full-blown argument. He wasn't as concerned about seeing Mom, except that she might get emotional and beg him to come home and make restitution. Why couldn't his folks allow him to go through rumschpringe the way other fellows his age did, without laying down so many rules and stipulations? Others he knew had trucks and cars. Why couldn't he?

Luke loosened his grip on the steering wheel. He needed to be calm when he arrived home.

As Grace stood at the kitchen sink, peeling potatoes for supper, she struggled to stay focused on the job at hand. For a long time after Carl had left this morning, she'd paced the floor, asking God to give her the wisdom to know how to tell Anna that her English grandfather had come for a visit. At least Grace hoped it was just for a visit. What if Carl had been lying when he'd said he hadn't come to take Anna away?

The back door opened and slammed shut. "Guess what, Mama?" Anna asked, as she burst into the kitchen. "Karen Miller's got twin baby sisters!"

"That's exciting news." Grace motioned to the umbrella stand near the door. "Put your umbrella and coat away, and then you can have some hot chocolate and cookies while you tell me about it."

"That sounds *appeditlich.*"

Grace smiled. "I think hot chocolate and

cookies are always delicious."

A short time later, they sat at the table, each holding a cup of hot chocolate with a plate of cookies between them.

Between bites of cookie and slurps of hot chocolate, Anna told Grace about Karen's news and that her parents had named the babies Lorine and Corine. When Anna finished her story, she turned to Grace and said, "I wish I had somethin' exciting to share with the kinner at school."

"Are you hoping another *boppli* will be added to our family?" Grace asked.

Anna shook her head. "Not unless it can be a baby sister this time."

Grace chuckled and patted Anna's hand. "If and when I have another boppli, it will be up to God to decide whether it'll be a buwe or a maedel."

Anna nodded and reached for another cookie. "Where's Daniel? How come he's not eatin' cookies with us?"

"Your little bruder was fussy most of the afternoon, so I put him down for a nap about an hour ago. He's still sleeping."

Anna's eyebrows drew together. "I'm glad I don't have to take naps anymore. When I was livin' with Poppy and Grandma Davis, I had to take a nap every day."

Grace flinched. Should she tell Anna

about Carl having been here earlier today? She'd wanted to discuss things with Cleon first and had hoped he would help her decide the best way to tell Anna. She'd gone out to the barn to speak with him earlier, but Dad had said Cleon was out making some deliveries.

Maybe I should tell Anna now. Grace opened her mouth, but a shrill cry coming from upstairs halted her words.

"Daniel's awake," Anna announced.

"You finish your cookies, and I'll go get him," Grace said with a nod. Maybe it was better that she hadn't said anything yet. It might be best to wait and talk to Cleon first.

Martha had just started down the road after leaving her job at the Schrocks' house, when a truck passed, going in the opposite direction. She thought she recognized the driver, and when he rolled down the window and motioned her to pull over, she knew it was Luke.

Martha guided her horse and buggy to the side of the road and waited for Luke to turn his truck around and park behind her. When he stepped up to the driver's side of her buggy, she opened the door.

"I'm glad to see you," he said breathlessly. "Something happened today, and I wanted to let you know."

"It's starting to rain," she said. "Why don't you get in and tell me about it?"

Luke climbed into the buggy as soon as Martha slid to the passenger's side. "I moved out of my folks' house this morning," he said.

Martha's mouth dropped open. "Why?"

"I had a disagreement with my daed because I got home late last night." Luke grunted. "He said if I didn't sell my truck and join the church, I'd have to move out."

"But that's lecherich. A lot of Amish fellows going through rumschpringe have cars or trucks."

Luke nodded. "It might seem ridiculous to you and me, but not to Pop. He's got old-fashioned ideas, and he's been after me to sell my truck ever since he found out I had one and kept it hidden in the woods." He grunted again. "I wish Toby hadn't told them I had it."

Martha's heart went out to Luke. She could see by the droop of his shoulders and the pinched look on his face that he was grieving over this conflict with his folks. "What are you going to do now? Have you found another place to stay?"

"Jah. John said I could sleep in the back room of his shop until I find something more permanent." He motioned to his truck. "I just came from my house, where I picked up my clothes and few personal items. Thankfully, my folks weren't at home, or I'm sure we'd have ended up in another disagreement."

She touched his arm. "I'm sorry, Luke."

"Maybe it's for the best," he said with a shrug. "Living away from home without Pop watching my every move will give me a better chance to play detective."

"I suppose. Even so —"

"What's new with you?" he asked, changing the subject. "Have you found more clues or done more investigating?"

She shook her head. "Not really, although I did see our neighbor, Ray Larson, looking over at our place this morning with his binoculars."

Luke's eyes narrowed. "Any idea why?"

"I went over there and asked. He said he was looking for some unusual bird he'd seen earlier."

"Did you believe him?"

"I guess so." Martha shivered, as a gust of wind blew in through the cracks around the opening of the buggy flap. "I know it's ridiculous, but I'm starting to think everyone I know is a suspect."

"Does that include me?"

She shook her head. "No, Luke. Not any-more."

Luke reached for Martha's hand. "It's nice to know at least one member of the Hostet-tler family believes I'm innocent. I just wish I could prove it to everyone else."

CHAPTER 26

Grace had just cleared their breakfast dishes from the table and was about to run some water into the sink, when a knock sounded on the back door. Her heart gave a lurch. Could that be Carl? He'd said he would return on Saturday, but she hadn't expected it would be this early or that she would feel so unprepared.

Thursday night, after Anna had gone to bed, Grace had told Cleon about Carl's visit. Cleon hadn't seemed too upset by the news. He'd even said he thought it might be good for Anna to spend some time with her English grandpa, since they had once been so close. Grace wasn't sure about that. She was still worried that even if Carl hadn't come to take Anna way, the child might want to go with him.

Grace had waited until last night to tell Anna about her grandfather's visit, when the child was preparing for bed. Anna had been so excited about the prospect of seeing her poppy that it had been hard for her to fall asleep. Grace half expected to find Anna up at the crack of dawn this morning, but Anna had slept longer than usual and had come down to breakfast still wearing her nightgown. Now the child was upstairs in her room getting dressed.

Another knock sounded at the door, a little louder this time. With a sigh, Grace went to answer it, wishing Cleon was here, but he'd gone to check on his bee boxes as soon as he'd finished breakfast.

When Grace opened the door a few seconds later, she found Carl standing on the porch holding a vinyl doll with bright red hair in his hands. "This is for Anna," he said. "She is here, I hope."

"She's upstairs getting dressed. We . . . uh . . . didn't expect you so soon." Grace opened the door wider. "If you'd like to wait for Anna in the kitchen, I'm sure she'll be down soon."

Carl seated himself at the table, and a few minutes later, Anna bounded into the room. "Poppy! You're really here!" She threw herself into his arms.

"Oh, I've missed you, Anna girl." He nuzzled her head with his chin. "But I hardly recognized you in those plain clothes."

"I dress Amish now." Anna kissed his cheek. "You look the same, only better."

"Why don't we go into the living room and sit down?" Grace suggested. "I think it will be easier for us to visit there."

Holding her grandfather's hand, Anna led the way. Grace followed. When they entered the living room, Grace took a seat in the rocking chair, and Carl sat on the sofa with Anna in his lap.

"Can you stay and visit all day, Poppy?" Anna gazed up at Carl with a look of adoration.

"I'd like to, Anna, but I have an appointment this afternoon."

Anna's lower lip protruded. "You're goin' home?"

He shook his head. "I'm going to see about renting a house in Berlin."

"Why would you need to rent a house if you're only here for a visit?" Grace asked.

"I'm thinking about moving here so I can be closer to Anna."

Grace's hands turned cold and clammy. Things were complicated enough in her life; she didn't need Carl moving to Holmes County and complicating them further.

"If you move to Berlin, I can see you all the time," Anna said excitedly. "Berlin's not far from here. Right, Mama?"

Grace opened her mouth to respond, but Daniel's shrill cry halted her words. "I need to tend to the baby," she said, looking at Carl.

"I didn't realize you had a baby."

"His name's Daniel, and he's my little brother," Anna answered for Grace. "Daniel still cries and wets his *windle* a lot."

Carl quirked an eyebrow as he looked back at Grace.

"Windle means diapers," she explained.

"Oh, I see."

Grace stood and held out her hand to Anna. "Why don't you come upstairs with me while I see about Daniel?"

Anna shook her head. "I wanna stay here with Poppy."

Grace struggled with the need to tend Daniel or remain in the living room. *What if Carl takes Anna while I'm upstairs? He has a car. He could get away quickly, and there wouldn't be a thing I could do about it.*

As if Carl could read her mind, he smiled and said, "Anna will be fine; I promise."

Daniel let out another ear-piercing scream, and Grace bolted for the stairs. She'd only gotten halfway up when someone knocked on the front door. Turning back around, she went to see who it was.

■ ■ ■ ■

Rosemary lifted her hand to knock on Grace's door for the third time, when the door suddenly swung open. Grace stood there with a panicked expression on her face.

"Is everything all right?" Rosemary asked, feeling immediate concern.

Grace touched her flushed cheeks. "Daniel's crying, and I need to go to him. But I've got company in the living room."

"Would you like me to entertain your company while you take care of Daniel?"

"I'd appreciate that." Grace led Rosemary into the living room, where a middle-aged man sat on the sofa with Anna in his lap. "Carl, this is my aunt Rosemary." She looked at Rosemary then nodded at Carl. "This is Anna's grandfather, Carl Davis."

"It's nice to meet you," Rosemary and Carl said in unison.

Daniel's howling increased, and Grace excused herself, leaving Rosemary alone with Carl and Anna. She took a seat in the chair opposite them.

"Do you live around here?" Carl asked.

"I'm Roman Hostettler's sister. I grew up in Holmes County but moved away when I was a young woman. I married an English man, and we moved to Idaho." She paused a moment to see if he would comment, but when he said nothing, she continued. "My husband died several months ago, so I came home to see my family."

"So you're just here for a visit?"

"No, I've recently purchased a house nearby. Where are you from?"

"I've been living in Nevada for the last several years, and I'm also widowed."

"Poppy came here to see me," Anna put in.

Rosemary smiled at the exuberance she saw on the child's face. Anna was obviously happy to see her English grandfather.

"Anna's mother was married to my son, Wade, at one time," Carl said. "Wade was killed in a car accident when Anna was a baby."

"Yes, I know about that."

Carl looked like he was about to say something more when Grace returned to the room, carrying Daniel.

"Can I hold him?" Rosemary asked.

Grace nodded and handed the little boy to Rosemary.

Rosemary rubbed her chin along the top of Daniel's downy head as she breathed in the sweet smell of him. Oh, how she wished she could have had more than one child, but she was grateful God had given her Ken.

"I hate to cut this visit short," Carl said looking at his watch, "but I'm supposed to meet a Realtor in Berlin in half an hour, and I don't want to be late." He placed Anna on the sofa and stood.

With a panicked expression, Anna grabbed his hand. "Please, Poppy, don't go away again!"

He bent down and gave her a hug. "I'm going to look at a house, but I'll be back to see you soon."

"You promise?"

"Yes, I promise."

Anna clung to Carl's hand as she walked him to the door. Grace followed.

When Grace and Anna returned to the living room, Grace nodded at Anna and said, "Why don't you take Daniel to the kitchen and see if you can find some cookies for the two of you?"

"I don't want any cookies. I want Poppy," Anna said tearfully.

"He said he'd come back soon."

Anna sniffed and swiped at her tearstained cheeks. "What if he doesn't? What if he goes away like he did before?"

Feeling the need to offer Grace some support, Rosemary jumped in. "Anna, your grandfather said he was going to look at a house to rent in Berlin. If he wasn't going to stay awhile, do you think he would do that?"

"I . . . I guess not."

Rosemary set Daniel on the floor and pulled Anna into her arms. "Your grandpa will be back soon, just like he promised." She gave the child's back a little pat. "Now take your brother into the kitchen like your mama said and find some cookies to eat."

"Okay." Anna grabbed Daniel's hand and scooted out of the room.

Grace released an audible sigh and collapsed onto the sofa.

Rosemary took a seat beside her. "You're not happy about Anna's grandpa coming to Holmes County, are you?"

Grace's eyes filled with tears. "I'm afraid he might try to take her again."

"Would he be renting a house in Berlin if kidnapping was on his mind?"

"I . . . I guess not."

"I think Carl Davis has plans to stay in Holmes County so he can be closer to Anna." Rosemary took Grace's hand and gave it a gentle squeeze. "The best thing you can do is try to relax and leave this in God's hands."

"It won't be easy," Grace said with a slow

nod, "but I'll try."

Martha left Spector's store in Berlin, where she had gone to buy material for a new dress, and headed across the parking lot to the hitching rail. She'd only taken a few steps, when she halted. Her horse and buggy were missing!

"What in all the world?" She gritted her teeth and tried to think. She was sure she'd tied her horse near the end of the hitching rail.

She looked around helplessly, but the horse and buggy were nowhere in sight. Could this be another attack or just a prank some kids had decided to play? Were other buggies missing, or had only hers been targeted?

With heart pounding and palms sweaty, Martha ran around to the front of the building, calling her horse's name. No sign of Gid or the buggy, either. She looked up and down the main street but saw nothing out of the ordinary.

Should I call the sheriff or maybe Aunt Rosemary? Yes, I'll use the phone at Spector's; Aunt Rosemary will know what to do.

Martha dashed back to Spector's and had just reached the parking lot when she spotted Luke and John getting out of John's

SUV. Luke waved at her, and as the two men started across the parking lot, Martha rushed up to them. "My horse and buggy are missing!"

Luke looked at her as if she'd lost her mind. "How could they be missing?"

"I don't know, but they are." Martha pointed across the parking lot. "I tied Gid to the hitching rail before I went into Spector's. When I came out again, Gid and my buggy were gone."

"Maybe you didn't tie the horse securely enough," John said.

"Yes, I did; I'm sure of it."

"Then he probably got restless and broke loose," John said.

"Or else someone untied the horse and let him go free," Luke put in. "That has been known to happen on occasion."

"What am I going to do?" Martha transferred her package from one hand to the other. "My horse could be most anywhere by now."

"If he broke free and no one's driving him, then he's probably headed for home," Luke said.

Hope welled in Martha's chest. "Do you think so?"

"Makes sense to me."

"I agree with Luke," John said with a nod.

"Let's get in my rig and look for your horse and buggy."

CHAPTER 27

"There they are, Luke! There's my horse and buggy!" Martha shouted as they headed out of Berlin in John's SUV.

"Can you tell if there's a driver in the buggy?" John asked, craning his neck.

"Doesn't look like it," Luke hollered.

Martha's heart pounded like a blacksmith's anvil. Gid ran wild, and the buggy swayed precariously. What if her horse veered into oncoming traffic and caused an accident? What if —

"Oh no, the buggy's going over!" Luke shouted.

Martha gasped as she watched her buggy topple onto its side. Gid continued to trot, dragging the buggy along.

John pulled his rig to the side of the road. They all jumped out and ran down the road after the runaway horse and buggy. About fifty feet beyond where the buggy had fallen over, Luke grabbed the horse's reins and got him stopped.

"Is Gid hurt?" Martha panted as she caught up to them.

"Doesn't seem to be," John said. "But I don't know about your buggy."

"Let's get it up and assess the damage." Luke handed the reins to Martha, and he and John set the buggy upright.

Martha breathed a sigh of relief when she saw that the only real damage was to the mirrors and blinkers on the right side, which had both been smashed.

"The rig should be okay to drive if you think you're up to driving it," John said to Martha.

She nodded slowly, although her hands shook so badly she wasn't sure she could hold the reins.

"I'll ride with Martha and drive the horse." Luke turned to John and said, "If you don't mind following so you can give me a ride back to your shop, that is."

John nodded. "Sure. No problem."

Martha smiled. "I appreciate you both helping me get home."

Roman was heading up to the house to see if Judith had supper started, when he spotted Martha's horse and buggy pulling into the yard. To his surprise, Luke was in the driver's seat, and Martha sat beside him. The horse was lathered up, and he noticed that the mirror and right blinker on the buggy had been smashed.

Roman rushed toward the buggy just as John Peterson's SUV came up the driveway. "What's going on?" he called as Luke stepped down from the buggy. "What happened to my daughter's rig, and why are you driving it instead of her?"

Martha scrambled out of the buggy, holding a package. She spoke before Luke could respond. "Gid broke free when I was at Spector's, and Luke and John helped me track him down." She motioned to the sweaty horse. "When we spotted him on the road a short ways out of town, he was running wild, and the buggy was being whipped from side to side."

"When the buggy flipped over," Luke added, "the horse dragged it a ways before we got him stopped."

Roman looked over at John, wondering if he would agree with what Luke had said.

John nodded. "It's true. It happened just the way Luke said."

"If I hadn't run into Luke and John in Spector's parking lot and if they hadn't offered to help me look for the horse, I don't know what would have happened." Martha looked over at Luke with a strange expression. Was it merely gratitude, or was there something else? Could Martha have a romantic interest in Luke?

Roman massaged his temples, hoping to clear his thinking. No, she was just reacting to the frightening situation; that had to be it. He looked first at John and then at Luke. "I . . . uh . . . appreciate you coming to the aid of my daughter."

"No problem," John said. "We were happy to do it."

"I'm just glad Martha and her horse and buggy are okay," Luke added, as he shuffled his feet a few times.

Martha took a step closer to Luke. There was that look again. Was it more than gratitude Roman saw on his daughter's face?

"You'd better get in the house and see about helping your mamm with supper," he said, nudging Martha's arm. "I'll put Gid in the barn and rub him down." He smiled at John and gave Luke a quick nod. "Again, I appreciate what you did."

"See you, John. See you, Luke." Martha gave Luke another smile and scurried into the house.

As Luke and John climbed into John's rig and drove away, Roman headed to the barn with the horse. *I sure hope Luke has no designs on my daughter. If he does, he's got a big surprise coming.*

Grace yawned and leaned her head against the back of the sofa. She was glad to have both children tucked into bed. Now maybe she and Cleon could have some time alone. They needed to talk. Ever since Carl's visit earlier today, she'd been a ball of nerves. What if Carl rented a house in Berlin and decided to stay in the area permanently? Would he want to see Anna all the time? What kind of influence would he have on the child? Grace feared that Anna might become dissatisfied with the Amish way of life if she spent too much time with Carl. What if, despite Carl's promise, he tried to take Anna away?

"Are you feeling okay tonight?" Cleon asked as he took a seat beside Grace. "You look all done in."

"I am awfully tired," she admitted. "It's been a very long day."

"Was Daniel fussy?"

"Jah. He's cutting another tooth." She released a sigh. "And then there's the problem with Anna."

"What problem is that?"

"When I tucked her in bed, all she could talk about was her poppy and how she

318

couldn't wait to see him again." She drew in a shuddering breath. "Oh, Cleon, what if he tries to influence her against the Amish ways?"

"Did he say anything that might make you think he would do that?"

Grace shook her head. "No, but I don't trust him. He and his wife took Anna from me once. I won't give him the opportunity to do it again."

"From what you've told me, taking Anna and not leaving an address or phone number where you could reach them was mostly his wife's doing."

"That's true. Even so —"

Cleon reached for her hand. "Anna is the man's only grandchild. Do you think it's fair to deprive her of spending time with him?"

Grace clenched her teeth so hard her jaw ached. "Do you want Anna to go away?"

Cleon's furrowed brow and the squint of his eyes let Grace know she'd said too much. "How can you even say such a thing? Of course I don't want Anna to go away."

"Are you sure? I mean, it wasn't too long ago that you and she didn't get along so well."

"Things are fine with me and Anna now; you know that. I love that little girl as if she were my own."

Tears clouded Grace's vision. "Maybe I'm being overly sensitive. I'm probably over-reacting to Carl's visit earlier today."

"Maybe you're trying too hard to protect Anna."

Heat flooded Grace's cheeks, and she sat up straight. "If caring about my daughter and seeing that she's safe is being overly protective, then so be it."

Cleon grunted. "This isn't getting us anywhere, Grace, and I don't want to argue."

"Neither do I."

"Then let's make a compromise."

"What kind of compromise?"

"Anna can spend time with Carl, but only when you, me, or someone from your family is with them. He can take her shopping or out to lunch, but someone from the family will accompany them." Cleon gently stroked her shoulder. "He's also welcome to come here to visit Anna. Agreed?"

She nodded slowly. "Jah, okay."

CHAPTER 28

Rosemary groaned as she bent to pull a clump of weeds from a flower bed near her house. This was the second week of March, and spring was on its way. So was a backache if she didn't take it a bit easier. She smiled, despite the knot that was beginning to form in her lower back. It felt good to be back in her home state, living close to Roman and his family. Ken and Sharon were getting along fine on their own, and in Ken's last letter, he'd said they were planning to build a new house in a few months.

A cool breeze rustled through the trees, and Rosemary turned her thoughts back to the weather. Now that the snow was gone, she planned to take a day sometime soon and drive up to Geauga County to see where Walt and his family lived.

Rosemary straightened when she heard a car pull into the driveway and was surprised when a middle-aged man with thinning hair got out and came up the sidewalk. She realized it was Carl Davis.

"Remember me?" he asked, stepping up to her.

"I remember, Carl. We met at Grace's."

He smiled and nodded. "I was driving down the road and spotted you standing in your yard, so I decided to stop and say hello, since we're almost neighbors."

Rosemary tipped her head. "Oh?"

"I'm renting a house about a mile from here."

"You're planning to stay in Holmes County then?"

He nodded. "Anna's my only granddaughter. I want to be close to her."

Rosemary's jaw clenched. She knew how Grace felt about Carl showing up out of the blue. She also knew Grace was afraid he might try to take Anna away from her again. But if Carl planned to stay in the area, then it wasn't likely he had kidnapping on his mind.

He shifted from one foot to the other. "I don't know how much Grace has told you about my wife and me taking Anna away from her, but —"

"You owe me no explanations," Rosemary said with a raised hand.

"I know I don't, but I was hoping once

you heard my story you might be willing to talk to Grace for me — smooth the way, if you will."

Irritation welled in Rosemary's soul. "Look, Mr. Davis, I barely know you, and I really don't think —"

"Won't you please hear me out?"

She motioned to the porch. "Shall we have a seat?"

Carl stepped onto the porch and lowered himself into one of the wicker chairs near the front door. Rosemary took the seat beside him.

"I never meant to hurt Grace by taking Anna," he said. "My wife convinced me that it was the best thing for the child." He clasped his hands around his knees and grimaced. "She said we'd be doing Grace a favor by removing the burden of raising a child without a father."

"Did you think to offer your son's widow a home, too?"

Carl dropped his gaze to the porch as he slowly shook his head.

"Why not?"

"Bonnie convinced me that Grace was an unfit mother and our son had told her that if something happened to him, he wanted us to raise Anna." He lifted his gaze to meet hers. "My wife was a very controlling woman. In order to keep the peace, I went along with most everything she wanted."

Rosemary swallowed hard. She could relate to Carl's last statement. She'd done many things during the time she'd been married to Bob in order to keep the peace. She knew well what it was like to be married to a control freak.

"Shortly after my wife died, I decided that Anna would be better off with her mother. I was having some health problems and didn't think I could care for the child on my own." Carl sucked in his bottom lip and released it again. "After my meeting with Grace the other day, I realized she felt threatened by my showing up and wanting to see Anna."

"That's understandable, don't you think?"

He nodded. "She has no reason to feel threatened. I'm not here to take Anna away. I just want to be close to my granddaughter. My health has improved, and I want to be able to do all the things for Anna that a grandparent should do."

"I understand."

"Do you really?"

"I believe so."

"Will you speak to Grace on my behalf? Will you assure her that I'm not here to make trouble for her or take Anna away?"

"I'll act as a go-between if necessary, but I think you should talk to Grace yourself and tell her what you've told me."

"Yes, yes, I'll do that."

"Grace and her family have been through enough with the attacks against them. Grace doesn't need anything else to stress about."

Carl's eyebrows pulled together. "Attacks? What kind of attacks are you talking about?"

"I figured Grace had probably written and told you."

Carl shook his head. "She only responded to a couple of my letters after I brought Anna to her, and she never mentioned any attacks having been made on her family." He leaned slightly forward, as deep creases formed in his forehead. "Can you tell me what happened?"

Rosemary cleared her throat a couple of times as she tried to formulate a proper response. How much should she share with this man she barely knew? If she told him the details of the attacks and he became concerned for Anna's safety, he might change his mind and try to take Anna away after all.

"For the last two years, my brother and his family have been the victims of some acts of vandalism," she began. "They don't know who did the attacks or why."

"What kinds of things have been done?"

"Break-ins, tools stolen, clothes cut in two, a fire started at Grace and Cleon's place, and —"

"Their house was set on fire?"

Rosemary nodded and drew in a deep breath. "Grace's sister Ruth and her first husband, Martin, also had their buggy rammed off the road, and Martin was killed in the accident. Of course we aren't sure the accident was related to the other attacks."

Carl's face blanched as he rose to his feet. "Grace should have told me about this! Anna's life could be in danger. It's my duty as her grandfather to see that she's protected from potential danger." Without another word, he rushed off the porch, climbed into his car, and sped down the driveway.

Rosemary gripped the armrests on her chair. "Oh, Lord, what have I done?"

"Cleon, what are you doing?" Grace asked when she entered the kitchen and spotted him sitting at the table with a pen and piece of paper. "I figured you had left for work by now."

"I'll be heading out soon. I wanted to make a list of some supplies I need for my beekeeping business first. I've thought about building a small shop near the front of our property, where I can sell honey and beeswax candles, but as long as your daed needs my help in his woodworking shop, I probably won't follow through with the idea."

Grace pulled out a chair and took a seat beside him. "If you really want to quit working for Dad and go out on your own, I'm sure he could find someone else to take your place in his shop."

Cleon shook his head. "I don't want to leave him in the lurch right now. He's been through enough with having to deal with all the attacks."

Grace shuddered. "That land developer is back in the area, you know, and he's after Dad to sell."

"That's about as likely to happen as one of Martha's hundlin giving birth to a baby bee." Cleon pushed away from the table and bent to give Grace a hug. "If there are any problems today, come out to the barn and get me, okay?"

"I will."

Cleon started for the door but turned back around. "I mean it, Grace. If you need me, I'll come."

Grace forced a smile. "I'm sure everything will be fine."

When Cleon headed out the door, Grace

went upstairs. She found Anna sitting on the floor in her room, playing with the doll Carl had given her. "Why aren't you dressed yet?" she asked. "Have you forgotten that you have school today?"

Anna dropped the doll and scrambled to her feet just as a shrill scream came from across the hall.

"I'd better tend to your bruder," Grace said, hurrying from the room.

A short time later, Grace had Daniel in his high chair, and Anna was seated at the table eating breakfast.

"When's Poppy coming to see me again?" Anna asked.

Grace shrugged and reached for a piece of toast.

"I hope he comes soon."

Grace made no comment, thinking Anna might change the subject if she didn't answer her question.

"I can't wait 'til school lets out for the summer," Anna continued. "Then I'll be able to see Poppy a lot. He's gonna move here, isn't he, Mama?"

"Maybe." Grace pointed to Anna's plate. "Finish eating and then clear your dishes. You don't want to be late for school."

Much to Grace's relief, Anna ate the rest of her breakfast in silence. When she finished, she put her dishes in the sink and grabbed her lunch pail off the counter. With a cheery smile, she said, "See you after school, Mama," and skipped out the door.

Grace had just started cleaning scrambled eggs off Daniel's face when she heard a car pull into the driveway. She finished up with Daniel, scooped him out of his chair, and headed for the door. When she opened it, she found Carl sitting in one of the wicker chairs, with Anna in his lap.

"What are you doing here, Carl?" Grace asked as stepped onto the porch and took a seat in the chair beside him, placing Daniel in her lap.

"Poppy wants me to see his new house," Anna said, her blue eyes twinkling like fireflies, and her lips curving upwards. "Can I go there now?"

Grace shook her head.

"How come?"

"Because you have to go to school, and if you don't leave now, you're going to be late. Aunt Martha's planning to give you a ride, and I'm sure she's waiting down by the barn with her horse and buggy by now."

"Can I go with Poppy after school?"

"No."

Anna opened her mouth as if to say more, but Carl spoke first. "Anna, why don't you run on now? I'll come again soon, and then we can talk some more."

Anna hesitated a moment but finally gave Carl a hug and headed down the driveway toward the barn.

Carl turned to face Grace. "We need to talk."

"About what?"

"About the attacks that have been made against your family and about the safety of my granddaughter."

"Who told you about the attacks?"

"It doesn't matter who told. What matters is that Anna might not be safe living here."

Grace's face heated up. "Are you saying my husband and I aren't capable of protecting our daughter?"

Carl squinted. "*Your* daughter, Grace. Anna's your daughter and *my* granddaughter, and I won't stand by and watch her be victimized by some lunatic who's determined to hurt your family. Therefore, I'd like Anna to move in with me for a while."

Her mouth dropped open. "What?"

"I'd like Anna to move in with me. Just until the attacker has been caught and I know it's safe for her to come back here."

"Absolutely not! Anna is not moving in with you!"

"I'll be back to see Anna sometime soon."

Carl reached into his pocket and pulled out a slip of paper. "Here's my new address and also my cell phone number, so if you change your mind about Anna moving in with me, bring her over or give me a call."

As Martha headed for town, a strange feeling came over her, as though something was wrong. Was it the way Gid pulled against the reins when she tried to make him run, or was it the absence of cars on the road that made her feel so odd? Usually at this time of the morning, several cars would be heading toward Berlin. Today, however, her horse and buggy seemed to be the only things moving on this stretch of road.

"Giddyap there, boy." Martha flicked the reins. "I thought you liked to trot."

The gelding whinnied and flipped his head from side to side.

"What's wrong with you, Gid? Are you getting old and lazy?" She snapped the reins again and was shocked when they broke in two. Gid bolted down the road as the buggy, now out of Martha's control, bounced and swayed behind him.

"Whoa! Hold up there!" she hollered.

The horse kept running, and all Martha could do was grip the edge of her seat and hope he would decide to stop before they ran off the road or were hit by some other vehicle.

She spotted a truck coming down the hill and said a prayer out loud. "Dear God, don't let Gid drag this buggy to the other side of the road."

"I've got to stop that horse!" Luke whipped his truck into the other lane and pulled ahead of Martha's horse. When he slowed his truck, the horse halted. A sense of relief shot through him as he shut off the engine and hopped out of the truck. He sprinted around and grabbed the horse's broken reins. "Are you okay?" he called to Martha.

"I'm fine. Shaken up a bit, but not hurt." She jumped down from the buggy and started toward him. "The horse's reins broke, and —"

"They didn't break, Martha. From what I can tell, they were cut."

Martha's eyes widened, and she gasped. "No wonder Gid was acting so skittish when I smacked the reins and tried to make him trot."

"Have you got any rope?"

"I think there's some in the buggy." Martha scurried around to the back of the buggy and returned a few minutes later with a piece of paper in her hands.

"Where's the rope?" Luke asked as she approached him.

"There wasn't any. I found this lying on the floor where the rope should have been."

Holding on to the horse, Luke took a step toward her. "What is it?"

"It's a note. I . . . I think it was written by the person who's been attacking my family."

"What's it say?"

"SOMEONE NEEDS TO PAY." Martha's voice quivered. "Oh, Luke, just when we think this nightmare might finally be over — just when my hopes begin to rise — something else happens to let us know that the attacker isn't done with us yet, and the hope I felt sinks like a rock thrown into the pond." She drew in a deep breath. "Someone cut Gid's reins, and if you hadn't happened along when you did and gotten the horse stopped . . ." Her voice faltered.

Luke let go of the broken reins and pulled Martha into his arms. His insides twisted with the thought of what could have happened to Martha. "I'm concerned for your safety," he said, gently patting her back.

Martha opened her mouth to say something, but Luke spoke again. "Are you going to tell your daed about this?"

"About the note or the cut reins?"

"Both."

She shrugged. "I suppose he needs to know about the reins, but I'm afraid to mention the note — at least not in front of my mamm."

"How come?"

"It'll upset her too much. She tries to hide it, but she's been a ball of nerves since the last few attacks."

"Then do whatever you think's best. Maybe you can talk to your daed about this when your mamm's not around." Luke motioned to Gid. "If you don't mind leaving your horse and buggy here, I'll drive you over to Abe's harness shop and we'll see about getting some new reins."

"Danki. I appreciate your help with this."

Luke struggled with the desire to kiss Martha, but a van came by just then, so he pulled away. The last thing he needed was for someone they knew to see them hugging or kissing. That kind of news would probably get back to Roman, and then both he and Martha would be in trouble. He gave her arm a gentle squeeze. "Let's go, shall we?"

CHAPTER 29

As Martha sat at the supper table, she thought about the events of the day: discovering her horse's reins had been cut, the note she'd found in the back of the buggy, the concern Luke had shown her today. She didn't see how anyone could think he had anything to do with the attacks. Luke was trying to help her find out who was behind them, and the handwriting on the note had obviously not been his. Besides, what opportunity would he have had to cut the reins, and for what reason? She knew she needed to tell Dad about this but wasn't sure what to do about Mom.

"You're looking very thoughtful there," Mom said, nudging Martha's arm. "You've hardly touched your chicken potpie."

"I'm not so hungry tonight. I've got a lot on my mind."

Dad grunted. "More than likely you're thinking about Luke Friesen. Probably wishing he'd give you another hug."

Martha's mouth dropped open, and Mom let out a gasp. "Roman, what are you saying?"

Dad picked up his spoon and gave his coffee a couple of stirs. "Toby King came by to see me today, and he had some story to tell."

"What story is that?" Mom asked.

"Said he'd been riding with Howard Kemper in his van and saw Luke and Martha standing beside her buggy. They were locked in each other's arms."

Martha nearly jumped out of her chair. "Dad, it wasn't like that. I can explain —"

"I should hope so!" Dad's face turned as red as an apple. "I'd like you to tell me and your mamm what you were doing with Luke today, and why you had your arms around each other."

"My horse's reins broke, and Luke offered to drive me over to Abe's place and get a new set of reins." She would explain that the reins were cut later, when she could talk to Dad alone.

"Did you ride in Luke's truck?"

Martha's heart started to pound. "You know about his truck?"

Dad's fist came down hard on the table, jostling the silverware and nearly knocking over his glass of water. "I know all about

Luke's truck! Toby filled me in on that bit of information, too."

Martha reached for her glass of water and took a drink. Her mouth felt so dry she could barely swallow. If Toby had told Dad about Luke's truck and said he'd seen the two of them hugging, then that must have been him riding in the vehicle that had passed when she and Luke had been talking beside her buggy. And if Toby had felt the need to blab that to Dad, then he really must have something against Luke.

"Have you and Luke been courting behind our backs?" Mom's question drove Martha's thoughts aside.

Martha wasn't sure how to respond. Even though she and Luke weren't officially courting, they had gone a few places together. He'd also said he wished they could court. She gulped down some more water. "No, we're . . . uh . . . not courting."

"Then why was he hugging you?" Dad asked.

"We weren't hugging. Luke was trying to comfort me."

"Comfort you?" Mom's eyebrows furrowed. "Why did you need comforting, Martha?"

"Because I was upset about my horse's reins having been cut," Martha blurted out.

"What?" Mom and Dad said in unison.

"I thought at first they were just broken, but Luke's the one who discovered they'd actually been cut, and then —" Martha saw Mom's hands begin to shake, and she caught herself in time before blurting out the part about the note she'd found in the back of her buggy.

"Ach, Martha," Mom said shakily. "You could have been hurt."

"We'll talk about the reins being cut later," Dad said, staring hard at Martha. "Right now I'd like to deal with the issue of Luke having his hands all over you."

Martha shook her head vigorously. "He didn't, Dad. Luke was just —"

Dad slammed his fist on the table again. "I will not allow it to happen a second time! I forbid you to see Luke again!"

Martha's eyes filled with tears as she pushed back her chair and rushed from the room.

Judith released a shuddering sigh. "Ach, Roman. Why'd you say such a thing to our daughter? Can't you see how much it hurt her?"

"I don't care if it did. She shouldn't be sneaking around and meeting up with Luke behind our backs." Roman grunted. "Hugging him right there on the side of the road where everyone could see. What was that girl thinking?"

"Maybe it's the way she said. Luke might have just given her a hug to comfort her."

"Over some broken reins?"

"They weren't broken. You heard what Martha said." Judith paused and drew in a quick breath. "Those reins were deliberately cut, Roman. It was another attack."

He grabbed his glass of water and took a drink. "I doubt Martha was upset enough to need the kind of comforting Luke was offering. I think Luke just used it as an opportunity to put our daughter in a compromising position and make her look bad."

"Why would he do that?"

"For the same reason he's been doing all those horrible things to us. He's trying to get even with me for firing him."

"Please don't start with that again, Roman." She touched his arm. "I thought you'd decided the land developer was probably behind the attacks."

"I said it *could* be the land developer, but I have no proof."

"We never will know for sure who's responsible until the sheriff catches him."

"Jah, right! Like Sheriff Osborn's going to camp out on our property and wait for someone to pull another prank."

"They aren't pranks, Roman. Whoever's behind the attacks is out for more than a good time."

"You're right about that." He scratched the side of his head. "Fact is, I've been thinking and praying about this a lot lately."

"Will you speak to the sheriff again and see if he has any leads?"

He shook his head. "I'm thinking I might do a little investigating on my own."

Her eyebrows lifted high on her forehead. "What kind of investigating?"

"I haven't come up with a plan yet, but when I do, you'll be the first to know. In the meantime, I've got other things that need to be done. I talked with Cleon this morning, and we've decided to get started on my new shop, hopefully in the next week or so."

"Will you have a work frolic then?"

He nodded. "Probably so. It'll be good to be in my own shop again. I've had about as much of working in that smelly barn with Martha's yappy dogs as I can take."

"I hope Poppy comes over to see me soon," Anna said as she swirled her noodles around on her plate with a fork. "I wanna show him Papa's bees."

"You know you're not to go near my bee

boxes," Cleon said with a shake of his head. "I've told you before that you might get stung."

Anna's lower lip protruded. "I never get to have any fun."

"There's nothing fun about seeing my bee boxes."

"Then how come you go out there all the time, Papa?"

"Because I have things that need to be done."

"What kind of things?"

"I have to check on the honeycombs, and when the time is right, I extract the honey."

Anna smacked her lips. "I love peanut butter and honey sandwiches. Sure wish we could've had that for supper tonight."

"You had a peanut butter and honey sandwich for lunch," Grace reminded the child.

"I could eat another one now. It might help me not miss Poppy so much."

Cleon reached over and patted Anna's hand. "He's going to be renting a place near Berlin, and that's not far away, Anna. I'm sure you'll be able to see him a lot this summer when you're out of school. Maybe your mamm will take you to see his new house sometime later this week."

Anna's face lit up. "How about tomorrow

after school?"

"We can talk about that later," Grace said.

Cleon turned to face Anna. "In the meantime, you need to finish eating your supper."

Anna's forehead wrinkled. "Daniel don't have to eat his supper."

Grace glanced over at her son, sitting in the high chair next to the table. "That's because he's already eaten. I fed him earlier, remember?"

"Then how comes he's sittin' in his chair with a cracker and a cup of milk?"

"So he can feel like part of the family and be near us," Cleon answered.

They ate in silence for the rest of the meal. Grace hoped Anna would be willing to take Daniel into the living room to play after supper, because she needed to talk to Cleon and tell him what had happened when Carl had shown up this morning saying Anna wasn't safe living with them.

"It's later now," Anna said. "Will you take me to see Poppy tomorrow after school?"

"I don't think so." Grace gritted her teeth. *I wish Wade's dad hadn't come back to Holmes County. I wish he would stay out of Anna's life.*

"How come?" Anna persisted.

"I've got too much to do tomorrow."

Anna gave Cleon an imploring look. "Will you drive me to Berlin so I can see Poppy?"

"Your daed will be working tomorrow afternoon," Grace said.

Anna bumped the tray on Daniel's high chair, and Daniel let out an ear-piercing wail. Grace grabbed a couple of napkins to wipe up the milk that had spilled out of his cup.

"Stop that *gegrisch!*" Anna said, covering her ears with the palms of her hands.

"He's only hollering because you bumped his tray and spilled his milk."

"He's hurtin' my ears." Anna pinched Daniel's arm, and he screamed even louder.

Grace's hands shook as she lifted Daniel from his chair and placed him in her lap. "Anna, tell your bruder you're sorry for pinching him."

Anna shook her head. "He's too young to know what I'm sayin'. Besides, he shouldn't have yelled in my ear like that."

"Either apologize or go to your room," Grace said through tight lips.

With tears in her eyes, Anna glanced over at Cleon.

"You'd better do as your mamm says," he said.

"But I haven't had my dessert."

Grace's face heated up. "Then apologize

to Daniel!"

Anna shook her head and dashed from the room.

Cleon's forehead wrinkled as he looked over at Grace. "Did you have to yell at her like that?"

Grace's defenses rose. "She acted like a pill throughout the meal, and when she pinched Daniel, I'd had enough."

"She's upset about not being able to see her grandpa tomorrow."

Grace wrapped her arms around Daniel and held him tightly, hoping the gesture might offer her some comfort. "I'm not sure Anna should ever see Carl."

"Why not? I thought we agreed that she could see him if someone in the family was with them."

"He found out about the attacks against my family, and he doesn't think Anna's safe living here." Grace gulped on the sob rising in her throat. "He said he wants Anna to move in with him."

A muscle on the side of Cleon's neck quivered, and he blinked rapidly. "I won't let that happen, Grace. I promise you'll never lose your daughter again."

CHAPTER 30

The following morning as Grace stood at the stove, stirring a pot of oatmeal, she thought about Carl's suggestion that Anna come to live with him, and it upset her all over again. She did want Anna to be safe, but not at the risk of letting Carl take control of her again. No, Anna's place was here, with them.

Forcing her thoughts aside, Grace turned from the stove, cupped her hands around her mouth, and called, "Anna, breakfast is ready!"

No response.

"Maybe she's in the bathroom," Cleon said as he stepped into the kitchen.

Grace shook her head. "I'm sure I would have heard her come down the stairs."

"Maybe she took them softly for a change." Cleon moved toward the high chair and ruffled Daniel's curly hair. "Or Anna might have come downstairs during one of this little guy's yelling matches. No one can hear much of anything when he gets to hollering."

Grace bit back a chuckle. Daniel had become pretty verbal lately. "Would you mind checking the bathroom to see if Anna's there while I finish making the pancakes?"

"Don't mind at all." Cleon left the room and returned a few seconds later. "No sign of Anna in the bathroom. Want me to check upstairs and see if she's still in her room?"

Grace nodded.

Cleon left again, and when he returned, he was frowning.

"What's wrong?"

"Anna's gone."

"Gone?"

"She's not in her room, and when I looked in her closet to see if she might be there, I discovered that her suitcase was missing."

Grace gasped. Had Anna been kidnapped, or had she run away?

As Luke bounced along in the passenger's seat of John's SUV, he was surprised when he spotted Grace's daughter, Anna, walking along the edge of the road in the opposite direction of the schoolhouse, lugging a small suitcase. "Hold up there, would you, John?

I know that little girl, and I'd like to find out where she's going with that suitcase."

When John slowed his rig and pulled to the shoulder of the road, Luke hopped out. "Where are you going, Anna?" he called.

Anna merely shrugged and kept on walking.

"The direction you're heading is not the way to the schoolhouse," Luke said, walking beside her.

"I know that."

"Would you like us to give you a ride to school?"

She shook her head.

"Then get in the car, and we'll take you home."

"I don't wanna go home. I'm goin' to see Poppy."

"Poppy?"

Anna nodded. "Poppy's my *grossdaadi,* and I wanna be with him."

Luke had never heard Anna refer to Grace's dad as "Poppy" before. Could Anna be talking about her other grandfather — the one she'd been with before she'd come to live with Grace?

"Where's your grossdaadi live?" Luke asked.

"In a house in Berlin. He's livin' there now."

"Do you know which house, Anna?"

She shook her head. "No, but I'll find him!"

Luke touched Anna's shoulder. "If you want to visit him, then you'd better ask your mamm, don't you think?"

Anna's blue eyes flashed angrily, and her chin jutted out. "Mama said no, but she can't stop me from bein' with Poppy. Nobody can keep us apart."

"I'm sure no one wants to keep you apart, Anna."

"Uh-huh. Poppy asked if I could go to his house to see him, and Mama said no, not today."

Luke was sure if Grace knew Anna was out on the road by herself, heading toward Berlin in search of her grandfather, she would be worried sick.

"Look, Anna, if you get in the car we can talk about this better."

Anna hesitated but finally climbed into John's rig. Luke grabbed her suitcase and climbed in, too. "Head for Cleon's place," he mouthed to John after he'd taken his seat and shut the door. John nodded and pulled onto the road.

Martha had just stepped out of the barn when she heard a vehicle pull into the yard.

Her breath caught in her throat when she saw Luke getting out of John Peterson's SUV. Didn't he know better than to come here uninvited? What if Dad came out of his shop and saw Luke and Martha together? After the scene Dad had made the other night when he'd confronted her about seeing Luke, Martha knew he would be hopping mad if Luke showed his face around here again. She still hadn't had the chance to speak to Dad alone and tell him about the note she'd found in the back of her buggy. She wasn't even sure she wanted to bring up the subject, for fear of riling Dad again.

Martha took a step toward Luke but halted when he turned and lifted Anna out of the SUV. "What in the world?" She rushed over to them. "What's Anna doing in John's rig? I figured she'd be home having breakfast or in Cleon's buggy on her way to school."

"That's what I thought, too, when I saw her walking along the edge of the road in the opposite direction of the schoolhouse." Luke nodded toward Grace and Cleon's place. "You want to come along while I walk Anna up to her house?"

Martha was about to reply, when Anna hollered, "I don't wanna go home! I wanna see Poppy!"

The child pivoted toward the road, but Martha reached out and grabbed her arm. "You can't go running off by yourself," she said firmly. "We'll go up to your house, let your mamm know you're okay, and then you can talk about seeing your grandpa."

Anna dug in her heels. "I need to see Poppy!"

Martha gritted her teeth. "You don't even know where he lives. You're coming with me!"

"Let me talk to her." Luke squatted beside Anna. "We know you want to see your grossdaadi, but let's go up to your house and talk to your mamm and daed a few minutes. I'm sure we can work things out."

Anna finally nodded and reached for Luke's hand.

Luke picked up Anna's suitcase, and as he and Anna started up the driveway, Martha turned to John, who still sat in his vehicle. "Thanks for bringing her home, John."

"Sure, no problem. We couldn't let the little tyke skip school and try to find her grandfather's house all alone."

"I appreciate that." Martha smiled. "Would you like to come up to the house with us?"

John shook his head. "I think I'll head to

the barn and see your dad. I heard he's planning to rebuild his shop soon."

Martha nodded. "Would you do me a favor, John?"

"What's that?"

"Would you please not mention anything to Dad about Luke being here?"

"How come?"

"Dad doesn't care much for Luke, and —"

"Sure, no problem. I won't say a word."

"Thank you." Martha turned and hurried up the driveway behind Luke and Anna.

When Grace heard footsteps on the back porch, she jerked open the door. There stood Anna holding Luke Friesen's hand. "Anna! Oh, Anna!" she cried.

"Where have you been?" Cleon asked, as he joined Grace on the porch, holding Daniel in his arms. "You sneaked out of the house without telling your mamm or me where you were going, and I was just getting ready to go out looking for you."

Anna gave no reply as Luke herded her up the stairs.

"John and I were heading to Berlin, and we saw her walking along the side of the road in the opposite direction of the schoolhouse," Luke said as they stepped onto the porch.

"She was going to see her grandpa Davis," Martha added as she followed behind Luke.

"What!" Grace and Cleon said in unison.

"I . . . I wanted to see Poppy." Anna's voice quivered, and her blue eyes filled with tears. "Poppy loves me."

Grace dropped to her knees and wrapped her arms around the child. "Oh, Anna, we love you, too."

"But we can't have you skipping school," Cleon said. "You don't even know where your grandpa Davis lives. You would have gotten lost on your own, and it's dangerous for you to be out by yourself like that."

Anna sniffed. "C–can I see Poppy after school today?"

"Not today." Grace patted Anna's back. "We'll see about going there some Saturday when you have no school."

When Grace and Cleon took Anna inside, Martha remained on the porch with Luke.

"Danki for bringing Anna home," she said, leaning on the railing as she faced Luke, who stood with his back to the door.

"It scared me when I saw her lugging a suitcase and heading in the direction of

Berlin by herself," he replied. "When I found out what she was up to, I figured her folks were probably worried and that we needed to get Anna home as quick as we could."

"You really do care about my family, don't you?"

"Of course I care." Luke glanced down the driveway, where John's rig was parked near the barn. "I even care about your daed. Although I'm sure he'd never believe that."

Martha grimaced. "Dad can be pretty stubborn at times. It's not easy to make him see that he's wrong about something."

"Well, he's wrong about me, and I aim to prove it. I just wish there were more clues that would help us find out who's behind the attacks." Luke grunted. "I don't think we've done such a good job of investigating things, Martha. To tell you the truth, I'm beginning to wonder if we'll ever find out who's behind the attacks."

"I have some information I think is worth thinking about," she said.

His eyebrows shot up. "You do?"

She nodded.

"What is it?"

Martha motioned for Luke to come closer. "I recently discovered that Ray Larson has set up a bird feeder close to our fence line that borders his property."

Luke's mouth fell open. "You don't really think your nice neighbor has anything to do with the attacks."

"I hope not, but when I asked Ray about the feeder, he said he'd put it there so he could watch certain birds." She frowned. "I think he might be watching us and not the birds. I'm hoping to find out what he's up to."

"How are you planning to do that? Since you're working for Irene more now than ever, you're not always home to keep an eye on things."

"That's true, but I'll watch when I am here, and —"

Luke held up one hand as Cleon stepped out the door.

"I didn't realize you were still here, Luke," Cleon said. "Figured you and John would be headed for work by now."

"He closed his shop for a few hours this morning," Luke replied. "The two of us were headed to town when we spotted Anna." He nodded toward the barn. "John's visiting Roman right now, so I figured I may as well hang around here 'til he's done."

"I'm heading to work at the barn myself," Cleon said. "Should I tell John you're waiting up here at the house, Luke?"

Luke nodded. "But I'd appreciate it if you didn't mention that I'm talking to Martha. Roman wouldn't like it."

Cleon gnawed on his lower lip but finally nodded.

"Maybe I should wait in John's rig," Luke said when Cleon stepped off the porch. "No point in borrowing trouble."

"Cleon said he wouldn't tell Dad you're with me."

"Even so, I think I'd better go." Luke turned and sprinted down the driveway.

Martha turned and started up the steps leading to her sister's house, figuring Grace probably needed a listening ear.

"How are things with you these days?" John asked Roman as he stood near one of the workbenches that had been set up in the barn.

Roman shrugged his shoulders. "Fair to middlin'."

"There haven't been any more attacks, I hope."

"Not for a while." Roman saw no need to mention that the reins of Martha's horse had been cut.

"That's good to hear. It's kind of worrisome to think there might be a deranged person running around our community, ready to terrorize some other unsuspecting family at any moment."

"So far, we're the only ones who have been attacked." Roman blew out his breath. "If the person behind the attacks was planning to hit other folks' homes, I'm sure they'd have done it by now."

"What about the vandalism done at some of the schools?"

"I'm sure those were done by pranksters. Same holds true for the other mischief that's been pulled."

"You're probably right about that," John said with a nod.

"So, what brings you by here this morning?"

"Luke and I were headed to Berlin and spotted your granddaughter Anna heading in that direction. After Luke talked with her awhile, we brought her back home."

Roman's forehead wrinkled. "Anna was heading to Berlin by herself?"

"That's right. She said she was going to see her grandpa."

"Carl Davis?"

John shrugged.

A car door slammed, and Roman glanced out the window. He spotted Luke getting into John's SUV.

John glanced out the window then, too.

"Guess I'd better get going."

"All right then. Thanks for bringing my granddaughter home."

"No problem. We were glad to do it." John headed for the door but turned back around. "Oh, I heard you were going to start building a new shop soon."

"That's right. Hope to get started on it in the next week or so."

"Let me know if you need any help."

"Thanks, John, I will."

Roman watched as John got into his truck. Despite the fact that he didn't care much for Luke, he was grateful he'd brought Anna home; he just couldn't muster up the words to say so.

CHAPTER 31

Crash! Bam! Thump, thump, thump!

Roman sat straight up in bed and snapped on the battery-operated light. His heart pounded as he looked at his and Judith's bedroom window. It had been shattered, and a brick lay on the floor near their dresser.

Judith bolted upright and let out an ear-piercing scream.

With no thought for the broken glass covering the floor, Roman rushed over to the window and pulled the curtain aside. The moon was hidden by clouds tonight, and the yard was shrouded in darkness.

"What is it, Roman? Do you see anyone out there?" Judith's voice quavered, and when Roman turned to look at her, he saw tears on her cheeks.

"It's too dark for me to see," he said, moving back to the bed. "I'm sure whoever threw that brick isn't hanging around so he can get caught. No doubt, the culprit's long gone."

"Oh, Roman," she sobbed, "I . . . I don't think I can take much more of this. I wish you c–could make it stop."

He lowered himself to the bed and took hold of her hand. "If there was something I could do about these horrible attacks, don't you think I would?"

Judith started rocking back and forth, holding her hands against her temples.

He touched her shoulder. "Judith, are you okay?"

No response.

"Judith, are you listening to me?"

She continued to rock, staring vacantly across the room.

Suddenly, Martha burst into the room. "Did you hear that big boom? It sounded like —" Her gaze went to the window, and then to the floor. "Did . . . did you see who threw that brick, Dad? Were either you or Mom hurt?"

Roman shook his head, but Judith continued to sit and rock as though in a daze.

Martha rushed over to the bed and took a seat beside her. "Mom, are you okay?"

"She's fine; just a little shook up is all."

Martha turned to face Roman. "Are — are you sure she's all right? She looks like she's in shock."

"She was talking to me a few seconds ago. She seemed kind of shaky, but I don't think she's in shock."

"Maybe Mom should lie down in bed."

"That might be a good idea." Roman helped Judith lie down, and he made sure her head was resting on a pillow. "Martha, why don't you run to the kitchen and get your mamm a cup of herbal tea?"

Martha hesitated a moment, took a quick glance at her mother, and bolted from the room.

Martha entered the kitchen, lit the gas lamp hanging above the table, and put a kettle of water on the stove to heat. Then she hurried across the room, grabbed a flashlight from the top drawer, and opened the back door. Clicking on the flashlight, she shone the beam of light around the yard. No sign of anyone. Of course that didn't mean no one was lurking in the shadows. If she hadn't been so concerned about Mom, she would have ventured into the yard and searched for the culprit who'd thrown that brick.

I'll never find out who's been doing these things to us if I don't find some clues, she fumed. *But I'd better not go outside and look for them now.*

Martha stepped back into the house and closed the door. She would look for some clues first thing in the morning. In the meantime, she needed to check on Mom and give her some tea.

"Where's your mamm? I figured she'd be here making breakfast," Dad said when he stepped into the kitchen after finishing his chores the following morning.

Martha turned from the stove, where she'd been frying bacon. "Mom's still in bed."

Dad's eyebrows shot up. "It's not like her to sleep so late."

"I'm not sure she's sleeping, Dad. I think she may still be upset over what happened last night with the brick."

"I can understand her being upset last night," Dad said as he washed his hands at the sink. "But I boarded up the window, cleaned up the glass, and promised to notify the sheriff, so there's no reason for her to be lying in bed feeling *naerfich.*"

Martha pursed her lips. "I think Mom has every right to feel nervous. These attacks have been going on too long, and it's enough to put anyone's nerves on edge."

"Which is why I agreed to notify the sheriff."

"When do you plan to call him?"

"Sometime today, but not until I've had some breakfast and have checked on your mamm."

Martha set a plate of toast on the table just as Dad took a seat. "Don't you think you ought to call the doctor and see about getting Mom in as soon as possible?"

He shrugged his shoulders. "I think she just needs a good rest. She's been working awfully hard around here lately, you know."

Martha released an exasperated sigh. "Mom's not in bed because she's tired and needs a good rest. She's —"

He held up one hand to silence her. "If she's not feeling better by noon, I'll take her to the clinic in town. In the meantime, I'm going up to Grace and Cleon's place to tell them what happened last night."

"Dad, what's wrong? You look like you didn't sleep a wink last night," Grace said when her father entered the kitchen as she was getting breakfast on the table.

He moaned and sank into a chair. "There was another attack during the night."

"Ach, no!" Grace gasped, and Cleon reached out to grab her hand.

"What happened?" Cleon asked.

"Someone threw a brick through our bedroom window."

"Were either of you hurt?"

Dad looked up at Grace and shook his head. "Not physically, anyway."

"What do you mean, Dad?"

He tugged his ear. "It's your mamm. She's not acting like herself at all."

"What's wrong with Mom? How's she acting?"

"Like she's in some kind of daze. Won't say a word to anyone and doesn't seem to know where she is."

Grace covered her mouth with the palm of her hand. "I knew it. I knew this was coming."

Dad looked up at her and tipped his head. "What's that supposed to mean?"

"Mom's been on edge ever since the attacks first began, but with each one that's happened, she's gotten worse." Grace slowly shook her head. "I'm afraid the brick being thrown through your window might have pushed her over the edge."

"I don't think so." Dad's eyelids blinked in rapid succession. "I'm sure she'll snap out of it soon and be back to her old self."

"Mom hasn't been her old self for a long time, Dad." Grace moved over to the row of wall pegs by the back door and grabbed a sweater.

"Where are you going?" Cleon asked.

"To see Mom, of course. Can you take care of things here while I'm gone?"

Cleon looked over at Dad. "What about work? Are you planning to open the shop today?"

Dad shook his head. "No, no. I think I'd better spend the day with Judith." He rose from his chair. "I'll walk back to the house with Grace now, and we'll let you know later how things are going."

Anna spoke up for the first time. "What about Poppy? Don't I get to see him today?"

"Not today, Anna," Cleon said. "Your grandma Hostettler is sick, and your mamm has to look after her."

Grace didn't wait to hear Anna's response. She rushed out the door with Dad behind her. *Oh, dear Lord,* she silently prayed, *please help my mamm.*

As Martha headed outside after the breakfast dishes were done, all she could think about was her mother lying in her room, refusing to get out of bed. Mom hadn't eaten anything from the breakfast tray Martha had prepared for her, nor had she spoken a word to either Martha or Dad.

Martha worried that Mom might be on the verge of a nervous breakdown.

"I hope Dad decides to take Mom to the doctor," Martha muttered as she zigzagged across the yard, searching for clues that might give some indication as to who had thrown the brick into her parents' room the night before. It wasn't fair, this nightmare they'd been living since the first act of vandalism that had taken place over two years ago. Martha was sure if it had been some kids playing pranks it would have ended long before now. No, someone was definitely trying to get even with someone in her family. The questions remained: who and why?

As Martha made her way along the edge of the flower bed near the house, she spotted an empty beer bottle lying in the grass. *Whoever threw that brick must have been drinking and dropped the beer bottle.*

She was about to head into the house when something shiny sticking out of the dirt caught her eye. She bent to investigate and discovered a ballpoint pen. She didn't recognize it as belonging to anyone in her family, but she thought she might have seen it, or at least one like it, somewhere before.

Clutching the pen tightly in her hand, she hurried back to the house to check on

Mom. She'd just entered the kitchen and had slipped the pen in a drawer, when Dad showed up with Grace.

"Where's Mom?" Grace asked with a panicked expression.

"She's in her room, resting," Martha replied.

Grace moved in that direction, but Martha stepped between her and the hallway door. "Why don't we let Dad check on Mom first? That will give the two of us a chance to talk."

Grace looked like she might argue, but she finally nodded and took a seat at the table.

Dad hurried down the hall toward his bedroom.

Martha took a seat beside Grace. "I think Mom needs to see the doctor. She's not doing well at all."

Grace's head moved slowly up and down. "Dad said she won't speak to anyone and acts like she doesn't know where she is."

"That's right. She's been like that since the brick was thrown through the window during the night."

"Is Dad going to phone the doctor?"

Martha shrugged. "He said that if Mom wasn't feeling better by noon, he would."

"If she's as bad as you say, then I don't

think we should wait that long, do you?"

"Probably not."

Grace pushed her chair away from the table and stood.

"Where are you going?"

"Into Mom's room to see for myself how she's doing." Deep wrinkles formed in Grace's forehead. "If I think she needs to see the doctor, I'm going to insist that Dad make the phone call right now."

Luke glanced at the clock on the far wall of John's shop. It was after eight and still no John. Luke didn't remember John saying the night before that he planned to run any errands this morning, but maybe something had come up at the last minute and John had decided to run into town.

"He should have called to let me know he was going to be late," Luke mumbled as he glanced at the phone sitting on John's desk. It had only rung once this morning, and that call had been a wrong number. "Guess I'd better get busy and find something to do, because when the boss does get here, I'm sure he won't be too happy if he sees me standing around."

For the next hour, Luke stayed busy staining a set of cabinets that were supposed to be finished by the end of the week. When those were done, he put the can of stain away and started sanding an antique rocking chair that had been brought into the shop the day before for restoration.

At nine thirty, the shop door opened, and John stepped into the room. "I overslept. Why didn't you call me?"

"Figured you might call me," Luke replied.

John's forehead wrinkled. "How could I call if I was sleeping?" He tromped across the room and dropped into the chair at his desk with a groan. "The battery in my stupid alarm clock must have gone dead, because it never rang this morning."

"I would have called if I'd known you'd just overslept, but I thought maybe you had run some errands in town."

"No errands today." John glanced across the room, where the coffeepot sat on a table. "Is there any coffee made?"

Luke nodded. "Made some first thing this morning."

"Good. A steaming cup of hot coffee is just what I need." John left his desk and ambled across the room, stretching his hands over his head and releasing a yawn. "I never feel right when I oversleep. It'll probably take my brain the rest of the day to thaw out so I can get some work done."

Luke gestured to the cabinets he'd just stained. "As you can see, I've got those ready to go." He pointed to the rocking chair. "I also started on that."

"Glad to hear it," John said as he poured himself a cup of coffee and added three teaspoons of sugar. Luke had never figured out why John liked his coffee so sweet. He preferred his black.

"Have you heard anything from your folks lately?" John asked when he returned to his desk.

"I saw Mom from a distance in town the other day but didn't get a chance to speak to her."

"Do you think your folks are still mad at you?"

"I'm not sure." Luke scrubbed his hand across his chin. "I think they're more disappointed than anything."

"Because you haven't joined the Amish church?"

Luke nodded. "By the time Dad was my age, he was already married, and Mom was expecting her first baby."

John took a swig of coffee. "How much longer do you plan to sleep in my back room?"

"Do you need me to find another place to stay? Because if you do —"

John lifted his hand. "I didn't say that. I just don't think it's an ideal living arrangement."

"I hope to have some answers soon. Then maybe I can make a decision that will give my parents some peace."

"What kind of answers are you talking about?"

"I'll explain things when I can." Luke motioned to the rocking chair. "In the meantime, I'd better get back to work on that."

John set his coffee cup down. "I'd better try to get something done myself."

CHAPTER 32

Martha paced the kitchen floor and kept glancing at the clock on the far wall as she waited for Dad and Grace to come out of Mom's room. By noon, Mom still hadn't responded to anything Dad or Grace had said to her, and at Grace's insistence, Dad had phoned the doctor and gotten Mom an appointment for this afternoon. Then he'd called Rosemary and asked if she would give them a ride to the doctor in Millersburg. Grace and Dad had gone into Mom's room forty-five minutes ago to help Mom get dressed.

What could be taking so long? she fretted. *Surely it couldn't take Mom this long to get dressed.*

Martha had known for some time that her mother was upset over the attacks that had been done to them. After the last several acts of vandalism, Mom had acted jittery for days. But she'd never freaked out like she had last night or gone into her own world, refusing to talk to anyone.

Martha sank into a chair at the table and let her head fall forward into her open palms. She feared the worst where her mother was concerned. Mom rarely got sick, and whenever she did, she usually bounced right back. What if Mom didn't bounce back this time? What if . . .

Martha jumped when she heard her parents' bedroom door open. She raced into the hallway and was pleased to see Mom standing there, fully dressed. Grace and Dad stood on either side of her with their arms around Mom's waist.

"How are you feeling?" Martha asked, rushing to her mother's side.

Mom blinked a couple of times and gave Martha a blank stare.

"She'll be better once she sees the doctor," Dad said with a nod.

"Would you like some lunch before you go?"

"I've already eaten," he replied.

"No, I meant Mom."

"She might feel better if she had something to eat," Grace said. "Would you like some tea and a boiled egg before you go, Mom?"

"I . . . don't care for any."

Hope welled in Martha's soul when Mom replied to Grace's question. If Mom was speaking again, maybe she would be all right and wouldn't need to see the doctor after all. She was about to voice that thought when a horn honked from outside.

"That must be Rosemary," Dad said. "We're supposed to be at the doctor's in half an hour, and if we don't go now, we'll be late. We can get something to eat on the way home." He ushered Mom quickly out the door, calling over his shoulder, "If you're coming with us, Martha, you'd better get a move on."

"She's going to be all right," Grace whispered as Martha headed out the door. "She *has* to be all right."

As Ruth washed the breakfast dishes while Esta dried, she glanced over her shoulder and smiled at Molly sitting on the floor, playing with one of her dolls.

"Can I go over to Anna's when we're done with the dishes?" Esta asked. "I want to take Winkie along and show her the new tricks I've been teaching him."

Ruth nodded. "I suppose it would be all right. But only if Gideon goes with you."

Esta wrinkled her nose. "How come he has to go along?"

"Because you'll need someone to drive the pony cart."

"I can drive it. Cinnamon's a tame pony and does just what I say."

"That may be, but I won't have you out on the road by yourself in the pony cart." Ruth added a few more squirts of detergent to her sink full of dishes. "Either Gideon goes along, or you'll have to stay home."

Esta's lower lip jutted out. "Gideon's always so cranky. Can't Josh go instead?"

The back door flew open, and Josh tore into the room. His face was red and his breathing labored. "You'd better come quick, Mama. Gideon fell on a broken beer bottle out by the barn, and he's bleedin' real bad!"

A broken beer bottle? Ruth had no idea how a beer bottle would have gotten there; no one in their family drank anything with alcohol in it. She supposed it could have belonged to one of the men who came to Abe's harness shop, but what would they have been doing up by the barn?

Shaking her head to clear her thoughts, Ruth opened a drawer and grabbed a clean dish towel. "Esta, stay with Molly while I check on Gideon," she instructed as she rushed out the back door.

Ruth found Gideon lying on the ground

not far from the barn, moaning and clutching his leg. Nearby lay the shattered remains of a beer bottle.

"Gideon, let me have a look at your leg," she instructed.

The boy groaned and pulled his bloody fingers away from the spot he'd been holding. Ruth bent for a closer look, and her stomach clenched when she saw how deep the cut was.

"You need to go to the hospital for stitches," she said, wrapping the towel securely around Gideon's leg.

"Can't you just slap a bandage on it?"

She shook her head. "The cut's too deep and wide for that. Besides, we can't take the risk of infection setting in."

"But Papa's gone shopping in Berlin today," Gideon said. "So how am I gonna get to the hospital?"

"I'll call for a ride and take you there myself."

Gideon looked like he might protest, but to Ruth's surprise, he nodded and said, "Jah, okay."

After Rosemary dropped Judith, Roman, and Martha off at the doctor's, she decided it was time to pay the sheriff another visit. He needed to know about this latest attack, and he needed to find a way to make the attacks stop. She hoped he was in his office today and not out patrolling.

When Rosemary entered the sheriff's office a short time later, she was relieved to find the sheriff there.

"What can I help you with?" he asked, as she took a seat on the other side of his desk.

"There's been another attack at my brother's house."

He lifted both arms and laced his fingers together as he placed his hands behind his head. "What's happened now?"

"Someone threw a brick through Roman and Judith's bedroom window last night."

"I see."

Irritation welled in Rosemary's chest. Didn't the man even care? Wasn't he concerned that someone may have gotten hurt?

"My brother and his wife are over at the doctor's right now," she said through tight lips.

"Was one of them hit by the brick?"

She shook her head. "But they could have been."

He dropped his arms and placed both hands on his desk. "If they weren't hurt, then why the trip to the doctor's?"

"Judith's been a nervous wreck since the last several attacks, and this one . . . well, it sort of put her over the edge."

He leaned slightly forward. "Did she suffer a nervous breakdown? Is that what you're saying?"

"We're not sure, but she wouldn't talk to anyone for a while, and —"

"I'm sorry to hear about the broken window and Mrs. Hostettler's shattered nerves, but unless I'm given some evidence to go on, there's really not much I can do."

Rosemary released an exasperated sigh. "It's my impression that you promised my brother you'd keep a closer eye on his place."

He gave a curt nod. "I did say that, but I'm a busy man. You can't expect me to spend all my on-duty hours camped across the road from the Hostettlers', waiting for the next attack to occur."

Rosemary's face heated up, and she gripped the strap on her purse. "You don't have to be so harsh."

"I'm just stating facts as I know them." Sheriff Osborn gave her a half smile. "As I'm sure you know, that brother of yours is a stubborn man. He's given me little or nothing to go on and rarely notifies me when there's been an attack."

"He planned to tell you about this one," she was quick to say. "He got detained when we had to take Judith to the doctor's."

The sheriff picked up his pen and jotted something on a piece of paper. "I'll stop by Roman's place later today and see what information I can get out of him."

"Will you check around the place for evidence?"

"Of course."

She rose from her chair. "Thank you, Sheriff."

As Rosemary left the sheriff's office, she felt a small sense of relief. At least he'd been notified about the brick and the broken window, and he was planning to speak to Roman about it. She knew Roman might not appreciate her having gone to the sheriff without his permission, but that didn't matter. They had to find out who was behind the attacks and, in the meantime, protect Roman's family.

As Rosemary headed to her car a few minutes later, she was surprised to see Carl Davis walking up the sidewalk across the street. She hadn't seen him since the day he'd stopped by her house, but she knew after talking with Grace the following day that Carl had suggested Anna come live with him so she would be safe. Of course Grace had vetoed that idea because she feared Carl might try to take Anna away again, and Rosemary couldn't blame her for that. She'd had the same thought when Carl had visited with her.

She hurried to her car, hoping Carl wouldn't see her. The last thing she needed was for him to find out about the latest attack. He'd probably be even more determined to take Anna from Grace.

Rosemary opened the door, slid quickly behind the wheel, and started the engine. A short time later, she pulled up to the doctor's office. She found Martha and Judith sitting in the waiting room, while Roman paced the floor.

"Where have you been?" he growled. "We've been waiting for thirty minutes!"

"I had an errand to run." She glanced at Judith then back at Roman. "What'd the doctor have to say?"

Roman shook his head and motioned to Judith. "I'll tell you later."

As Ruth sat in the backseat of Donna Larson's car, with Gideon at her side, her mind replayed the events that had happened since she'd found Gideon on the ground with a cut leg. After she'd taken him into the house, she'd gone to Abe's shop and phoned Aunt Rosemary, hoping she'd be free to give them a ride to Millersburg. Aunt Rosemary obviously wasn't at home, for all Ruth had gotten was the answering machine. Then she'd called Donna Larson and was relieved when Donna answered and said she'd be glad to give them a ride to the hospital. Since Ivan was alone in the harness shop, she didn't feel free to ask him to go up to the house to watch the children while she was gone, so she'd left a message on her folks' answering machine, asking if either Mom or Martha might be free to watch the children. In the meantime, she'd put Esta and Josh in charge of the younger ones, which she hoped hadn't been a mistake.

The trees lining the road blurred as they sped along in Donna's car, and Ruth offered a silent prayer. *Dear Lord, please protect the kinner while I'm gone.*

A short time later, Donna pulled up to the hospital emergency entrance. "I'll let you and Gideon out here and then find a place to park."

"We could be awhile," Ruth replied. "If you have some errands to run while you're in town, you'll probably have time to do them."

"I might run over to the post office, but I shouldn't be long. I'll come inside and check on you as soon as I get back."

"Thanks." Ruth opened the car door and

stepped out; then she turned to help Gideon. Hobbling on one foot, he gave no resistance as she led him into the emergency room. Once he was seated, she went to the front desk.

"If you'd like to have a seat, someone will be with you soon," the woman behind the desk said after Ruth had filled out some paperwork.

Ruth took a seat next to Gideon. "It's going to be okay," she whispered.

"I–I'm scared of gettin' stitches." His chin quivered slightly. "It's gonna make my leg hurt worse; I just know it."

Ruth reached over and touched his arm. "When I was a little girl, I fell and broke my arm. I was scared then, too."

"You were?"

She nodded. "But my mamm was with me when I went to the hospital, and I knew God was with me, too."

Gideon looked over at her with tears clinging to his lashes and smiled. "Danki for comin' with me today, Mama."

Ruth swallowed against the lump lodged in her throat as she gently squeezed his fingers. At least one good thing had come from Gideon's accident.

CHAPTER 33

That evening after supper, Martha decided to ride her bike over to Abe and Ruth's so she could tell them what had been going on with their mother. Since Ruth had been depressed for several months after Martin's death, Martha hoped Ruth might have some suggestions as to what they could do to help Mom.

As she peddled her bike along the shoulder of the road, her thoughts wandered. The attacks that had begun over two years ago with the break-in of their house and then Dad's shop had gone on far too long. They needed to find out who was responsible for the attacks and make them stop. If they didn't, someone else might get hurt or end up dead, like Martin. Martha had been trying for several months to figure out who the attacker was, but she was no further along in finding him now than she had been when she'd first decided to do some detective work. The only thing she was sure of was that Luke was not the attacker. He wouldn't be helping her if he were. Martha was certain that Luke wanted to find out who the attacker was as much as she did, if for no other reason than to clear his name with Dad.

A horn honked from behind, and Martha jumped. Her bike swerved to the right, but she righted it before running into the ditch. She glanced over her shoulder and was surprised to see John Peterson's SUV pull alongside of her.

He leaned over and rolled down the window on the passenger's side. "Need a ride?"

She pointed to her bike. "Thanks anyway, but I've got a ride."

He smiled. "I can see that. I just thought if you had a ways to go, I'd put your bike in the back of my rig and I could give you ride to wherever you're going."

"I'm heading over to Abe and Ruth's place, so I don't have much farther to go."

John's smile widened. "No, I guess you don't. How are things with the Wengerds these days? I haven't talked to Abe in a while."

"Last I heard, things were fine and dandy with my sister and her husband." Martha

grimaced. "My family's still having problems, though."

"What kind of problems? Have there been
more attacks?"

She nodded. "Someone threw a brick
through my folks' bedroom window last
night, and Mom's been pretty upset ever
since." No point in giving John all the
details. Martha was sure her dad wouldn't
like it if everyone in the area knew Mom
was on the verge of a nervous breakdown.

"That's too bad. No one was hurt, I
hope."

"No, but they could have been."

"Did your dad report it to the sheriff?"

"Aunt Rosemary did while Dad and Mom
were at the doctor's."

"What were they doing at the doctor's?"

"As I said before, Mom was pretty upset,
and Dad wanted her to get something from
the doctor to help settle her nerves."

"That makes good sense. I'll drop by your
dad's shop soon to see if there's anything I
can do to help."

"I'm sure he'd appreciate that."

"I'll let you get to your sister's, and I'd
better get home myself. It's been a long day,
and I'm bushed."

"Okay. Thanks for stopping, John."

"Sure thing." John rolled up the window

and pulled back onto the road.

Martha smiled. Even in the face of adversity, it was nice to know they had caring neighbors like Donna and Ray Larson and John Peterson.

Ruth had just stepped onto the porch to check on the children playing in the yard when she spotted Martha peddling up the driveway on her bike. "It's good to see you," she called as Martha climbed off the bike and leaned it against the barn. "I left a message on the folks' answering machine earlier, but you must not have gotten it until now."

"What message was that?" Martha asked as she stepped onto the porch.

"The one about me needing you or Mom to come over here and watch the kinner while I took Gideon to the hospital for stitches."

Martha's forehead wrinkled. "What happened to Gideon? Is he all right?"

Ruth nodded. "He cut his leg on a broken beer bottle someone threw in our yard, but he'll be fine." She took a seat in one of the porch chairs and motioned Martha to do the same. "I called Donna Larson for a ride to the hospital, and then we took Gideon in for stitches."

"Who watched the kinner?" Martha asked,

glancing at the children playing in the yard.

"I figured you or Mom would be coming over, so I left Esta and Josh in charge of the two younger ones. But when I got home, I found out that Ivan had closed the shop and come up to the house to watch them himself."

"What about Abe? Where was he when all this happened?"

"He'd gone to Berlin to get some things he needed in his shop."

Martha moaned. "What a *verhuddelt* day this has been for all of us."

"How has the day been mixed-up for you?"

"Someone threw a brick through Mom and Dad's window last night."

"Ach, that's *baremlich!* Were either of them hurt?"

"Not physically. The worst part was how Mom reacted to it. She was so upset that she didn't want to get out of bed this morning. Except for a couple of words, she wouldn't say much to Dad, Grace, or me, either."

Ruth covered her mouth with her hand as she struggled to control her emotions. "How's Mom doing now?" she asked.

"Well, Dad called Aunt Rosemary this afternoon, and we took Mom to see the doctor."

"What'd the doctor have to say?"

"He thinks Mom's on the verge of a nervous breakdown."

"Ach, no!"

Martha nodded. "The doctor wanted to put Mom in the hospital, but Dad said no to that idea. So the doctor gave Mom a prescription for something to help her relax and said she needed to rest."

Ruth jumped up from her chair. "I'd better go over there now and see how she's doing. Maybe she needs my help. Maybe —"

Martha put a restraining hand on Ruth's arm. "She's already in bed. There's nothing you can do right now except pray."

Ruth swallowed around the lump in her throat. "Has the sheriff been notified?"

"Jah. Aunt Rosemary went to see him while Dad, Mom, and I were at the doctor's."

"Is the sheriff going to come out and check for evidence?"

Martha shrugged. "I don't know about that, but I did find a couple of things on my own when I was looking around outside this morning."

"What'd you find?"

"There was a ballpoint pen lying in the

flower bed, and not far from it was a beer bottle."

"A beer bottle?"

Martha nodded.

"Gideon fell on a beer bottle this morning. That's how he cut his leg." Ruth rocked back and forth in her chair as she mulled things over. "You don't suppose —"

"That the beer bottle Gideon fell on was left by the same person who dropped a beer bottle at our place?" Martha said, finishing Ruth's sentence.

"That's exactly what I was thinking." Ruth bit down on her lip so hard she tasted blood. "I wonder if the person who threw the brick into Mom and Dad's window came over here last night with the intent of doing the same thing but got scared off by Winkie. I did hear the dog barking once during the night."

Martha shrugged. "I suppose that's possible, but I'm wondering why none of my dogs barked last night. If they'd heard an intruder, I'm sure they would have been howling like crazy."

"I think Abe needs to know about this," Ruth said as she moved toward the door. "He's in the living room, rocking Molly to sleep."

"It'll be dark soon, so I'd best be getting

home," Martha said. "I'll say hello to the kinner and be on my way."

"Tell Dad I'll be over to see Mom in the morning," Ruth called over her shoulder.

On an impulse after John had closed his shop for the day, Luke decided to go for a ride in his truck. It had been a long, busy day, and he needed to relax — needed to get out of the small room in the back of John's shop where he'd been staying at night since he'd moved out of his folks' house.

Maybe I'll drive over to Walnut Creek and see what's doin', Luke told himself as he started down the road in that direction.

He'd only gone a little ways when he spotted Martha riding her bike along the shoulder of the road. He pulled over behind her and tooted his horn.

Martha stopped the bike and got off.

Luke turned off the engine and hopped out of the truck. He swallowed hard when he saw how flushed Martha's cheeks were. Several strands of dark hair had escaped her kapp, no doubt from the wind. It was all he could do to keep from pulling her into his arms and kissing those rosy cheeks.

"Where're you headed?" he asked.

"I just came from Ruth and Abe's place, and now I'm headed home. I'm really glad to see you, Luke. We need to —"

"You're losin' daylight," Luke interrupted. He looked up at the darkening sky. "It's not good for you to be out on the road alone." He motioned to the back of his truck. "Why don't you let me put your bike in there and give you a lift home?"

Martha hesitated as she glanced around kind of nervouslike. Was she worried someone they knew might drive by and see her talking to him? Probably so, he decided, since she didn't want her dad to know they'd been seeing each other. Luke was on the verge of telling her to forget the offer of a ride and suggesting he follow behind her bike in his truck, when she said, "I'd be happy for a ride home. It'll give us a chance to talk."

Luke lifted the bike with ease and set it in the back of his pickup. "Aren't you worried what your daed will think when I bring you home?" he asked as Martha opened the door and climbed into the passenger's seat.

"I figured you could drop me and my bike off at the end of our driveway. That way, Dad will be none the wiser."

"Guess that makes good sense." Luke skirted around to the driver's seat and started up the truck. Before he pulled onto the road, he turned to Martha and said,

"I've got to tell you, though, I'm getting tired of sneaking around in order to see you. Every time we want to see each other, we have to meet some place in secret." He thumped the steering wheel with his knuckles. "It's not right that a fellow in love has to sneak around to see his *aldi.*"

Martha's mouth dropped open, and her eyes widened. "Did you mean what you just said?"

"What? That I'm sick of sneaking around in order to see you?"

She shook her head. "The part about being in love and me being your girlfriend."

Luke reached across the seat and took hold of her hand. "It's true, Martha. I'm in love with you."

She sat there several seconds, staring at his fingers, intertwined with hers. "I . . . I love you, too, Luke, but I don't know if I can ever truly be your aldi."

"Because of your daed?"

She nodded. "If we could just find out who's behind the attacks —"

Luke stopped her words with a kiss. Her favorable response made him wish all the more that he had the right to court her.

"Oh, Luke," she murmured, pulling slowly away, "I'm afraid things will never be the way we want them to be. You see, what I wanted you to know is that there's been another attack, and even though I found some evidence, I still don't know who threw the brick."

Luke squinted as he studied her face. "What are you talking about? What evidence? What brick?"

"Last night, someone threw a brick through my folks' bedroom window. No one was hurt, but it left Mom really shaken." Martha paused to take in a quick breath. "This morning, I was looking around the place for evidence, and I found a ballpoint pen and a beer bottle that I believe the attacker must have dropped. The pen came from the Farmstead Restaurant, so whoever dropped it probably has eaten there."

"What'd you do with the evidence?"

"I threw the beer bottle out and put the pen in a kitchen drawer."

"Did your daed call the sheriff?"

"My aunt Rosemary spoke to the sheriff while Dad and I sat with Mom at the doctor's."

Luke's brows furrowed. "What was she doing at the doctor's?"

"This morning, Mom wouldn't respond to Dad or me, so we knew she needed to see the doctor."

Luke sat silently, trying to digest all that

Martha had said. "What did the doctor say about your mamm?"

"He thinks she might be having a nervous breakdown, so he prescribed some medicine to calm her down and said she needed to rest." Martha squeezed Luke's fingers. "I'm afraid if the attacks don't stop soon, Mom might get worse and never fully recover."

Luke groaned as he leaned against his seat. "Your mamm's mental condition is one more reason why we need to find out who's behind the attacks. I don't know about you, but I plan to step up my investigation."

"What are you planning to do?"

"I don't know, but when I come up with a sensible plan, I'll let you know."

Martha drew in her bottom lip. "What if we never find out who's doing these horrible things to my family? What if —"

Luke put one finger against her lips. " 'With God, all things are possible.' Isn't that what the Bible says?"

She nodded slowly. "It's hard to hope and have the faith to believe when things keep going from bad to worse."

"Don't give up," he said as he pulled onto the road. "Maybe by the time we meet again, I'll have come up with a better plan."

CHAPTER 34

The following morning, Roman looked out the kitchen window and spotted Sheriff Osborn's car pulling in. As the sheriff stepped onto the porch, Roman went to open the door.

"Your sister came by my office yesterday and said someone had thrown a brick through your bedroom window," the sheriff said.

"Took you long enough to get here," Roman mumbled.

The sheriff stiffened. "I'm doing the best I can."

"Jah, well, I don't see how you're ever going to find out who's responsible for the attacks that have been done here if you don't keep a closer watch on our place." Roman grunted. "Doesn't make much sense for us to notify you when something happens if you don't care enough to check things out right away."

"It's not that I don't care. If you'll recall, you haven't always notified me right away."

"That may be true, but you were notified this time, and you don't show up until today."

The sheriff cleared his throat a few times and raised himself to his full height. "I'm a busy man, and I don't have time to stand around here all day debating the issue with you. I came to see if I could find any evidence, and that's what I plan to do." He moved toward the porch steps. "You want to show me exactly which window the brick came through?"

"Jah, sure." Roman followed the sheriff down the steps, and they walked across the grass. "That's the one." Roman pointed to the first floor window he'd patched with a piece of plywood.

"I'll take a look around out here in the yard," the sheriff said. "There might be some footprints showing or some other evidence that could help me find out who threw that brick."

Roman stood off to one side as Sheriff Osborn studied the lawn and the ground beneath the bedroom window. After several minutes of looking, the sheriff shook his head and said, "No footprints in the flower beds, and it would be hard to spot any in the grass unless there was snow on the ground. Don't see anything lying around that might give me any clues, either." He glanced at the house. "Mind if I have a word with your wife?"

Roman shook his head. "That's not possible."

"Why not?"

"Judith's asleep in our room right now."

"I can come by later this afternoon."

"No, I . . . I don't think Judith will be up to talking to you at all." Roman rubbed the back of his head. "You see, Judith kind of went into shock after the brick flew through the window, and I had to take her to the doctor's yesterday."

The sheriff nodded. "Yes, your sister mentioned that."

"The doctor gave Judith some medicine to take — something to calm her nerves and allow her to sleep." Roman continued to rub the spot on the back of his head. "Even if she was feeling up to talking to you today, she wouldn't have anything more to say than I've already told you."

"How about your daughter, Martha? Was she at home when this happened?"

Roman nodded.

"Is she here now?"

He nodded again.

"Mind if I speak with her?"

Roman moved toward the house. "I'll get her now."

Martha had just slipped a batch of sticky buns into the oven when the back door opened and Dad stepped into the kitchen. "Sheriff Osborn's here," he said. "He wants to speak with you."

Martha's forehead wrinkled. "What does he want?"

"Said he wants to question you about the brick being thrown through our bedroom window. Guess he wants to know if you heard or saw anything suspicious."

Martha nibbled on her bottom lip as she contemplated how much she should tell the sheriff. Not that she knew that much, really. She'd been asleep when the incident happened and hadn't seen anyone in the yard. But she had found that beer bottle and the ballpoint pen when she'd looked around the yard yesterday morning.

Dad rubbed the back of his head and squinted like he might be in pain.

"Have you got a headache?" she asked.

"Jah. Feels like a bunch of horses have been stamping on the back of my head. When things calm down around here, I may have to see the chiropractor."

"That's probably a good idea."

He inched toward the door. "Are you comin' or not?"

Martha nodded. "I'll be right there. Just let me set the timer so these buns don't burn."

"I'll see you outside then."

Moments later, Martha went outside. "My dad says you want to speak to me," she said to the sheriff, who stood on the porch, leaning against the railing.

He nodded. "Just wondered if you saw or heard anything the other night when the brick was thrown through your folks' bedroom window."

"The only thing I heard was the loud noise from the window being broken."

"Did you find any evidence?"

Martha wasn't sure how she should answer the sheriff's question. She didn't want to lie, but she didn't feel she should tell him about the pen she'd put in the kitchen drawer, either. Not with him being on their list of suspects. "I . . . uh . . . found a broken beer bottle in the yard."

"Where is it now?"

"I threw it away so no one would step on it."

"That's just great." The sheriff moaned. "I thought I told you before not to touch any evidence you found after one of these attacks. How are we supposed to check for fingerprints if you toss the evidence?"

Martha's face heated up. "I'm sorry."

"Please remember, the next time you find any evidence, leave it there, and call me right away."

Ruth's heartbeat matched the rhythm of the horse's hooves as she traveled down the road toward her folks' place in one of Abe's buggies. She'd left Molly and Owen with Aunt Rosemary for a few hours so she could see how Mom was doing. She feared if the attacks didn't stop, Mom might never be the same.

As Ruth approached her parents' driveway, she spotted Sheriff Osborn's car pulling out. He glanced her way, lifted one hand in a quick wave, and tore off down the road.

I wonder if the sheriff came to talk to Dad about the brick being thrown through their window. Hopefully he'll be able to find out who's behind these attacks and put a stop to them, once and for all.

Just as Ruth pulled her horse and buggy up to the hitching rail, Cleon stepped out of the barn. "If you're going to be here awhile, I'll put your horse in the corral," he offered.

"Danki," she said with a smile. "I came to check on Mom, so I'll probably be here a few hours."

Cleon's forehead creased. "She's not been the same since that brick was thrown through your folks' bedroom window. I think it really put her over the edge."

Ruth nodded. "She's been getting more nervous after each attack."

"The sheriff came to see your daed this morning, so maybe he'll have some answers soon," Cleon said as he helped Ruth out of the buggy.

"I hope that's the case." She slowly shook her head. "These horrible attacks have gone on long enough. We all need some answers."

"You're right about that." Cleon started to unhitch the horse. "When I get your horse put away, I'll be in the barn working with your daed. When you're ready to go home, come get me, and I'll take care of hitching your horse to the buggy again."

"I will. Danki." Ruth hurried toward the house. When she entered the kitchen a few minutes later, she was surprised to see Mom fully dressed and sitting at the table, drinking a cup of tea. "It's good to see you up," Ruth said, bending to give her mother a hug. "I thought I might find you in bed."

Mom stared at Ruth as though she was

looking right through her and said in a placid tone of voice, "I'm having a cup of tea."

Ruth nodded and looked over at Martha, who sat in a chair on the other side of the table.

"We need to talk," Martha whispered.

"Talk . . . talk . . ." Mom shook her head. "No, I'm too tired to talk."

Martha slid her chair back and stood in front of Mom. "Why don't I walk you down to your room so you can rest awhile?" she said, placing one hand on Mom's shoulder.

Mom stood silently and walked slowly out of the room. Martha followed.

Ruth sighed and reached for the teapot sitting in the middle of the table. Mom might be up and dressed, but she was definitely not herself.

Martha returned to the kitchen a few minutes later and took a seat. "I'm glad you came by. As I said, we need to talk."

"About Mom, you mean?"

Martha nodded.

"If Grace is at home, maybe we should see if she'd like to be in on this discussion. Dad, too, for that matter," Ruth quickly added.

"I've already talked to Grace, but I need your input before we can talk to Dad."

Ruth leaned forward with her elbows on the table. "Mom's not doing well at all, is she?"

Martha shook her head. "If not for the medication the doctor put her on, she wouldn't even be out of bed or saying much of anything to us."

"But the little she said to me didn't make much sense. It was as though she hasn't a care in the world — like she's in a daze or something."

"Exactly." Martha poured herself a cup of tea and took a sip. "The medication is helping Mom get out of bed, but it's keeping her so doped up that she can barely respond to things going on around her. She can't spend the rest of her life taking medication for her nerves, and we can't continue to live our lives in fear that there will be another attack."

Ruth fingered her untouched cup of tea. "Is there anything we can do about this?"

"I think the first thing we need to do is figure out some way to help Mom — something that doesn't involve her taking a lot of medication to keep her calmed down."

"Do you have any ideas?"

Martha nodded. "When I spoke with Grace last night, she suggested we send Mom up to Geauga County to stay with

Dad's brother, Walt, and his wife, Mary, for a while."

Ruth rubbed her chin as she contemplated the idea. "How's that going to help?"

"Mom will be safe at Walt's place, and if any more attacks take place here, she won't know about them or have to deal with the fear of what might happen." Martha picked up the jar of honey sitting on the table, added a bit to her cup of tea, and stirred it around with her spoon. "I think if Mom has some time away from all this, her nerves might heal."

"What's Dad think about the idea?"

"Neither Grace nor I have said anything to him yet. We wanted to get your opinion first."

Ruth nodded. "I'm all for it. Even if Mom's nervous condition doesn't improve up at Walt's, at least we'll know she's in a safe place."

Martha pushed away from the table. "While Mom's taking her nap, maybe I'll go up to Grace's house and get her; then the three of us can have a little talk with Dad."

Chapter 35

Roman looked up when the barn door opened, and his eyebrows furrowed when all three of his daughters stepped up to his desk.

"What are you three doing out here, and who's keeping an eye on your mamm?" he asked.

"Mom's taking a nap, and we decided this was a good time for us to talk to you about something," Grace said as she shifted a sleeping Daniel in her arms.

He stood and motioned to his chair. "I'm sure that boy's getting heavy. Maybe you'd better sit here."

"Better yet, let me take him," Cleon said stepping up to Grace. "I'll sit with him over at my workbench, so you're free to talk with your daed and sisters."

"Danki." Grace handed their son to him.

"What's this all about?" Roman asked, lowering himself into the chair again.

"It's about Mom," Martha spoke up. "We think she needs to go away for a while."

His forehead wrinkled. "Go away?"

All three sisters nodded.

"We were thinking it might be good if you took Mom up to Geauga County to stay with Uncle Walt and Aunt Mary," Ruth said.

He leaned forward, placing his elbows on his desk. "How's that gonna help anything?"

"Mom will be safe from the attacks there," Martha said. "Being in a safe place with people she knows might help her nerves to settle."

Grace nodded. "Maybe she'll be able to get off the medication that's making her act so spacey and out of touch with what's going on around her."

Roman sat massaging his forehead as he contemplated the idea. Maybe taking Judith to Geauga County would be a good thing. He could let people know that he planned to take Judith to visit his brother, Walt, for a few days and that he would be staying there with her until she got settled in and used to the idea of being away from home. Hopefully, the culprit would hear that Roman was leaving and plan another attack, believing that no one was at the Hostettler home. Roman would return home sooner than planned without telling anyone. Then he'd hide out in the house. With any luck, he could catch the person in the act. Of course this plan would mean that he'd have to get Martha out of the house, too.

Roman looked up and smiled at his daughters. "I think you've got a good idea. I'll get in touch with Walt right away and see if it's agreeable with them. If it is, I'll see if Rosemary's free to drive us up there. She's been wanting to go up to Geauga County to see where Walt lives, anyway. We can spend a few days having a little family reunion," he added.

"I'm glad you're in agreement with this," Ruth said with a look of relief.

"Of course this means I'll have to put my plans to begin building the new shop on hold awhile longer, but that's not as important as getting your mamm away from here right now." He looked over at Martha. "I think it would be a good idea if you went with us to Walt's."

Her mouth dropped open. "How come?"

"I wouldn't feel comfortable leaving you home alone. It might not be safe."

"But I can't go," she argued. "I'm needed here to care for my dogs. Not to mention my job at Irene's."

"Martha can stay with us," Grace was quick to say. "That way, you won't have to worry about her being alone in the house, and she'll be able to fulfill her responsibilities to Irene and still care for her dogs."

Roman nodded. "That sounds fine to me." He looked back at Martha. "You can go to the barn to do what you need to do with the dogs whenever Cleon's around, but I don't want you going there alone. And no going into the house while I'm gone, either. Is that clear?"

"Jah," Martha said with a slow nod. He could tell by her frown that she wasn't happy about it.

"When do you think you'll be able to leave for Geauga County?" Grace asked.

He shrugged. "I'd like to head out tomorrow morning, but that will depend on whether Rosemary's available to take us or not."

"If she's not, maybe you can hire Ray Larson to drive you and Mom up there," Ruth suggested. "He's driven you plenty of other places."

"That's true," Roman said with a nod. "But Rosemary's been wanting to see Walt and his family, so I think it would be best to wait until she's free to drive us."

"I have several errands I need to run in Millersburg, and I'll probably be gone the rest of the day," John said as he slung his jacket over his shoulder and headed for the door. "See if you can get those cabinets finished up while I'm gone, okay?"

Luke nodded. "Unless we get a bunch of customers, I should have them finished by closing time."

"Great. See you tomorrow then."

A short time later, the shop door opened, and in walked Rod and Tim, two of the English fellows Luke had been hanging out with for some time.

"What are you up to?" Tim asked, coming to stand near Luke.

"I'm trying to finish up a set of cabinets for my boss," Luke replied.

Rod glanced around. "Where is your boss, anyway?"

"He had an appointment in Millersburg today." Luke dipped his paintbrush into the can of stain. "So what are you two doing here?"

"Came by to see if you'd like to go to New Philly with us. There's a new sports bar that just opened there, and we thought —"

Luke shook his head and pointed to the cabinets. "You'd better count me out. I've got work to do."

Rod stuck his head close to Luke. "Since your boss ain't here, then you oughta be able to take off a little early, don't ya think?"

"Not if I want to keep my job."

"Puh!" Tim grunted. "You're such an old stick-in-the-mud these days. Haven't wanted to do anything fun since you started hanging around that little gal who raises dogs."

Luke grimaced. He'd never told Tim or Rod that he'd been seeing Martha.

"Don't look so stunned." Rod leaned over and rapped Luke on the head. "There isn't much that goes on around here that me and Tim don't know about."

"Do you know that Martha's folks had a brick thrown through their bedroom window the other night?" Luke asked pointedly.

Rod looked at Tim then back at Luke. "Nope. Never heard a thing."

Luke spread some stain over one of the cabinet doors as he contemplated what to say next. If Rod and Tim were responsible for the attacks, they'd probably never admit it, but he felt that he needed to ask.

"I know you two have pulled a couple of pranks around here over the last few years," he began. "I thought you might have had something to do with the brick that was thrown."

Rod shook his head. "Nope. The only pranks we've been involved in were some outhouse tipping and vandalism at a few of the local schools. We've had nothing to do with what's been done at the Hostettlers.' " He looked over at Tim. "Ain't that right, Tim?"

Tim nodded. "We might like to have a little fun now and then, but we're not stupid enough to single anyone out or do anything that might get the law on us."

"The law could get on you for vandalism at the schools if they knew you were the ones who'd done it," Luke reminded.

Rod squinted his dark eyes at Luke. "Who's gonna tell — you?"

Luke shook his head.

Tim grunted and poked Rod's arm. "Lay off Luke, would ya? He's never given us any reason not to trust him, so don't be accusing him now."

Rod scowled at Tim. "I never said I didn't trust him. Just wanted to know if he was planning to rat on us or not."

"Doesn't sound like he is to me." Tim looked back at Luke. "Do you want to go to New Philly with us or not?"

"I appreciate the offer, but I'd better not. Don't want to risk getting my boss mad at me for sloughing off."

Rod nudged Tim's arm. "Let's go then. We're burning daylight."

Tim nodded and headed across the room. "See you soon, Luke," he called as they went out the door.

Luke grimaced. If Rod and Tim knew he'd been hanging around with them all this time just so he could find out if they were the ones responsible for the attacks, who knew what they might do?

I just don't think either Rod or Tim has anything to do with those attacks, Luke thought as he continued his work. *It's got to be someone who has a grudge against someone in Martha's family.*

Luke sucked in his breath. An image of Toby flashed into his mind. *He may not have any specific grudge against the Hostettlers, but he does have a grudge against me. I think I'll go over to Toby's house after I close the shop for the day and have a little talk with him. It's time we get a few things straightened out between us. If Toby's responsible for the attacks, maybe I can get him to admit what he's done.*

CHAPTER 36

That evening after work, Luke headed straight over to Toby's. As he climbed the back porch stairs, he prayed that God would give him the right words.

He lifted his hand to knock on the screen door, but the door swung open before his knuckles connected with the wood. Sadie stood on the other side of the door, her apron covered with a dusting of flour. "Luke! I'm surprised to see you," she said. "I heard a buggy rumble into the yard and figured it must be Toby."

"Toby's not here?"

Sadie shook her head. "He hasn't come home from work yet." She motioned to one of the wooden chairs sitting near the door. "If you'd like to wait for him, I'm sure he'll be here soon."

Luke shifted from one foot to the other as he contemplated what to do. Sadie seemed uncomfortable, so maybe it would be best if he came back some other time. Or he could try to catch Toby over at Keim Lumber. Maybe he hadn't left yet. He smiled at Sadie and said, "I think I'll head over to Charm and see if I can catch Toby before he gets off work."

"He might have already left," she said. "Are you sure you wouldn't rather wait for him here?"

Luke rubbed his chin thoughtfully and shook his head. "I'd better not." He turned and was about to step off the porch, when Sadie said, "I saw Martha earlier today when I stopped by their place to look at one of her pups as a possible birthday present for my mamm."

"How are things with her?" Luke asked.

"Okay with the kennel business but not so good with her mamm."

"She told you about the brick and Judith's reaction to it?"

Sadie nodded, her dark eyes looking ever so serious. "I guess Judith has been getting more nervous after each of the attacks. This one must have put her over the edge."

"That's what I understand. From what I heard, the doctor had to put her on medication in order to calm her down."

"Jah, and now Roman's decided to take Judith away for a while. Martha said they're hoping a change of scenery and being in a safe place might help heal her shattered nerves."

"Where are they going, do you know?"

"To Geauga County, where Roman's brother, Walt, lives."

"Is Martha going with them?"

Sadie shook her head. "She said she has to be nearby to care for her dogs, and she's got that part-time job with Irene to worry about."

Alarm flooded Luke's soul. If Martha wasn't going with her folks, did that mean she would be home alone? He was about to ask when Sadie said, "Martha plans to stay at Grace and Cleon's place while her folks are gone."

Luke blew out his breath. "That's good to hear."

Sadie tipped her head and smiled at him. "You love her, don't you?"

"Who?"

"Martha, of course. That's who we've been talking about, right?"

He nodded as a flush of heat covered his face. "I do care for her," he admitted. "For all the good it's doing me."

"You mean because of her daed?"

"Jah." He stared at the floorboards beneath his feet. "Unless I can prove to Roman that I've had nothing to do with the attacks, I'm afraid there's no chance of Martha and me ever being together as a couple."

Sadie touched his arm. "Where there's a will, there's a way. Where love's involved, there's always hope." She giggled, kind of embarrassed-like. "Look at Toby and me. For a long while, I thought we'd never get married, but look at us now. We're an old married couple."

"Come on, Sadie, you and Toby haven't even been married a year yet."

She smiled. "That's true, but there are days when it feels like we have."

Luke wasn't sure what Sadie meant by that, but he didn't feel he had the right to ask. Besides, he needed to get back in his buggy and head for Charm if he was going to catch Toby before he left work.

"I'd best be on my way," he said, turning to go. "If I should miss Toby, would you let him know I was here and that I'd like the chance to speak with him soon?"

"Jah, sure." Sadie gave Luke another smile and stepped into the house.

As Luke headed for the buggy, an idea popped into his head. If no one would be at Roman's house for several days, it would be the perfect time to go over there and look around. He might camp out in the barn for a few days. If the culprit showed up at the Hostettlers' again, Luke hoped he might catch him in the act.

Luke unhooked his horse from the hitching rail and was about to climb into his buggy, when Toby showed up. *Good. That'll save me a trip to Charm.*

Toby scowled as he climbed down from his buggy. "What are you doin' here, Luke?"

"I came to speak with you, but when Sadie said you weren't home from work yet, I decided to head over to Keim Lumber and see if I could catch you there."

"What did you want to talk to me about?" Toby asked as he unhitched his horse.

"It's about the attacks that have been going on at the Hostettlers'."

Toby grunted. "You'd know more about that than me."

Luke balled his fingers into the palms of his hands. "What makes you so sure I'm the one behind the attacks, and how come you've been trying to make it look as if I'm the guilty one?"

"You've been irritated with Roman ever since he fired you." Toby led his horse to the barn, and Luke followed.

"I'll admit, I was irritated at first, but I've got a better job now working for John. I'm not carrying a grudge against Roman. I'm not the one responsible for any of the attacks against them." Luke ground his teeth together. "You, on the other hand, have been carrying a grudge against me for some time, and it makes me wonder if —"

"If what?" Toby put the horse inside its stall and leveled Luke with a piercing look. "What are you accusing me of?"

"For some time now, you've been bad-mouthing me to my folks, to Roman, and to anyone who'll listen." Luke's voice shook as he struggled to keep control of his emotions. He should have had this discussion with Toby a long time ago.

Toby grabbed a brush from the shelf overhead and started grooming his horse.

"You know, Toby," Luke went on to say, "instead of pointing fingers at me, you ought to be more concerned about making yourself look innocent."

"Innocent of what? I've done nothin' wrong."

Luke grunted. "You think running off at the mouth and telling tales about me isn't wrong?"

Toby's face turned bright red. "Well, I —"

"I have to wonder if it's not you who's been terrorizing the Hostettler family."

"Me? What reason would I have to hurt the Hostettlers?"

Luke shrugged. "The only thing I can think of is that you did it to get even with me."

"Huh?"

"You thought that if you could make it look like I was the one doing the attacks, then I'd be in trouble with the Hostettlers — not to mention the law."

Toby shook his head. "No way! You don't know what you're talking about, and you sure have no proof of such a crazy notion."

Luke nodded. "I think I do have some proof."

"Wh–what kind of proof?" Toby sputtered.

"Martha and I have found some evidence, and a couple of the items point to you."

The color in Toby's cheeks deepened. "I don't know what you're talking about. What kind of evidence did you find that points to me?"

"A work glove and a ballpoint pen."

"What?"

"I said —"

Toby held up one hand. "I know what you said. I just can't figure out what a pen and a glove would have to do with me."

"A work glove," Luke said through clenched teeth. "Just like the ones you wear at Keim Lumber."

Toby's eyebrows furrowed. "I told you

that I'd lost my glove, so what does that prove? And I don't know anything about a pen."

"The pen Martha found came from the Farmstead Restaurant in Berlin. I know you eat there a lot, so you could have picked up the pen during one of your meals."

Toby shook his head. "I had nothing to do with any of those attacks, and unless you can prove otherwise, I'd appreciate it if you'd stay away from me!"

"Fine then!" Luke started to walk away but turned back. "Just remember one thing. I'll be watching you, Toby!"

Martha was about to leave Irene's for the day, when she spotted Luke's buggy coming up the driveway. She stepped up to his buggy when he pulled up at the hitching rail. "This is a surprise," she said. "I didn't expect to see you today."

"I wasn't sure if you were working for Irene today or not, but I thought I'd stop by, just in case." Luke's face was bright red, and he swiped his hand across his forehead, glistening with sweat.

Alarm rose in Martha's chest. "What's wrong? You look really upset."

He nodded. "I just came from Toby and Sadie's place, and I wanted you to know what all was said before you heard Toby's version of things."

Martha's forehead wrinkled. "What are you talking about?"

Luke motioned to his buggy. "Let's have a seat, and I'll tell you what happened."

"Okay." Martha stepped into the passenger's side of Luke's buggy, and he slipped in beside her.

Luke cleared his throat a few times and reached for her hand. "Do you still believe I'm innocent of the attacks against your family?"

"Of course I do. I trust you, Luke. Really, I do."

"Good." He drew in a quick breath and released a puff of air that lifted the hair off his forehead. "I've told you before that I think Toby might be the one doing the attacks and that he's been doing them in order to get even with me. In the process, he's trying to make me look guilty."

"I thought you were thinking those rowdy English fellows you've been hanging around with might be responsible for the attacks."

"I did think that at first, but not anymore. As time's gone on, I've become more and more convinced that the attacks have been done by Toby." Luke chewed on his bottom lip and grimaced. "Remember that work glove we found that looked like one of Toby's?"

She nodded.

"And then there was that ballpoint pen you found. It had the name of the Farmstead Restaurant on it. Toby eats there a lot. I wouldn't be surprised if that pen was his."

Martha groaned. "I hate to think our own bishop's son could have done anything so terrible. He's a baptized member in our church, not to mention that he's married to Ruth's best friend."

"I know, I know." Luke sat staring at the floor. Finally, he lifted his gaze and turned to face her. "I had it out with Toby . . . told him what I suspect."

"What'd he say?"

"He denied it, of course. Said if I thought he was the one doing the attacks, I'd have to prove it." Luke's eyes narrowed. "Which is exactly what I plan to do, and I think it might be soon."

"Why?"

"Before Toby got home from work, I spoke with Sadie. She mentioned that she'd talked to you earlier today when she came over to your place to look at a puppy."

"That's right," Martha said with a nod.

"Sadie told me your daed's planning to take your mamm and go up to Geauga

County with the hope that it will settle her nerves."

"Jah. I'd planned to tell you all this as soon as I saw you again. I guess Sadie beat me to it, though."

"It doesn't matter how or when I found out," Luke said. "The important thing is that I know."

"Why's it important for you to know?"

"Because having your house sit empty for several days is exactly what I need."

"Huh?"

"I'm planning to hide out in the barn during the nights your folks are gone, and if the attacker comes around again, I'll hopefully catch him in the act."

Martha's mouth fell open. "Are — are you sure that's a good idea? I mean, what if someone sees you there, or what if —"

"You worry too much. I'll be just fine." Luke leaned over and gave her a kiss.

Rosemary glanced in the rearview mirror at Judith asleep in the backseat of her car; then she looked over at Roman, sitting up front in the passenger seat, chewing on his fingernails. "You're not nervous about taking Judith to Walt and Mary's place are you?" she asked.

"Huh?" He dropped his hands to his lap.

"Uh . . . no, I'm just . . . well, I've come up with a plan, and —" He turned and looked over his shoulder. "Good, Judith's asleep. I'm glad we decided to head out this evening rather than wait until tomorrow morning."

"I suppose it is a good idea to get Judith away from home as soon as we can."

Roman glanced in the back again. "I wouldn't want her to hear what I'm about to say." He turned toward the front and rubbed the bridge of his nose. "Not that she'd probably give much response. That medication the doctor prescribed keeps her so calm and relaxed she barely notices what's going on around her."

Rosemary nodded. "Maybe after some time at Walt and Mary's, she'll relax and her medication can be cut in half."

"I'm hoping that's the case."

"How long are you planning to stay in Geauga County?"

"Uh . . . that's what I wanted to talk to you about. I'm only planning to spend the night, and then I'll ride home with you after supper tomorrow evening."

"Roman, I hardly think one night at Walt's place is going to put Judith at ease enough to return home."

He shook his head. "Judith will stay with Walt as long as necessary. I'll be going home tomorrow with you."

"You're leaving Judith alone?"

"She won't be alone; she'll be in good hands with our brother and his wife. When I talked with Walt on the phone last night, he said Judith could stay with them for as long as necessary."

"Is this about you not wanting to be gone from your business?"

"No." Roman's voice lowered, and he cast another quick glance over his shoulder.

Rosemary looked in her rearview mirror again. Judith was still asleep. "What is it you're not telling me, brother?"

"I'm planning to return home and hide out in the house, hoping there will be another attack."

"What?" Her mouth dropped open. "Why on earth would you want another attack to occur?"

"So I can catch the one doing it." Roman pursed his lips. "I told as many people as I could think of that I'm taking Judith to my brother's place and that we'll be gone for several days. I did it in hopes that the word would get back to the one doing the attacks and he'll think with no one at home that he'll have the perfect opportunity to attack again."

She slowly shook her head and groaned.

"That's the most foolhardy thing I've ever heard you say. It could be downright dangerous."

He folded his arms in a stubborn pose. "I don't care if it is. I'm tired of these attacks, and I've decided it's time to take matters into my own hands."

"What about trusting God to take care of your family?"

"I am trusting God. I'm trusting Him to help me learn who the attacker is and bring these harassments to an end."

CHAPTER 37

Grace had just said good-bye to Anna, who was being driven to school in Martha's buggy, when she spotted Sheriff Osborn's car coming up their driveway. "I wonder what he wants," she murmured.

"Who?" Cleon called from the kitchen doorway.

"Sheriff Osborn. He's heading this way."

Grace stepped outside, and Cleon joined her on the porch. A few minutes later, the sheriff parked his car and got out. "I was down at Roman's house looking for him, but no one was there," he called. "Thought maybe he might be up here."

Cleon shook his head. "Roman's out of town."

Sheriff Osborn stepped onto the porch. "For how long?"

"Several days, I believe," Grace said. "He took Mom up to Geauga County to his brother's place for a while."

"Hmm . . . I see. Well, I just wanted your dad to know that I've been doing more investigating lately, and I've ruled out several of his original suspects." The sheriff leaned on the porch railing. "I think I might know who's responsible for the attacks, but I won't know for sure until I follow up on a couple more leads."

"What kind of leads?" Cleon asked.

"I'd rather not say anything more until I know something definite and the criminal's been caught." The sheriff raked his fingers through the back of his hair. "With your folks being gone for several days, it might be an open invitation for another attack, so I'm planning to keep a close watch on their place — hopefully catch the attacker in the act."

Grace drew in a deep breath and released it slowly as a sense of hope filled her soul. Was it possible? Did the sheriff really know who had done the attacks? It would be such a relief for all of them if the person was caught. Maybe it would happen while Mom and Dad were gone. Maybe soon the family would find some peace.

As Martha guided her horse and buggy down the road toward Anna's school, she thought about her folks being gone and how this would be the perfect chance to do some investigating without anyone knowing what she was doing or asking a bunch of questions. She planned to keep a close watch on things. If the attacker struck again, she would hopefully see who it was.

"Mama said she would take me over to Poppy's new house soon, but probably not 'til Grandpa and Grandma Hostettler get back from Geauga County."

Martha reached across the seat and touched Anna's hand. "I know you want to see your poppy again."

"Jah." Anna fiddled with the strap on her backpack. "Is Grandma Hostettler gonna die?"

Anna's unexpected question took Martha by surprise. "Ach, no, Anna. What makes you ask such a thing?"

Tiny wrinkles marred Anna's forehead. "Mama says Grandma's sick, and when my other *grossmudder* got sick, she died."

Feeling the need to reassure the child, Martha reached across the seat and took Anna's hand. "Grandma Hostettler's not going to die. She just needs to rest and calm her nerves. That's why Grandpa and Aunt Rosemary took her up to Geauga County to see my uncle Walt and aunt Mary."

A look of relief flooded Anna's face, and

she smiled. "When they get back home, will Grandma be better?"

"I hope so, Anna. I surely do."

Anna remained silent for the rest of the ride, and Martha hoped it was because the child's mind was at ease.

Now if someone could only put my mind at ease.

As Luke headed down the road in his truck toward John's shop, he glanced at the clock on the dash and grimaced. It was getting close to the time when he should be opening the shop, and if John showed up and Luke wasn't there, he'd have some explaining to do. Since he was supposed to be sleeping in the back of the shop, John would expect him to be there and to open the place on time.

Maybe I should tell John where I spent last night. Luke shook his head. *No, John's a gabber. He might say something to one of his customers.*

Luke had told John last night that Roman was planning to take Judith up to Geauga County and would be gone several days, but he didn't want anyone but Martha knowing he'd spent last night in Roman's barn and planned to continue doing so until Roman returned home. If the attacker heard that Roman and Judith were out of town, that could be a good thing, because he'd probably think he had free run of the place. But if the attacker thought anyone was hiding out with the intent of discovering who was responsible for the attacks, it could prove to be disastrous.

Luke had just passed the Amish schoolhouse when he noticed Martha's buggy pulling out of the parking lot. Figuring she must have driven Anna to school, he waited until her buggy was ahead of him; then he pulled up beside her and waved her off the road.

"Wie geht's?" Martha asked when he stepped up to her buggy.

"I'm kind of sore and stiff after sleeping in your daed's barn all night." Luke reached around to rub a sore spot in his lower back.

Her mouth fell open. "You stayed there last night?"

He nodded. "Said I was going to, didn't I?"

"Well, jah, but I figured you wouldn't start sleeping there until I could get you a key to open the padlock so you'd be able to get into the barn." Her forehead wrinkled. "How did you get into the barn, anyhow?"

"I brought my ladder along and went in through the small window that opens into the hayloft."

She slowly shook her head. "I might have known you'd pull something like that."

He offered her a sheepish grin. "I'm surprised you didn't know I had slept there."

"How would I know? I stayed up at Grace and Cleon's place last night, and there isn't a good view of my daed's barn from there. Just the rooftop can be seen from the second floor."

"I knew you were staying at Grace's, but I figured you'd show up at the barn to feed your dogs this morning and that you'd find me sleeping in the hayloft."

She shook her head. "Grace asked me to take Anna to school this morning. She was running late, so I decided the dogs could wait to be fed until I got back from the schoolhouse."

"Ah, I see."

"Did you see or hear anything unusual during the night?" she asked.

"Nope, and it wasn't because I was in a deep sleep, either." He grunted and rubbed his back again. "What little sleep I did get was not restful. I think I'll take the mattress off the cot I've been using in John's back room and take that with me when I sleep in the barn tonight."

Martha reached into her handbag and handed him a key. "You'd better take this with you then, because it would be kind of hard to carry the mattress up the ladder and squeeze it through the window."

"Good thinking." Luke took the key and shoved it in his pants pocket, but as he thought things through, his eyebrows drew together. "If I take your key, then how are you gonna get into the barn when you need to?"

"Cleon has a key. I'll ask to use his."

"Won't he think it's a bit strange that you'd need his key when you have one of your own?"

"I'll tell him it was in my purse but it's not there now."

"You'd tell your brother-in-law a lie?"

"I wouldn't really be lying, because the key won't be in my purse — it'll be in your pocket."

Luke chuckled. "Good point. No wonder I fell in love with you — you're a real schmaert woman."

Martha's cheeks turned pink, and if a car hadn't been passing just then, he would have kissed her.

"I'd best be on my way," Luke finally said. "I need to get to work before John gets there, or he'll want to know why I didn't sleep in his back room last night."

"John doesn't know what you're planning to do?"

He shook his head. "Figured the fewer people who knew about my plan, the better. No point getting the word spread around that someone's hiding out in your daed's barn hoping to catch the attacker."

"You think John would blab if you asked him not to?"

"Probably not intentionally, but he's quite the gabber. Who knows what he might let slip to his customers?"

Martha nodded. "Maybe it's best that you don't say anything then."

He smiled. "On that note, I'd better be off. Maybe I'll see you in the morning."

"If I get out to the barn to feed my dogs before you leave." She reached out and touched his arm. "Please be careful, Luke. I couldn't stand it if anything happened to you."

Luke clasped her hand. "You be careful, too."

CHAPTER 38

"Are you sure it's going to work out for you to stay here?" Rosemary asked as she pulled along the shoulder of the road several feet from Roman's driveway.

Roman nodded. "I'll be fine."

"Does Cleon know what you're planning to do?" she asked.

He nodded. "He's agreed to keep quiet about it."

"What if something happens while you're asleep?"

"I'll stay awake at night and try to sleep during the day. Cleon will be at the shop in the barn most of the day. I doubt anyone would be dumb enough to come around then, anyway."

"I suppose you're right." Rosemary leaned across the seat and gave him a hug. "Please be careful, and if you need anything, I'm only a phone call away."

"I'll remember that. Thanks for driving

me and Judith up to Walt's place. I feel a lot better knowing I've left her in good hands."

"You're welcome."

Roman opened the car door and stepped into the night. As Rosemary drove away, he sent up a silent prayer. *Lord, please help Judith get better soon, and help me to find out who's behind the attacks.*

Luke pulled his truck off the road and parked it behind a clump of bushes about a quarter of a mile from the Hostettlers' place. He didn't dare drive it onto their property and give away the fact that he was there.

He reached under the seat and grabbed a flashlight. "Oh no," he groaned. "I forgot to bring that mattress with me."

Luke hesitated, wondering if he should go back to John's shop and get the mattress. He decided it would take too much time. It was dark, and he needed to get to the barn and keep watch as soon as possible.

"I guess one more night on a bed of straw won't kill me," he muttered as he started in the direction of the Hostettlers', being careful to stay hidden behind the trees. Some time later, he came to their driveway, but rather than walking up it, he stayed off to one side where a hedge of bushes grew.

He continued his walk up the driveway until he came to the barn; then he slipped his hand into his pants pocket and withdrew the key Martha had given him that morning. He'd just unlocked the padlock on the door, when he heard a noise. It sounded like a door had slammed up at Roman's house. But how could that be? No one was supposed to be at home there.

Swish! Luke jumped when an owl flew past his head, and he dropped the key.

Thump . . . thump . . . thump . . . Another noise came from the house, and he whirled in that direction.

I'd better check things out before I get settled in the barn.

Using only the light of the moon, Luke crept along the edge of the lawn. He was almost to the house when he felt someone's hand touch his shoulder.

"What do you think you're doing?"

Luke's mouth went dry as he whirled around. Holding the flashlight in front of him, he directed the beam of light at the man who'd startled him. "Roman! What are you doing here? I thought you'd taken Judith to Geauga County."

"I did take her, but I came back so I could keep an eye on my place." Roman's eyes narrowed as he glared at Luke. "What I'd like to know is what *you're* doing on my property in the middle of the night." A muscle on the side of Roman's neck quivered as he held his hand in front of his face. "For heaven's sake, put that flashlight down! You're gonna blind me with it!"

"Sorry," Luke mumbled as he lowered the flashlight.

"You came here to do another act of vandalism, didn't you?"

"No, I —"

"I'll just bet you didn't. What other reason would you have for sneaking around my place in the dark?"

"I was heading for the barn so I could —"

"What? Do something to one of the animals there?"

Luke opened his mouth to reply, but Roman rushed on. "I've spent the last couple of years trying to deal with these attacks by choosing to look the other way, but I've come to the conclusion that there are times when God expects people to put feet to their prayers."

"What's that supposed to mean?"

"It means, I left Judith in Geauga County and came back home so I could keep an eye on our place and hopefully catch whoever's been doing the attacks to us." Roman leaned so close that Luke could feel his hot breath blowing on his neck. "It looks like the Lord's finally answered my prayers and has helped me learn who the culprit is." He grabbed Luke's arm before Luke could offer a word in his own defense. "You're comin' with me."

"To where?"

"To the phone shed. I'm calling the sheriff to let him know I caught you trespassing on my property in the middle of the night. I'm going to tell him that I think you were about to commit another act of vandalism."

Luke shook his head. "No, that's not why I'm here. I —" He glanced around nervously, hoping no one had seen the two of them out here. If the attacker had decided to strike again and had found them standing out here on the lawn, he'd be long gone.

"Look," Luke said in the calmest voice he could muster, "why don't the two of us go into your house and talk things through? If you'd just give me a chance to explain things to you —"

"You can explain it to the sheriff!"

"I'll tell you what. If you promise to hear me out, and then if you decide I'm still the guilty party, I'll phone the sheriff myself."

"Fine then." Holding onto Luke's arm, Roman led the way to his house. Once they were in kitchen, he turned to Luke and said,

"All right now, let's hear your story."

Luke took a seat at the kitchen table and proceeded to tell Roman how for the last several months he and Martha had been trying to find out who was responsible for the attacks. He ended by saying that he'd spent last night in Roman's barn and had planned to sleep there again tonight, hoping the attacker would show up so he could catch him in the act of committing another crime.

"That's some story you told."

The room was dark so Luke couldn't see Roman's face clearly, but he knew from the tone of Roman's voice that he didn't believe him.

"It's the truth; just ask Martha if you don't believe me."

"I'm not asking my daughter anything that has to do with you." Roman grunted. "Besides, I told her to stay away from you some time ago, and I don't think she'd go against my wishes."

"She didn't deliberately go against your wishes, but she wants these attacks to come to an end as much as I do."

"As much as you do? What reason would you have for wanting the attacks to end?"

"Because I'm in love with Martha, and she loves me. I'd like your permission to court her."

"That will never happen!"

Luke swallowed around the lump in his throat. This wasn't going well, and if he couldn't convince Roman that he and Martha had been working together and that he wasn't the one responsible for the attacks, he'd probably be heading for jail before the night was over.

"If Martha and I aren't working together, then why'd she give me this?" Luke reached into his pocket to retrieve the key Martha had given him but found it empty. That's when he remembered that he'd dropped the key by the barn.

"What's in your pocket?"

"Nothing. I mean, I did have a key to your barn, but I dropped it."

"How'd you get a key to unlock my barn?"

"Martha gave it to me so I could get inside to spend the night."

"I don't think my daughter would be dumb enough to give anyone outside of our family a key to my barn."

"She did give me the key. Let's go to the barn now, and I'll look for it."

"I think you're trying to pull a fast one; that's what I think."

"No, I'm not. Please, let's go to the barn."

"Give me a few minutes to think about

this some more."

Martha woke up in a cold sweat. She'd been dreaming that someone had broken into the barn, taken the wrench and glove she'd hidden in the hayloft, and had set the barn on fire. What if it was true? What if —

She threw the covers aside, jumped out of bed, and raced to the window. From the second floor guest room at Grace's house, she could only see the top of Dad's barn. No smoke or flames shot out from it.

Martha leaned against the window ledge. That dream had been so real. She drew in a deep breath and tried to relax. What she needed most was some assurance that she was doing the right thing in trying to solve the mystery of the attacks.

Last night, before Martha had gone to bed, Grace had told her that the sheriff had stopped by that day and said he thought he might know who was responsible for the attacks and that he'd let them know more when he could.

Martha shuddered as a new realization hit her. If the sheriff thought he was getting close to catching the one responsible, then he couldn't be the culprit.

She turned on the battery-operated lamp by her bed and picked up the Bible lying on the nightstand. How long had it been since she'd read God's Word and sought guidance from Him?

She opened the Bible to Proverbs, one of her favorite books. Her gaze went to the third chapter, verses 5 and 6. She read the passage out loud. " 'Trust in the Lord with all thine heart; and lean not unto thine own understanding. In all thy ways acknowledge him, and he shall direct thy paths.' "

"I haven't been doing that, Lord," she murmured. "I've been trying to take matters into my own hands and haven't trusted You to direct my paths. Maybe what I need to do is go out to the barn, get the evidence I have hidden in the hayloft, and take it to the sheriff in the morning."

Martha removed her nightgown, put on a dress, slipped into her sneakers, and tied a black scarf over her head. If Luke was in the barn, as he said he would be, she wanted to explain to him her decision to turn over the evidence to the sheriff.

With that settled in her mind, she grabbed the flashlight from her nightstand and tiptoed out of the room so she wouldn't wake Cleon, Grace, or the children.

Downstairs, she slipped quietly out the back door and hurried into the night air.

She found the barn unlocked and figured

Luke must be inside, but when she stepped through the doorway, a sudden chill shot up her spine. She thought about that morning several months ago when she'd been doused with white paint because someone had rigged a bucket of paint above the door. Instinctively, she looked up. There was nothing.

I'm just being paranoid, she told herself. *Everything's fine.* "*Be of good courage, and he shall strengthen your heart, all ye that hope in the Lord,*" she quoted from Psalm 31:24. It was a verse she'd learned as a child.

"Luke, are you awake?" she called, shining her flashlight toward the hayloft.

Woof! Woof!

"Quiet, Heidi; it's only me." Martha recognized her female sheltie's bark and figured she must have taken the dog by surprise when she'd entered the barn.

Holding the flashlight in front of her, she moved toward the back of the barn where the kennels were located. Heidi wagged her tail when she saw Martha, and Martha was glad to see that everything was okay. She just needed to talk to Luke and get the evidence she'd hidden under the mound of hay in the loft.

She reached through the wire fence and patted the top of the dog's head. "Go back to sleep, girl. I'll see you in the morning."

Martha made her way to the ladder leading to the hayloft and climbed up. "Luke, are you up here?"

No response.

She shinned the light around but saw no sign of him. *I wonder where he could be? Maybe he's in one of the empty stalls.*

She dug through the mound of hay, opened the box, and picked up the wrench and glove.

Thump! Thump!

"Luke, is that you?"

No response.

There was a muffled grunt, and then an arm reached out and grabbed her around the waist.

"Luke, I —"

Slap!

Martha gasped as a hand connected to her face. She dropped the glove, but her fingers tightened around the wrench.

"You're gonna pay for every year I suffered. You and your family are gonna pay!"

Martha swallowed against the bitter taste of bile rising in her throat. Even without seeing the man's face, she knew who it was.

CHAPTER 39

Rosemary punched her pillow and tried to find a comfortable position. She'd been tossing and turning in bed for nearly two hours. She couldn't seem to relax, couldn't keep the negative thoughts out of her head. What if Judith never got better? What if the attacks continued and they never found out who was doing them? What if Roman had put himself in danger by hiding out at his house?

The words of Romans 12:12 popped into her head: *"Rejoicing in hope; patient in tribulation; continuing instant in prayer."*

Rosemary slipped from her bed and went down on her knees. "Heavenly Father, the attacks against my brother and his family have affected each one in a different way. I pray that You will give everyone a sense of peace and the faith to put their hope in You. Help them learn patience in waiting for answers and remind us all that our strength comes from You. Amen."

As Rosemary got to her feet, she made a decision. She would get dressed and drive over to Roman's house. Since she couldn't sleep anyhow, the least she could do was keep him company during his nighttime vigil.

"Did ya hear what I said? You're gonna pay — each and every one of you has gotta pay!"

"What are you talking about?" Martha pointed the flashlight at John. "Why are you dressed in Amish clothes?"

He yanked on her arm, pulling her over to a bale of hay, and shoved her down. She smelled alcohol on his breath, and his clothes reeked of smoke. How odd. She'd never known him to drink or smoke. But then, she didn't really know him that well. None of them did. John had moved to the area a few years ago and opened a woodworking shop nearby. He'd been helpful and kind — like any good neighbor should — but they didn't really know him.

John sank down beside Martha and clutched at his head. "He . . . he made me do it."

"Who made you do what, John?" Martha hoped her voice sounded calmer than she felt.

"It . . . it's Roman's fault — Harold said so."

"Who's Harold?"

John groaned. "Said it was 'cause I liked wood. Said I reminded him of Roman."

Martha had no idea what John was talking about or why he was dressed in Amish clothes, but she knew by the tone of John's voice that he was deeply troubled.

"Say, where'd you get that?" John pointed to the object Martha held in her hand.

She glanced at the wrench and wondered if she dared —

"I said, where'd you get that?" He leaned closer and snatched the wrench out of her hand.

"I . . . uh . . . Luke found it in the field after my dad's shop was blown up." *Luke. Oh, Luke, where are you?* Martha shined the flashlight around the hayloft. She couldn't see a mattress. If Luke was here, there should be a mattress. But if Luke wasn't here, why had she found the barn door unlocked? The padlock wasn't broken. Could John have crawled up a ladder and entered the barn through the small window in the hayloft like Luke had last night? Or could he . . .

"Gimme that!" John snatched the flashlight out of Martha's hands, clicked it off, and tossed it on the floor. "What was Luke doin' in the field with Harold's wrench?"

"Who is Harold?"

"Harold Crawford — my stepdad." John sounded more coherent. Maybe the effects of the alcohol were beginning to wear off.

"Did the wrench belong to your stepdad?"

"Harold's dead. Mom gave me his tools. Guess she figured I needed somethin' to remember him by." John's tone was bitter, and a groan escaped his lips. "I've got a lot more'n a few tools to remember Harold by."

A shaft of light from the moon shone in through the hayloft window, and Martha's mouth went dry as she saw John run his fingers over the bridge of his crooked nose. A nose that had obviously been broken at some point.

She looked at the wrench in his hands and thought about the initials she'd seen engraved there. *H. C. Those must stand for Harold Crawford.*

Martha didn't understand why John had brought up his stepdad, or how the man's wrench had ended up in their field. She was about to ask, when John leaned forward and began to sob. "No! No! Don't hit me no more, Harold. Ple–ease it's not my fault. I didn't do nothin' wrong."

Martha wasn't sure what to do. John was

clearly upset, but he'd also been drinking. Should she try to run away from him or stay here and try to offer comfort?

She reached out and touched John's shoulder. "Did your stepdad abuse you, John?"

John's head jerked up, and he leaned so close to Martha that she could feel and smell his hot, putrid breath on her face. "Harold — worked for Roman — 'til he got fired." His words were short and choppy, and he spoke to Martha as if she were a stranger.

"Who got fired?" Martha asked.

"Harold."

"My dad fired your stepdad?"

"Roman fired Harold."

"How come?"

John rubbed his forehead with one hand and clung to the wrench with the other hand. "Harold came to work late — after he'd been drinkin'." He paused, drew in a quick breath, and released it with a shudder. "Got fired — went out drinkin' some more — came home — beat the stuffing outta me and Mom."

Martha gasped as a light began to dawn, but John spoke again before she could comment. "Harold begged Roman — 'Gimme my job back' — Roman said no — Harold drank even more."

"Did Harold try to find another job?"

"Said he couldn't find one. Moved us to Oregon 'cause that's where his brother lived. Said he might have a job for Harold." John clutched Martha's arm, and his nails dug into her flesh. "Harold hated Roman for firin' him. I hate Roman, too! It's *his* fault Harold drank. It's *his* fault Harold beat me and Mom when he got drunk." John touched the side of his nose again. "I never shed a tear at his funeral, neither."

"I'm sorry you and your mother were mistreated, but —"

"Roman's gotta pay! It's Roman's fault Harold couldn't find a job. It's Roman's fault Harold hated me! Roman's gotta pay for every year we suffered!"

Martha's heart pounded so hard she heard it echo in her head. "Are . . . are you the one who's done all those horrible things to us?" she asked, already knowing the answer but not wanting to believe it. Ever since John had moved to Holmes County and opened his own woodworking business, he'd been nice to them, loaning Dad tools, buying Martha's dog, and offering his assistance in any way it was needed. It was unthinkable that he could have done such hateful things. It was as if he were two different people — one kind and helpful, the other hateful and full of revenge. John Peterson was a sick man who obviously needed help.

"I did most of those things." John emitted a high-pitched laugh. "Made it look like it was Luke."

It was all coming together. John had befriended Luke and then tried to make it look like Luke had been the culprit so no one would suspect it was John.

"Why did you come here tonight?" Martha dared to ask.

"Came to burn this barn down; that's why I came."

Martha's palms grew sweaty as she thought about the dream she'd had where the barn was on fire. Had it been a warning of things to come?

"You can't do this, John." Martha struggled not to cry. She had to remain calm. She couldn't let him know how frightened she felt.

Dear God, she silently prayed, *show me what to do.*

"Who's gonna stop me from burnin' the barn?" Before Martha could respond, John grabbed her around the neck and jerked her to his side. "If you tell Harold, you're gonna burn, too."

■ ■ ■ ■

"I wish you'd believe me, Roman," Luke said as he paced in front of the kitchen table. Even though it was dark in the kitchen and Roman couldn't see Luke's face, he could tell by the tone of his voice that he was agitated.

Well, I'm agitated, too. I can't believe that one of our own could stoop so low as to attack a fellow Amish man. Roman gritted his teeth and clasped his fingers tightly together. *And I can't believe one of my own daughters would betray me by falling for the one who's been attacking us.*

"I'd really like to go look for that key," Luke said.

Roman was about to reply when the back door opened and clicked shut.

"Roman, are you here?"

"I'm in the kitchen," Roman replied, recognizing his sister's voice.

"It's dark in here. How come you don't have a gas lamp lit?"

"Didn't think it'd be a good idea to light up the place and let anyone know I was here."

"Oh, right." Rosemary's voice grew closer as she moved across the room.

452

"Hello, Rosemary."

"Luke? Is that you?"

"Jah."

"What's going on here?"

Roman could see Rosemary's silhouette as she came closer. "Luke and I are havin' a little discussion," he mumbled. "I caught him sneaking around in the yard."

"I wasn't sneaking," Luke defended himself. "I was just checking things out by the house; then I was going to the barn to spend the night so I could keep an eye on things, when Roman came up and startled me."

"You were planning to sleep in the barn?" Rosemary's tone was one of disbelief.

"That's right. I knew Roman and Judith were gone, so I figured I'd take advantage of the fact that nobody was around and hide out in the barn a few nights."

"Whatever for?"

"He made up some wild story about him and Martha working together to find out who's been attacking us," Roman said before Luke could respond. "Did you ever hear such a tale?"

Rosemary cleared her throat a couple of times. "Actually, Martha did tell me she and Luke —"

"I know, I know. She and Luke are *in love*."

"It's true we are," Luke spoke again. "That's one of the reasons I need to clear my name and find out who's responsible."

Rosemary moved over to the table and placed her hand on Roman's shoulder. "Before you interrupted me, I was going to say that Martha told me she and Luke were doing some investigating because they wanted to find out who was behind the attacks. I believe Luke when he says he was planning to sleep in the barn so he could keep a watch on things. Maybe we should go up to Grace and Cleon's place and ask Martha to confirm what Luke's said," she suggested.

Roman shook his head. "No way! It's the middle of the night, and I'm not waking my daughter out of a sound sleep so she can tell me how much she loves Luke." He grunted. "She'd probably say most anything to keep him out of trouble."

"Then at least let's go out to the barn so I can look for the key I dropped," Luke said.

"What key?" Rosemary asked.

"The key to the padlock that locks the barn. Martha gave it to me so I could get inside at night."

Rosemary touched Roman's shoulder again and gave it a gentle squeeze. "I think we should see if the key is there, don't you?"

Roman ground his teeth as he mulled things over. Should he go look for the key to please Rosemary, or should he phone the sheriff?

CHAPTER 40

John slipped the wrench into his pants pocket and stood. "There's been enough talk!" He reached into his shirt pocket and withdrew a cigarette lighter; then he bent down and grabbed a handful of hay. "If ya don't wanna burn with the barn, then you'd better get outa here now."

Martha squeezed her eyes shut and started to pray. *Please, God, don't let John do this. Give me the right words to say.* She opened her eyes and drew in a deep breath. "I . . . I don't know all the details of how things were between my dad and your stepdad, but I'm sorry your stepdad took his anger out on you and your mother."

The stubble of hay crackled under John's feet as he shifted his position. "Roman's gonna be sorry." His voice cracked. "He ruined my life. He's gotta pay."

"Your life's not ruined, John. You have a good business, a well-trained dog that's devoted to you, and you've got your whole life ahead of you. If you'd just —"

"Shut up!" John flicked the lighter, and a glow of light illuminated his face. Deep lines etched his forehead. His eyes looked red and swollen. He pointed to the hayloft ladder. "Go down!"

Martha did as he requested, praying with each step she took. There had to be a way to get through to John. She couldn't let him burn Dad's barn. Her throat felt clogged as she thought about her dogs in their kennels near the back of the barn. She had to save them — Dad's horses, too. Maybe if she made a run for the door, she could dash up the hill to Cleon and Grace's place and get help before it was too late. Or should she stay and keep talking to John — try to make him see the error of his ways? After all, John needed saving, too.

When John stepped off the bottom rung of the ladder behind her, she turned to him and said, "Luke really likes you, John. He's said many times what a good boss you are. He enjoys working for you."

"Luke's a good guy, not like Roman."

Martha cringed. If John liked Luke so much, then why had he tried to make Luke look like the one who'd done the attacks?

"My dad's not a bad person, John," she

said. "It's not his fault your stepdad drank or beat you."

"Uh-huh. Harold said it was. Someone's gotta pay."

"Harold said that because he couldn't face up to his own problems," Martha said. "It was Harold's drinking that got him fired, and he beat you and your mother because he needed help for his drinking problem and uncontrollable temper, not because my dad fired him." She paused to gauge John's reaction, but he said nothing.

"Do you believe in God, John?"

He rocked back and forth on his heels. "Mom did. She read her Bible. She prayed when Harold got drunk." He snorted. "For all the good it did her! God never answered Mom's prayers. God didn't care about us. If He had, He would've done somethin' to make Harold stop. Roman needs to pay."

"God doesn't *make* us do anything," Martha said, carefully choosing her words. "He gave us a free will to choose between right and wrong. You can't blame my dad for the actions of your stepdad, either. Harold chose to drink and abuse his family; nobody made him do it."

John gave no reply, but he made no move to light the barn on fire, either. He snapped the cigarette lighter closed and shoved it in his pocket. Martha took that as a good sign and continued with what she felt God had laid on her heart.

"Instead of hating your stepdad and my dad, you need to forgive them."

John shook his head. "I can't."

"In your strength, you can't, but with God's help, you can. In Matthew 6:14, God's Word says: 'For if ye forgive men their trespasses, your heavenly Father will also forgive you.' " Martha touched John's arm. "The things you've done to my family are wrong. The only way you'll ever find peace in your heart is to seek God's forgiveness."

John drew in a ragged breath and blew it out with another snort. "There's only one way to find peace. I've gotta end it all."

End it all? Was John saying he planned to commit suicide? Was he going to burn the barn with him in it? Or was he planning to do worse things to them?

As Roman, Luke, and Rosemary approached the barn, Roman noticed that the door was slightly open. He turned to Luke. "Did you unlock the lock before you dropped the key?"

Luke nodded. "Said I did, didn't I?"

"Did you open the door?"

"No, I never got that far."

Roman frowned. "But it's open now, so that means someone must be in the barn." He turned to Rosemary. "You'd better stay out here. Luke and I will go in and see what's up."

She touched his arm. "Listen, I hear voices. Do you hear them, Roman?"

He tipped his head and listened. "You're right. Someone must be inside."

"Maybe it's Cleon and Martha. Could be they came to feed her dogs," Rosemary said.

"At this hour?" Roman blew out an exasperated breath.

"I'm going in," Luke said, pushing past them.

As soon as Roman stepped inside, he realized that one of the voices was Martha's.

"She's talking to someone," Luke whispered as they crept along in the dark.

"Maybe it's Cleon." Roman followed the sounds of Martha's voice. As they drew closer, he saw the back of her head. He shined his flashlight in that direction, and she turned to face him.

A man dressed in Amish clothes stepped out from behind Martha.

Luke rushed forward. "John! What are you doing in Roman's barn in the middle of the night, wearing Amish clothes?"

"That's what I'm wondering, too," Roman said.

John kicked a hunk of straw with the toe of his boot and mumbled, "Came to burn down the barn."

Rosemary gasped, and Roman gripped the flashlight so hard his fingers ached. "You were going to do what?"

John's finger shook as he pointed it at Roman. "Came to make you pay for what you did to me and Mom!"

Roman's forehead wrinkled as he slowly shook his head. "I don't understand. I've never done anything to you. I don't even know your mother."

"John's stepdad used to work for you," Martha spoke up. "I guess he had a drinking problem and you fired him because of it." Her voice was thick with emotion. "John said his stepdad used to beat him and his mother, and —"

Roman's jaw dropped. "Harold Crawford? Was he your stepdad, John?"

John nodded. "I vowed to make you pay for turnin' the only man I'd ever known as a father into an evil monster."

"So you're the one who did these things against the Hostettlers?" Luke stepped between John and Martha. "And you tried to make it look as if it was me?"

"That's right. Roman's gotta pay for every

461

year Harold smacked me and Mom around."

Roman trembled as he struggled to keep his emotions under control. Violence went against the Amish ways, but at this moment, he wanted to do something that would make John pay for all the horrible things he had done to Roman's family.

"I was just telling John that he doesn't have to hate you or his stepdad," Martha said. "I told him he could ask God to forgive his sins and choose to forgive those who have hurt him."

"Martha's right," Luke added. "You can release your pain to God and forgive Roman, your stepdad, and yourself."

John's gaze went to Martha, back to Luke, and finally to Roman. With a shuddering sob, he dropped to his knees.

Martha and Luke went down beside him, each with their hands on John's trembling shoulders.

Rosemary touched Roman's arm. "Let's move over there." She motioned to the other side of the barn. "Let's give Martha and Luke a chance to talk to John."

Roman hesitated but finally nodded. He lit one of the gas lamps hanging from the rafters and followed Rosemary across the barn.

She stopped near one of the stalls and turned to face him. "Are you finally convinced that Luke's not holding a grudge against you?"

He nodded and swallowed hard, unable to speak around the thick lump in his throat.

"What are you going to do about John?" she asked.

"What do you mean?"

"John needs help for his emotional problems. And he'll have to pay for his deeds. Do you want me to phone the sheriff?"

Roman was about to reply when he heard a car pull into the yard. He opened the barn door and stepped out just as Sheriff Osborn got out of his car.

"Roman, what are you doing here?" the sheriff asked. "I heard that you took your wife up to Geauga County."

"I did, but I left her with my brother and came back so I could keep an eye on my place." Roman moved over to stand by the sheriff. "Did someone call and ask you to come over here?"

The sheriff shook his head. "I was out patrolling tonight, and since I was in the area and knew you were gone, I decided to swing by your place and check on things. Then I spotted two black trucks parked out by the road — one about a quarter of a mile from here and one on the other side of your driveway. It made me suspicious. When I came up the driveway, I spotted a car parked near your house."

"That's my sister's car," Roman said.

"Where is she?"

Roman pointed to the barn. "In there, with Martha, Luke Friesen, and John Peterson."

The sheriff's bushy eyebrows pulled together. "What's going on?"

Roman drew in a quick breath and told the sheriff everything that had transpired since he'd caught Luke in the yard. He ended by saying, "John confessed to the attacks against us."

The sheriff grunted. "I figured as much. I've been watching John for some time and waiting for him to make his next move so I could catch him in the act. He'll pay for his crimes; I can assure you of that."

"I won't press charges against him — it's not the Amish way," Roman was quick to say.

"I realize that, but if John's the one who killed Martin, then the state will press charges. He can't be allowed to get away with the other things he's done to your family, either."

"I'm not saying he should get away with

464

it," Roman said. "I'm just saying I won't press charges."

The sheriff nodded. "Let me worry about the details." He walked swiftly toward the barn, and Roman followed. They found John still on his knees with Martha, Luke, and Rosemary standing around him in a circle.

"John says he knows he'll have to pay for what he's done," Martha said when she spotted the sheriff walking toward them with Dad at his side.

"You got that right," the sheriff said with a nod. He read John his rights and handcuffed him. "I'll drop by some time tomorrow to ask a few more questions," he said to Dad as he led a very quiet and remorseful-looking John out of the barn.

"Flo. I've gotta get Flo," John mumbled as he approached the sheriff's car. "I can't leave my dog alone."

"Don't worry about Flo," Luke called to John. "I'll take care of her for you."

As the sheriff's car headed down the driveway, Dad swiped a hand across his face. "Whew! After all this time of living in fear and wondering when and where the next attack might occur, I can't believe it's finally over."

"Maybe now things will get back to normal and we'll know some peace," Martha said.

"Speaking of peace," Luke said, "I'll need to make my peace with Toby, since I now know he had nothing to do with the attacks."

"And speaking of peace —" Rosemary nudged Dad's arm. "Isn't there something you'd like to say to Luke?"

The rhythm of Martha's heartbeat picked up as she waited to see how Dad would respond. He needed to apologize to Luke, but because Dad was a stubborn man, it was hard for him to admit when he was wrong.

Dad cleared his throat and took a step toward Luke. "My sister's right: I do have something to say to you."

Luke stared at the floor.

"I need to ask your forgiveness, Luke." Dad's voice quavered, and Martha wondered if he might break down in tears. This whole ordeal had to have been terribly stressful on him.

"No need to apologize," Luke said in a voice barely above a whisper. "What's done is done. It's in the past now."

Dad shook his head. "I do need to apologize. I was wrong about you, Luke, and I . . .

I ask your forgiveness."

Luke lifted his gaze and stared at Dad. He, too, seemed to be struggling with his emotions. "I accept your apology."

"There's something else I'd like to say," Dad said.

"What's that?"

"Now that John will be going to jail, his shop will be closing down. So, I . . . I was wondering if you'd like to come back to work for me."

"Well, I —"

"Don't worry. I've learned my lesson. I promise not to be so harsh and demanding. If you've got an idea you want to share about woodworking, I'll listen."

"Jah, I would like to come back to work for you, Roman." Luke looked over at Martha and said, "But there's something I'd like even more."

"What's that?" Dad asked.

"I'd like permission to court Martha."

Martha held her breath as she waited for Dad's reply.

Dad stood, mulling things over. Finally, he nodded and said, "You've got my permission, but on one condition."

Luke tipped his head to one side. "What's that?"

"That you sell your truck, get baptized,

and join the church."

Luke smiled. "No problem there. That's exactly what I'd planned to do once my name was cleared."

Martha threw herself into Dad's arms and gave him a hug. "Now we just need to get Mom well so she can come home where she belongs."

"That's right," Aunt Rosemary spoke up. "And if I'm not mistaken, you'll probably need your mother's help making a wedding dress soon."

Martha's cheeks burned hot as she looked over at Luke. She was relieved when he stepped forward and whispered in her ear, "You're definitely going to need a wedding dress."

EPILOGUE

Six months later

As Martha sat at the corner table with her groom and their attendants, her heart swelled with joy. She'd just become Luke's wife, and now that the attacks were behind them, her family had finally found a sense of peace. Sheriff Osborn had come by the other day and given Dad a letter from John, who was still in jail. John admitted that he'd been drinking the night Martin was killed but said he hadn't rammed the buggy with the intent of killing anyone. He also said he'd been reading his Bible every day and that his faith was growing. He'd also been getting some counseling, which was helping him deal with his past and the abuse he'd suffered from his stepdad. John ended the letter by saying that he planned to move back to Oregon when his jail time had been served, and he apologized for all the horrible things he had done.

Martha was glad John was doing well, and she knew that, despite what John had done, God wanted her to forgive him. She also knew that in order to heal, she must forgive.

She glanced across the room to where Mom and Dad sat talking with Luke's parents. Although quiet and reserved, Mom was feeling much better these days. She no longer needed medication for her nerves, and the smile on her face as she leaned close to Dad told Martha that Mom was happy and at peace.

Martha shivered when Luke's warm breath tickled her ear as he leaned close and whispered, "Have you noticed how happy Cleon looks today? I think he was relieved when your daed said he was free to quit working at the shop with us and go out on his own with his honey and candle-making business."

"I'm happy for Cleon and also for his brother Ivan. He and Amanda make a wonderful couple."

Martha motioned to Grace, sitting beside Cleon with Daniel in her lap. "I'm also happy to see Grace looking so peaceful. Now that the attacks have ended and things are better between her and Carl Davis, she always seems to be wearing a smile."

Martha glanced at the table where Aunt

Rosemary sat beside her son and his wife. She was glad Ken and Sharon had been able to take vacation time and come to Holmes County for her wedding. Aunt Rosemary was all smiles as she visited with them.

"Did I tell you my cousin Ken and his wife are expecting a baby?" Martha asked.

"You have mentioned that a time or two," Luke said with a chuckle. "I'm glad for them and will be even happier when our time comes."

"Jah, me, too." Martha's gaze went to her aunt again. "Aunt Rosemary's real good with kinner. I think she'll make a fine gross-mudder, don't you?"

"I'm sure she will. She's also a good cook, so she'll probably do real well taking over your place at Irene's with all the dinners she serves." Luke motioned to Carl Davis, who sat on the other side of Rosemary with Anna by his side. "From what I hear, your aunt's been seeing a lot of Carl lately, which may be another reason she's wearing such a big smile today."

"Maybe there'll be another wedding in our family sometime soon."

"You mean Rosemary and Carl?"

Martha nodded. "They seem to have a lot in common."

Luke reached for her hand. "Like us, you

mean? We both enjoy being outdoors, we like to go fishing, and we take pleasure in working together with the dogs in your kennel business."

Martha smiled. "I appreciate the time you took to make me those new dog runs. Now, not only can I raise my dogs, but I can board and groom other dogs, as well."

He gently squeezed her fingers. "A man will do most anything for the woman he loves."

Her cheeks warmed. No matter how long she and Luke were married, she didn't think she would ever get tired of hearing him say he loved her.

"You two look happier than a couple of kids with a box of candy," Toby said as he and Sadie stepped up to the corner table. "I'm glad everything's worked out so well for you."

"Jah, and for you and me, too," Luke said with a nod. "For quite a while there, I thought our friendship might be over."

Toby clasped Luke's arm. "I feel bad for the trouble I caused. I don't know how I could have ever thought you were behind the attacks on the Hostettlers."

Luke grimaced. "I can't believe I thought it was you, either."

"That's in the past, and we've made our

peace, so let's look to the future," Toby said.

"Jah, I agree."

As the men continued to visit, Martha turned to Sadie and said, "How are you feeling these days?"

Sadie's smile seemed to light up the room. "Other than some bouts of heartburn and a bit of morning sickness, I'm feeling right as rain."

"Are you getting anxious for your boppli to be born?"

"Oh, jah." Sadie placed one hand on her bulging stomach. "February can't come soon enough for me." She leaned closer to Martha and whispered, "I'm glad things have worked out for you and Luke. You both deserve to be happy."

"Danki." Martha glanced across the room to where Ruth and Abe sat with their family. God had blessed Ruth when she'd married Abe.

Sadie nudged Toby's arm. "Should we go back to our table now and let the bride and groom visit with their other guests?"

"Jah, sure." Toby smiled at Luke. "I'll talk to you later."

Toby and Sadie had no sooner gone back to their table when Ray and Donna Larson stopped by. "We wanted to offer our congratulations on your marriage," Ray said.

"And say how much we're going to miss you, Martha, now that you won't be our neighbor anymore," Donna put in.

Martha smiled. "I won't be living that far away — just a few miles down the road in the house Dad, Luke, and Cleon built for us on the backside of Luke's folks' property."

Donna patted Martha's arm. "Do come by and see us whenever you can."

"We will," Martha and Luke said in unison.

"We left your wedding present on the back porch," Ray said. "It's a birdhouse that will attract the martins that come into our area every spring."

"Thank you. That's very nice." As Martha watched the Larsons walk away, she thanked God that her suspicions concerning Ray had been wrong. Ray and Donna had been good neighbors for many years.

"There's sure a lot of food here today," Luke said, pushing Martha's thoughts aside. "I'll be so full by the end of the day that I probably won't have to eat for a week."

She snickered and poked him in the ribs. "If I know you, come tomorrow morning, you'll be the first one at the breakfast table."

He laughed and motioned to the table where his folks sat with Martha's parents.

"From the looks of my daed's plate, I'd say he's eating more than his share today."

"I guess you take after him then, huh?"

Luke shrugged as his face sobered. "I hope not too much."

"What do you mean?"

"When we have kinner of our own, I hope I never distrust them the way my daed did me when I was going through rumschpringe."

She touched his arm. "Things are better between you and your folks now, so it might be best to keep your focus on that."

Luke smiled and took her hand. "How'd I find myself such a schmaert wife?"

"The same way I found such a smart man. I'm thankful God brought us together," she said.

He nodded. "And I'm thankful you never quit believing in me or lost hope that God would answer your prayers."

Martha released a contented sigh as she leaned her head on Luke's shoulder. Whatever they might have to face in the future, she could be at peace, knowing their love for God and for each other would see them through.

ABOUT THE AUTHOR

Wanda E. Brunstetter enjoys writing about the Amish because they live a peaceful, simple life. Wanda's interest in the Amish and other Plain communities began when she married her husband, Richard, who grew up in a Mennonite church in Pennsylvania. Wanda has made numerous trips to Lancaster County and has several friends and family members living near that area. She and her husband have also traveled to other parts of the country, meeting various Amish families and getting to know them personally. She hopes her readers will learn to love the wonderful Amish people as much as she does.

Wanda and her husband have been married over forty years. They have two grown children and six grandchildren. In her spare time, Wanda enjoys photography, ventriloquism, gardening, reading, stamping, and having fun with her family.

In addition to her novels, Wanda has written several novellas, stories, articles, poems, and puppet scripts.

Visit Wanda's Web site at www.wanda brunstetter.com and feel free to e-mail her at wanda@wandabrunstetter.com.